MW01167479

THE MORAL IS...

Some of My Best Stories and Fables

THOMAS THORSEN

outskirtspress
DENVER, COLORADO

THE MORAL IS...

Some of My Best
Stories and Fables

Author Photo © 2015 by Inge Thorsen. All rights reserved - used with permission.

Outskirts Press, Inc.
http://www.outskirtspress.com

ISBN: 978-1-4787-3996-8
Hard Cover ISBN: 978-1-4787-4120-6

Outskirts Press and the "OP" logo are trademarks belonging to Outskirts Press, Inc.

PRINTED IN THE UNITED STATES OF AMERICA

Table Of Contents

Foreword

While Thomas was teaching Engineering and Mathematics, he did love to write too. Around 1972, he found out that he could write short stories or fables. He had a special kind of humor and writing these stories seemed to give him a lot of pleasure.

During the last two years of his life, I discovered a great number of these stories on our computer. They were written anywhere between 1972 and 2010. I promised him that I would get them all together, as best I could, and put them into a book for everyone to read. He really liked that idea.

So, here are most of them, ENJOY!

Inge Thorsen

Acknowledgement

A special thanks to our friends at the Palos Verdes Senior writers group for all the encouragement and help I received while trying to keep my promise to my husband, Thomas. Thanks also to our son Steven who helped me put it all together.

A Matter Of Outlook

A WISE MAN lived on a mountaintop. For years, he said nothing. He stared deeply into space, oblivious of his surroundings. Pilgrims came to him to be in the presence of a wise or even holy, man.

One day, his contemplations were concluded and he spoke: "Man means nothing. He is born, he lives, and he dies. Who cares? Nothing he can do is of any significance. He is insignificant beyond any measure. A trifle; a figment of nothingness; a pathetic wisp of nothing." And the wise man went on and on in the same vein. His message was so depressing, so devoid of hope that no longer did pilgrims come to his mountaintop. During a storm, he was struck and killed by lightning. In time, his cadaver lost its flesh. Another violent storm blew his bones and his skull halfway down the mountainside. Later, avalanches and rock slides ground them to dust.

On another mountaintop lived another wise man. After staring deeply into space for many years, he also spoke: "Man is indestructible! His spirit will live forever. Cherish life; nothing in this universe has greater value. Each moment of life is a moment of joy! Worship the spirit of life within you. Man is the center of the universe. He shall endure!"

Pilgrims came flocking to his mountaintop, rejoicing in his message. By word of mouth, his fame and his message became known the world over. When his days ran out, he was struck and killed by

Lightning. His grateful followers put him in a casket of gold and he was entombed in a deep grotto in his beloved mountain. Here, pilgrims still come to seek solace and inspiration in the study of his life sayings.

> **Moral:** Pessimism will grind anybody to dust.
> Optimism will put you into a better-than-average casket.

A Space Story

PAULINE WAS HER name, the trampoline was her game. She was dedicated to a life on the trampoline. She began her jumping as a kid; by the time she had reached the age of four, she hit the ceiling in her parents' apartment. To keep her occupied, her parents nailed a trampoline to the ceiling right above the one on the floor. Pauline bounced as a yo-yo between the floor and the ceiling so fast that she was just a blur. It was hard to tell exactly where she was at any given moment.

In her early teens, her parents rented one of the elevator shafts in the apartment building where the family lived. Pauline's growing strength and the sophisticated trampolines she had acquired by now, let her bounce between basement and penthouse with the greatest of ease. An amazing performer she was; you could open elevator doors at any floor and you saw a constant blur before your eyes and you heard a swish-swoosh sound. There were those who maintained that she swished going up and that she swooshed going down. Others had the opposite opinion.

When Pauline came of age, the Space Age also came of age. Men, but not women, began to visit the moon and next would visit and colonize Mars and other heavenly bodies. The fury of the Women Movement knew few bounds. As a pacifier for Pauline and her fellow sisters, moon-faring men put a trampoline on the Moon and that not a moment too soon. Pauline grabbed the opportunity and bounced between Moon and Earth, landing on the Moon more regularly and far more often that any man could hope to do. Soon, she grew tired of this constant, monotonous travel between an uninteresting pair of planets and a satellite. Pauline set her sights on Mars and beyond.

But, men had not yet visited Mars and Mars was barren of trampolines. Pauline was impatient and decided not to wait. She would bring a trampoline with her and throw it down on Mars just before she arrived there herself. In her eagerness and impatience, she miscalculated her course and missed Mars. She is now swish-swooshing through the solar system and beyond. Some say she is swishing when she is leaving and swooshing when she reenters. Others have the opposite opinion, but reasonable men can differ.

Moral: What reasonable men can't differ about these days is that it is hard to keep women down; it is hardly worth the trouble.

Alberts, Chap. 1 ... or, Now What?

THE OTHER DAY I watched a game show on TV. For each question that you could answer correctly, the more you would win; fair enough and simple enough to catch the attention of a large enough audience. Then, at about halfway into the show, a new contestant walked onto the set and the contestant was me. He used my name, he looked like me, he seemed to be my age, he dressed like me, and during the warm-up period he told the same stories that I would tell now and then. Yet, it wasn't me. I would never try to get on a game show. If I had tried, I would not have been selected as a contestant. If I had been selected, I would have flunked out on the first question, being too nervous to maintain a functioning brain. But this fellow did very well. He kept going on answering every question correctly, no matter how difficult they were. At the end, he or I had won enough to live a life of virtue, or at least leisure, for some years.

Now what? I had won a small fortune even though I hadn't won it. Of course, the show was taped, so technically I could have watched myself later. But, surely, I would have remembered if I had been a contestant on the show. I called the local station and the network and asked how to contact myself. Those who answered, however, could not grasp what I tried to tell them.

Now what? I considered calling reporters at the local papers, but when I considered the probable reactions, I realized it was not a good idea. So I filed a missing person's report at the local police station. After a few days, they told me that I had been found and was living at the address they gave. The address was mine.

Now what? I put ads in the local papers offering a generous award for any information about him that was me. No one answered, possibly because I couldn't give an accurate description of myself. My next step was to explore the city on foot, hoping for a miracle. I thought I saw myself here and there in the distance, but as I got closer, I could tell it wasn't me.

Now what? Maybe we are twins the two of us. There have been many incidents in which identical twins were separated at birth, each twin given to separate sets of adoptive parents. Even when brought up separately, studies have shown that these twins as adults are remarkably alike aside from appearance. They tend to be engaged in the same kind of work, have the same interests, have the same temperament, have similar political affiliations, and tend to choose spouses of similar backgrounds. This gave me an idea. I checked the phone books for my possible twin, but we both had unlisted numbers, confirming these studies.

Now what? I set out again to locate my possible twin. Since he had received a monetary award sufficient to lead a life of virtue, or at least a life of leisure, for several years, I began to haunt the playgrounds of the rich and famous in the city's downtown area where virtue and leisure coexisted. One evening, in the lobby of a high-class hotel, I heard "Oh, Albert!" and next I was greeted effusively and lovingly as well as embraced and kissed by a young lady. She reminded me of Victoria, the queen, in her very young years, of course. As with that other Victoria, she took the initiative and we retired to her suite. I, as Albert, had a hard time following her conversation about what we had done or not done here and there and other places. After a while, Victoria seemed to lose her ardor as if a suspicion was lurking in her mind. I prayed that the real Albert would please show up and put an end to this affair.

Now what? Leaving Victoria, I decided to await any further developments in the hotel lobby. Eve after eve, no Victoria and no Albert. One evening, almost despairing by now, I looked at a game show on a TV monitor, different from that other show. Then, suddenly, there he was again, I or Albert or whoever. Before I could react myself, I heard from another part of the lobby where another TV was located: "That's me! But it is not me!" My reaction to this incident was that this development made everything too complicated for a simple mind like mine. After all, now there could be an Albert I (myself) and, possibly, an Albert II and an Albert III. I decided I didn't want to know the Albert looking at the other TV monitor. From a possible set of triplets, I could now face a possible set of quintuples of Alberts. How could I possibly deal with that? I was curious, of course, about that other Albert in the lobby. What Albert number would I be to him? Would he be trying to locate other Alberts as I had done? Perhaps he would be trying to locate me? If he found me, would I tell Albert III to get lost? Would I tell him to go looking for Albert II instead? Besides, there were probably lots of others who didn't even know they were Alberts. Consider also that if Victoria hadn't called me Albert, I wouldn't have known that I was an Albert even though my name is Albert. All this confusion is like worms in a computer, those that eat away at its innards and spread confusion worldwide.

So I went home with many questions still unanswered. I suppose I took the easy way out of this mess. I probably should have warned the world of the danger of being overrun by Alberts. However, as I could be regarded as being a member, however reluctantly, of the conspiracy, I let the urge to confess pass. I went to bed dreading the possibility that Albert IV and Albert V and who knows how many more would appear in my dreams. During pre-sleep period, I asked myself: How can we defend ourselves? What can we do about all these Alberts?

Moral, Chap. 1: Have yourself copyrighted and trademarked.

Alberts, Chap. 2 … or, So What?

AS THE DAYS slid by, all my anxieties about the Albert matter almost slid away too. Then, my anxieties slid into uneasiness. This uneasiness would not pass away, however. So what? - you may think; everybody is uneasy about something. Eventually, I told my mother about my uneasiness about the Albert matter. I asked her: "When I was born was I the only person involved in the birth process, not counting you?" "Of course", she said, "don't you think I would have noticed?" "Still, being under the influence of sedatives; that could diminish your recall of details." I had told her that I estimated that there were at least half a dozen Alberts, real or imagined, walking around. My mother said that had she given birth to identical sextuplets, she would have been famous and so would be the nurses, the doctors and the hospital. Think of books, movies, and sextuplets exhibitions. Why would anybody be interested in concealing such an event? My father agreed with the statement of my mother and he had not been sedated.

One day, I had to take a business trip to London. I knew, of course, that London was the location of Albert Hall, the concert hall named in honor of Queen Victoria's consort Prince Albert. Still ruminating in some recesses of my subconscious was the Alberts matter. One day, in a break from business, I decided to have a look at

Albert Hall. I intended to ask the doorman at the prestigious hotel where I was staying: "Where is Albert Hall?" What came out of my mouth, however, was: "Where is Albert?" The doorman answered that Albert was at home with the flu. The next day I asked him the same question; Albert still had the flu. Then the doorman looked at me - really looked at me - and he said: "If I didn't know any better, I would say *you* were Albert, except for your accent, of course". Finally, Albert's flu had run its course and the doorman introduced us to each other. We were indeed both an Albert from the knotting of our ties to the color of our shoes. Being both Albert, we didn't really have much to talk about and if we did talk we said the same things at the same time. So, who was I and who was he - or vice versa?

It is difficult to talk to yourself in any meaningful way. Here I was and here he was. We finally agreed, after some initial difficulties, to ignore the fact that we were one and, possibly, the same person and try to untangle our thoughts and to consider our predicament. We further agreed that one of us, or the other, was Albert I ("I") and one of us was Albert IB ("he"), where B stands for British. Then we sat together in the lobby of our prestigious hotel where we enjoyed comfortably cushioned chairs. For one reason or another, we fell into a discussion of FDR's Civilian Conservation Corps, or CCC for short. Afterwards, we went to the bar to enjoy certified citrus cocktails. Later in the evening, we spent some time with a chaperoned Czech couple, both of them females probably. Then it was time for bed and sweet dreams. I dreamed, and he too probably, that I was a Chinese capitalist conspirator trying to flee the mainland.

So what? You may think again. But when I woke up in the morning, this "Chinese capitalist conspirator" phrase was still with me - and very forcefully so. It is my habit, and probably Albert IB's also, that each morning I review my dreams of the past night for any clues as to where I might be headed in the future. I was struck by the various CCC events of recent memory. In particular, a bell rang very clearly as I recalled the "Chinese capitalist conspirator" phrase, certainly another CCC incident. "Conspirator implies Conspiracy" which in turn implies an "illegal conspirator". So what was the dream telling me? It was telling me, first, that there was conspiracy somewhere and, second, that the conspiracy had something to do with a CCC abbreviation; think Civilian Conservation Corps again. Of course, there was nothing sinister about this Corps. Albert IB and I (Albert I) went through the various CCC expressions we could think of. It didn't take long before we came up with "Central Cloning Conspiracy", "Central Cloning Council", and "Central Cloning Committee". Of these three, Albert IB strongly recommended the last one and I saw no reason not to concur. If you were to hatch a conspiracy, you wouldn't call it a conspiracy, you would choose something neutral such as council or committee. The choice, then, was committee which, while neutral, was still descriptive. By this logical process, I, or Albert I, or he, Albert IB arrived at the existence of the Central Cloning Committee. Then what?

We and the world were facing a conspiracy organized by the Central Cloning Committee or CCC. In Scotland, of course, a scientific team had cloned Dolly the sheep. If you can clone sheep, you certainly can clone human beings since human beings are not yet fully evolved - in contrast to the fully evolved sheep. Since mankind rejects such a view, the cloning of human beings had to be done in the deepest secrecy, hence the need for CCC. Why would you want to clone human beings? Why not wait until human evolution is completed and then clone? The answer, of course, is that while you wait for evolution to arrive at its conclusion, you should begin practicing so as to be ready for that event. Both Albert I or I and Albert IB or he was startled by our conclusion about us not being fully evolved, but facts are facts; you can't successfully argue against them.

Next question: why did CCC pick the name Albert since most Alberts are not cloned? Because, probably, whatever name that you may choose, you would have to face the same situation, except possibly with the name Fhistac. Furthermore, Albert is never mentioned in the Scriptures or in Shakespeare's works. Albert is the sort of name which you can get lost in a crowd with. Another question: How were the Alberts distributed over the Earth? If you put too many Alberts in one place, the cloning would become obvious. We estimated that a distribution of one or two Alberts per ten million of population or one or two Alberts per 10,000 square miles would be about the upper limit. But CCC overlooked the fact that since the Alberts are so much alike, they tended to be attracted to each other - somehow - as had happened in Los Angeles, California and London, England. Still, cloned or not, you had to be developed in a womb. How could a mother know that she was about to give birth to an Albert? But suppose she did know! Or, someone somehow persuaded the mother - and the father too - to pick the name Albert? CCC must have had a means of persuasion. Simple enough, the CCC would provide and implant a clone in the womb provided the child was to be named Albert at birth. In other words, the CCC would supply you with a male heir that you otherwise could not have had due to infertility.

Both Albert I and Albert IB were from single-child families. I called my mother in Los Angeles and Albert IB called his mother in Liverpool. Faced with the facts, both mothers admitted to having taken part in the CCC's cloning program.

My business in London came to its conclusion. I had always wanted to jump off the London Bridge into the Thames. I did, I was promptly arrested and speedily deported to the United States. Could all this have happened to anybody but an Albert? So what!

Moral, Chap. 2: Applied logic is mankind's gift to itself.

Alberts, Chap. 3 ... or, Then What?

SO, BY VERY logical deductions, we - Albert I and Albert IB - had concluded the existence of the Central Cloning Committee. Then what? For example, who were the members of the committee, where was the committee's headquarters, how often did the committee meet, who financed it, and where was the cloning done?

Thus far, we had only uncovered Alberts who were about our age, say in the lower thirties. Members of the committee had to be of an age sufficient to have acquired the necessary scientific knowledge, maturity and reputations. They also would have to be, at that stage, in their beginning thirties which means that these scientists now had to be about 65 years of age. Now, of retirement age, they would look back on their cloning work and wonder what had happened to their many offspring. Still unclear is whether they cloned themselves or did the cloning at random. How did they decide who to clone? It is fair to assume that the investigators were male; they would necessarily have feelings of guilt because of abandoning their sons, all those Alberts.

On this foundation, we - again Albert I and Albert 1B - were ready to build the structures required to locate members of the Central Cloning Committee. We had the advantage of being from two different countries with different cultures. On my side, Los

Angeles, California was an open, spirited place that would hardly blink at the idea of cloning. So, despite my innate shyness, I began running around announcing "I am cloned! I am cloned!" That earned me a line or two in the local papers and a word or two by the news outlets, morning as well as evening. And it worked! One day, I got a call, very circumstantial; would I as Albert care to have a talk with him? To avoid attracting any attention due to my local celebrity, we agreed to meet at the stratospheric ride at a local amusement park. We would recognize each other by wearing glasses. I went on the ride several times, but a lot of people wore glasses so that effort was inconclusive. On the last ride, a mature man fell out of his seat and hit the ground head first. It was reported later this mature man had survived the accident but he had lost his memory.

Albert IB in London took a different approach. He went to the Speakers' Corner in Hyde Park where he kept saying to his audience that "I am not cloned! I am not cloned!" Then he listed the many reasons why he was not cloned while at the same time giving them his phone number. For some reason, his denial of being cloned attracted some attention in the media. One day, he too got a call and was asked to meet with somebody at "Harrods", the premier department store in London at a table in its cafeteria. They would recognize each other by not carrying an umbrella. Albert IB sat down at a table next to a mature man without an umbrella. Before the two could interact, a chandelier fell on the mature man. It was later reported that he survived the accident but had lost his memory. By now, both I and Albert IB sensed that we were up against not just a committee but a conspiracy. For a while, Albert IB joined me in Los Angeles where he felt safer; nothing bad ever happened in my native city. We advertised in the major papers both in California and London. The ad read: "To those it may concern. Substantial awards offered for information on the current status of the Central Cloning Committee's pension fund". Obviously, we cleverly played on the fears of those now approaching their retirement age. From the many inquiries we received, the two of us interviewed the most likely suspects. There was a fellow who claimed to have been the committee's accountant in the U.S.; he had papers, true or false, that seemed to be legitimate. We gave him a section of the U.S. tax code and asked him to explain it to us. He couldn't, so no pension for him. We were obviously at dead ends.

Albert IB, now in London, called me to tell me about a note he had received, telling him to go to a little shoe shop around the corner from his rented rooms. The note told him to find a shoe box containing brown shoes, size 9 of the Valkyrie brand. There would be a note in the left shoe giving him further instructions. The further instructions told him to fly immediately to Los Angeles where further instructions awaited.

That same day, I got a similar note. I was told to go to the little shoe store around the corner from my condominium. There would be a note in a shoe box containing black shoes size 10 of the Lorelie brand. The note would be a in the right shoe. It said that I should fly to London where further instructions awaited. In fact I didn't have to wait that long; I had a drink or two on the plane and on the swizzle sticks there were messages that gave the same instructions as in the right black shoe of size 10. When I arrived in London I had to promise the British immigration officials that I would not jump into the Thames. I took this to mean that I should forthwith proceed to London Bridge and wait for further instructions. I strolled around the bridge for a while and then a shabbily dressed mean-looking fellow came up to me and told me to jump into the river. A man's word being his bond and all that, I refused. The fellow grabbed me and threw me into the Thames. Fairly instantly a large crowd gathered on the bridge and along the bank of the river along with television and movie cameras. Many of the passengers of the jumbo jet must have read that stuff on their swizzle sticks and gotten curious. When

I reached shore, I was given a round of applause from the crowds. What surprised me the most was a glimpse of Albert IB among the spectators - at least I was almost certain that it was him.

I wondered then and I wonder now why would all these people go to all that trouble, expense, and planning. For money? For the challenge of it all? For entertainment? To prove to themselves that they were smarter than I was? Why had Albert IB led me down the primrose path to the Central Cloning Committee? And how about Mommy and Daddy; why would they go along with such a plot? How could they? For money? For the excitement of it all? Or, was it just a practical joke? They had fooled me now and then when I was an innocent kid and even as an immature adult.

I couldn't understand the whole thing. All this running around, putting messages in left and right shoes and on swizzle sticks. All these actors, suitable dressed up and made up to look like me: Albert IB, Albert II, Albert III and so on. And, don't forget Victoria, my one-night stand. Why would anybody want to clone, so to speak, such a insignificant fellow like me? What was the point in trying to fool me? The whole thing was improbable and implausible bordering on the impossible.

Obviously, it didn't make sense and hence it couldn't be true. Consequently, the central Cloning Committee did exist some thirty years ago and it still exists today requiring a large organization, promoting and performing cloning of humans, while at the same time denying it and making whoever opposes them in any way look foolish and somewhat crazy. All these efforts to disprove that the Central Cloning Committee ever existed proves that the Committee did exist then and that it exists now.

Moral: Consider the paradox: "This Statement Is False".

Amateur Logic

IN MANY PROSPECTUSES distributed by investment funds to present their financial information and data, the last page or two may have the statement: "This page intentionally left blank", i.e.

This page

intentionally

left blank

But, the page is obviously not blank, hence leading us to the Thorsen Paradox. To avoid the paradox, the preceding page could have this note: "*Next* page intentionally left blank." This means of avoiding the paradox, then, is an illustration of the Gödel Incompleteness Theorem (proved in 1931) which states, paraphrased, that in any logical system there are questions which can only be decided by using data from outside that system. In this case, one must appeal to the preceding page.

Moral: Not all paradoxes are logical.

Another Night,
Another Dream

I WAS DRIVING downhill at a very high speed. Some neighbors who witnessed this gross violation of the local speed limit expressed with their faces, consternation, disapproval, concern, bewilderment among other displays of human emotions.

After all this speeding, I parked the car in a parking lot, undecided about what to do next. After what seemed like a short time interval, a car parked next to mine. A woman driver got out and accused me of having made a long scratch mark on the right side of her car. She insisted that she had to be compensated immediately or else. The "else" was not specified. In the other driver's opinion the compensation should be based on the length of the scratch. This whole scratch business seemed rather dubious to me. It couldn't have happened when I was driving at a high speed downhill nor could it have happened now that my car was standing still.

Still, the lady in the car next to me kept on insisting that she had to be compensated immediately in cash or else. I suggested that we let our insurance companies unravel this whole thing with the two of us not having to give it a second thought. She became very upset, apparently spooked by the prospect of facing insurance estimators. I pointed out to the lady that I carried very little cash with me. In fact, it was so little that I had parked in the parking lot trying to think of some way of earning some cash somewhere. So I pointed out to the lady that if we skipped my cash problem and the venality of insurance estimators we could go straight to the courts - the higher the better - where she would certainly get a much better settlement than I could give her. Either that or I would give her whatever cash I had today and then tomorrow I would introduce her to an insurance estimator that had helped me in the past.

She seemed doubtful. She pointed out to me that she was suspicious and perplexed that I would recommend to her an alternative that could be very costly for me. It did not seem logical, she said. I said that I preferred it that way. Satisfying the opposition - in the long run - is to satisfy myself. I found a piece of paper and gave it to her with a summary of what we had accomplished so far, almost guarantying her success in court.

She was still doubtful. After all, how can you trust a guy with hardly any cash in his pockets? And she went on and on with all the suspicions that she harbored. Finally I had enough. I tried to snatch from her my written proposal that she held in her hand or hands. Then she really got upset. The more I grabbed, the more she held onto that piece of paper. Getting more and more annoyed, even frantic, I made a lunge to retrieve what was mine. Rather than grasping air or paper or her hands, my hands touched hard surfaces, like a floor or a wall. How could that be? So I made another lunge, but again I felt I was touching more floors or more walls or imitations thereof.

Perplexed as I was, I was still capable of rational thoughts and behavior. What is the use of floors? They are used for putting things on them, such as furniture such as beds or tables or whatnot. What are walls used for? They provide surfaces where you can hang up things like pictures of landscapes or pictures of your grandparents and stuff like that. But back to floors; despite such things as tables and chairs, the most obvious and useful furniture suited for a floor are beds where we spend half our lives. So I made a final lunge and then I felt the outline of a bed. My desperate lunges must have scared away the lady with the car with the scratch. I never heard from her again. I wonder why.

The American
Pedestrian Association

THE AMERICAN PEDESTRIAN Association, or APA, was chartered some years ago to serve and to protect the American pedestrian. At any given time, there are more pedestrians walking than there are motorists driving; a possible exception being the hour or two after midnight. The association serves as a counterweight to other associations that cater to non-pedestrians. As is well known, pedestrians killed in accidents far exceed those who die from various kinds of cancers. One purpose, then, of APA is to educate the general public about pedestrian safety.

The pedestrian safety issue must be viewed as a political problem. Congress and the state legislatures must be lobbied into an awareness of the issues involved. A good example is the lack of will to act on pedestrian concerns. Motorists are protected by airbags and other devices derived from research with dummies in staged accidents. To APA's knowledge, there is no equivalent research on devices appropriate for pedestrians. If a pedestrian is run down in a marked crosswalk, that person has no defense at all. Cars are used as missiles against innocent pedestrians. If air bags were incorporated in a pedestrian's clothing at various sensitive points, fatality rates would be drastically reduced. In addition, based on research for the Early Warning Missile Defense System, the capability exists to incorporate similar early-warning systems into every car on the roads. Untold billions of the taxpayers' money has so far been shoveled into this research with little to show for it. However, if the cars manufactured in this nation had early warning systems installed, pedestrians would be warned of any incoming cars and fatalities would be negligible.

A basic concern of APA is: who is a pedestrian? Is a motorist a pedestrian just because he or she has to walk to his or her car parked outside their residences? In other words, there must be a minimum number of steps taken or a minimum distance covered before a person can qualify as a pedestrian. Hence, a true pedestrian must be equipped with a pedometer. A pedometer is to the pedestrian as the odometer is to the motorist. The minimum distance covered in one day should be about one mile. The assumption is that the distance is walked not run. For example, if a person runs a marathon, about 26 miles, that person is not a pedestrian. However, if you walked 26 miles in one day you are a pedestrian. It follows that the pedestrians' pedometers must be able to distinguish between walking and running. Also, just walking in circles does not qualify toward the rewards of pedestrian status; distances walked must be more or less straight forward.

Having discussed collisions between motorists and pedestrians, how about collisions between two or more pedestrians? The usual guide is English common law as practiced in various parts of the nation. In any case, pedestrians ought to carry pedestrian collision insurance with a low deductible. Some parts of the human body are more prone to damage than other parts; hence insurance companies will give deep discounts if these parts of the body are protected, such as airbags incorporated in the clothing. Another problem is the problem of the uninsured pedestrian.

Besides the various requirements discussed above, membership in APA requires payment of dues. So, join today and let us march forward together not too slow, not too fast, not too short, but long is OK. Of course, no motorists or runners need apply.

Moral: Common-interest associations are interesting.

Art And Artists...
Or Perplexity

ART IS ART and more art is more art. Each day, the global output of art objects is immense; to even put a number on it is impossible. Where there is art there are artists. Some produce art objects for their own enjoyment while other artists get paid for their artistic labor. However, there is not enough money, even on a global scale, to buy even a small fraction of the art produced. Consequently, there is discontent, hunger for recognition, an early onset of madness, alcoholism, despair, and above all perplexity.

Artists as a rule are perplexed. Since they know that their art is superior to all other art, they are perplexed that anybody would pay attention to all that other stuff and even be willing to pay for it. Consequently, some artists try to avoid perplexity by not producing art, although it is very hard to do these days. Even bird droppings, beginning with those of humming birds, can be artful. No two bird droppings are alike; it is just a matter of choosing the most artful arrangements of droppings.

All this art clutter, that is art produced by other artists, makes it difficult for the individual artist to be noticed, to be appreciated, and to get paid for art work. Being a long-ago dead artist can solve these problems. Of all the art produced in Antiquity, so little remains due to wars, earthquakes, and general mayhem that there is no need to distinguish between good or bad art. Next consider, briefly, the Renaissance. A lot of art was produced at that time, but only a fraction survives. This fraction, of course, is admired by everybody.

Next, skip to modern times where it is possible to be alive and still be an artist. The difficulty now is to be noticed by any of the several billions roaming the earth. There are the modern inventions of art museums, with art curators, where stuff is bought and then stored away in various basements. Getting to know curators, then, is one way. Another method is to connect with art patrons, wealthy individuals with bad consciences trying to minimize guilt feelings. They will buy art and at times even look at it. An artist, then, should get acquainted with possible patrons, but that is difficult. These men and women are so different that no single approach can be recommended. Some like art while others love tennis.

So, the dilemma remains: how to be noticed and get a reputation. As a recent survey of artists revealed, that is a matter of luck. This survey validates common sense. No wonder that perplexity affects the artistic community.

Moral: Vanity, all is vanity - - - or just luck.

Ballet And Sex Discrimination

WE ALL HAVE a sex of one kind or another, so we're all discriminated against in one way or another. Consider a general statement followed by a specific statement: Why can't a woman be more like a man? (to quote somebody). Why can't a ballerina be more like a ballerino? (to create a new word.). In other words, we want to inquire into the topic of sex discrimination as practiced in the strenuous art of ballet. Who does the heavy lifting? The ballerino does. In any classical and mainstream ballet, there comes a time, even several times, when the ballerino lifts the ballerina off the floor in one way or another. While the ballerina can relax, the ballerino must not only lift her up all by himself, but also move his feet in accordance with the choreography. The obvious question is: why can't a ballerina lift a ballerino?

After the lift, there comes a time when the ballerino stands still while he supports the ballerina so that she can swivel around on tippy-toes without losing her balance. There is no recorded instance ever of a ballerina supporting a ballerino while he swiveled. So why can't a ballerina be more like a ballerino? The next question: Why can't a *pas de deux* be sex neutral? There are, of course, all kinds of objections why this should not be so. First, the conventions of ballet go back hundreds of years. You shouldn't fiddle with traditions that old in any meaningful way. Second, a ballerina may not be strong enough to lift a ballerino. So, why can't the ballerinas do some weight lift-ing? Even such a common-sense observation is rejected out of hand. Well, if the ballerina is not strong enough to lift the ballerino why not replace the *pas de deux* with a *pas de trois*. That is, why can't two ballerinas support one ballerino?

Another source of sex discrimination in ballet is the traditional costumes. The costumes put on by ballerinos are not flattering to the male form. The lower half of them looks like tight sleepwear and reveals that embarrassing hump that leaves so little to imagina-tion; it is rather indiscreet. In contrast, the ballerina's outfits hide any humps with fluffy stuff here and there. It is an obvious case of wardrobe discrimination.

The standard objection to the scheme above is that the male is heavier than the female, assuming that the ages are comparable. The next objection is that why shouldn't the female be allowed to wear fluffy stuff, it looks so feminine. But, that is the whole point, there shouldn't be any emphasis on femininity any more than there should be any emphasis on masculinity. The only fair way to settle this dispute is for the dancers to be dressed in a unisex way so that the audience can see the art rather than the artifice. There is no denying, then, that ballerinos are discriminated against as compared to ballerinas.

Also, consider mixed-pair figure skating. Again, the male part-ner does most of the work. He has to lift the female over his head while he also has to keep on skating. After all the lifts comes the death-spiral routine. As the female bends more and more over back-wards until her hair touches the ice, the male has to hold on to her hand for dear life or she spins out of control and slides on her back on the ice until she hits the judges' box and the pair earn a zero score. Again, why can't the female lift the male over her head and why can't the female hold onto the male so he can do the death-spiral thing too. Further, it is obvious that the female of the pair gets the most attention even though it is the male that keeps the pair going. And, of course, the male of the pair is dressed in long black pants and a white long-armed shirt without distinction. The female of the pair gets to wear all the fancy fluffy stuff. Again, rank discrimination against the male.

(a rhyme or a poem?)

Battle In An Apple

A worm
Used an apple
As his dorm.

Another worm
With a different dapple
Also invaded this solid form.

Such were their needs
That they fought a battle
Between skin and seeds
Until the apple became a rattle.

Hunger made them into string-like things
So neither one would ever get his wings.
Neither one would ever fly
As a moth or as a butterfly
Soon they would both expire
In their little, hollow empire.

A Note: The composition above cannot possibly be called a poem because:

(1) it seems to make sense.
(2) it didn't write itself.

Being Psychic

NOT SO LONG ago, I rented a small office fronting a busy thoroughfare. A small sign was put up with the statement *"I Am A Psychic"* followed by the small print as it were, *"Futures Foretold And How To Avoid Them."*

A week went by and everybody I knew, both inside and outside the family, asked how many futures I had foretold during that seven-day interval and, of course, how much money I had made. I had to remind all these individuals that on the opening of my office, I had foretold that none would show up the first week.

Then I foretold that during the second week, no one would show up to ask about any foretelling. As I knew already, nobody showed up. That being so, it made no sense to open for business when nobody was going to show up.

Week after week, I foretold that no one would show up. I was always right. Unavoidably, words spread that I was a psychic that had foretold what would happen, week and week without fail.

One week, though, I had a customer late one Friday evening and that customer sort of blemished my record; I had not foretold him. Assuming this customer was just a fluke, I discarded his whole appearance. Inconsistent data are no data as far I was concerned. How can you be a successful psychic if your data base is not correct?

Came the dawn of the following Monday. More customers

showed up which was very bewildering to me as a psychic. My reputation as a psychic was rapidly and surely being ruined. And for what? Did they really need a psychic?

So, how to be foretelling and still be accepted as a foreteller? The answer, of course is, that whatever is obvious is obvious and hence does not need any explanations. In other phrases, the first weeks of a foreteller's foretelling are necessarily foretold by other psychics because the future is the same no matter who does the foretelling or foretelling would not be possible, at least not consistent foretelling. In regard to this circular argument, answers can be found anywhere on the periphery of the reasoning circle.

But, back to the beginning to arrive at the conclusion which is that to be a psychic it is enough to be psychic. No wonder, then, that eventually that office fronting a busy thoroughfare did a thriving business as any psychic could have foretold.

Once you get a reputation, it is impossible to shake it off - no matter what.

Bellyview Versus Bellvue

THE IDEA HAS been ventured that the beast of administrations is the soft underbelly of US education. At ground level, the grunts have the bellyview of the beast while the upper echelons can ride on the back of the beast. The view at ground level, with its circumscribed horizon, is toward survival; not to be crushed by the feet of the beast. The view from the back of the beast is toward Bellevue. That is, the generic name for wealth, respect, and prestige, despite its connotation - in some places - of mental distress or malfunction.

Educational administrators would rather not bother with teachers and students, only in some abstract sense are these two groups necessary for education. The purpose of education is to support educational administration which is more interesting and rewarding. Why bother with people who only want to teach; those people with no ambition, those people barely qualified to grip pieces of chalk and doodle on blackboards.

Consider students. Only a few are interested in learning educational administration. They seem to be more interested in subjects like computers, science, art, literature, sports, films, etc, all activities that dull your mind. The ideal situation would probably be one administrator per student, but society seems to hold on to a different, and misplaced, point of view due to their lack of understanding of educational administration.

Good educational administration requires good or excellent pay; that is the only way to attract qualified administrators. This in turn requires that teachers' salaries must be kept as low as possible. The most cost-effective schoolteachers are part-timers who are short of any educational administration credentials and who are supported financially by family and friends. The least cost-effective teachers are those who, despite all efforts of educational administrations, persist in continuing to teach year after year despite the best efforts of educational administrators in urging them to pursue other careers outside education or at least show some ambition to become educational administrators.

So, like an elephant the beast lumbers on, stepping on the ground-level grunts while carrying on its back the upper echelons toward their view of Bellevue. The grunts must be satisfied with the bellyview.

November 13th 2004

A Big Bang

THE STICK COMPANY makes - not surprisingly - sticks. Big ones and little ones, short ones and long ones, heavy ones and light ones. The history of the company is somewhat murky in that none of the founders left any direct proof that they had started the company nor that they had even ever lived. The few files from the initial phase of the company's existence seemed to have gone up in smoke, literally. There was a big fire, so big in fact that it was covered by the national and international media. Puzzling questions came up now and then and later about the company and its man power. Among them were: Where are the people who operated it? Who owned it? Where are they now if they were not at the company headquarters? Can anybody remember if they had ever worked at the company? Did the company have any branches anywhere else?

But, back to the big fire; after the fire had cooled down, there was a search for bodies but none were ever found. Neither were there any melted-down wedding rings or any remnants of metallic devices used to hold the parts of shoes together. Bodies or no bodies, rings or no rings, it was nevertheless decided to have a memorial event. Hundreds of mourners attended; they came from next door to the company as well as from far, far away. Strangely, only a few mourners noticed that they did not know each other and fewer yet did not know why they were attending the memorial. From casual small talks among those few, it could be concluded that all of them were unemployed.

That was 25 years ago. By now, the Stick Company was back in business as never before making all those sticks, long and short, heavy and light, big and small and so on. As the company gained its former stature as *the* stick company, it was determined by somebody somewhere that there was to be a memorial event to whatever happened a quarter of a century ago at that big fire. For some reason, I was appointed to be a member of the planning committee. It was probably due to my outstanding position within the community. Even so, I had hardly ever been on any civic committees of any kind and I was not quite sure what to expect. It was such an unusual assignment. On the other hand, I had had an experience lately that should make up for my inexperience. One of my dreams was so unusual that it gathered public inquiries as was only proper even though I felt that it was an invasion of my privacy. But, I insisted that I was to be a member of a board of inquiry as opposed to a planning committee. The details of such a dream should not get lost in the intricacies and unexpected twists and turns of committee work.

The dream begins with a big bang that keeps banging away, bringing activity to where before there had been nothing at all. It was as if the universe as we know it today had been created in my head and then spread outwards to the great unknown. As the proceedings of my board of inquiry advanced, there was a question whether this big bang that kept on banging away, had any similarity with the big fire at the Stick Company. For example, there were no traces of human remains, not even melted-down wedding rings or nails used to hold shoes together and all the other stuff you expect to find after a fire such as scorched fragments of baby pictures and other items of sentimental value. In short, it was if humanity had not yet made its appearance in the universe. And yet, the Stick Company was there and somebody had to have run the business and produce all those sticks that the company was supposed to be making. Next, all this business of people not knowing each other and yet all of them coming to the same place at the same time, the place of the memorial, and being interested in more or less the same thing.

And here we are 25 years later or sooner and we have to acknowledge there is more than an accidental connection between the Stick Company and the dream in my head that was so vivid that so many felt they had to look at it. It is true, of course, that as a general proposition, the universe doesn't really want to look at itself; it is too busy looking at something else. Once again, we have to acknowledge that not everything is as obvious as we want it to be. That dream in my head, or mind, seems to have ignited the universe's creation. From which it followed that committees of inquiry sort of joined the two world views together. It is easy to conjecture that since there is only one I, there must be other I's as well. But, that is like saying that the creation happened only once or at least there was only one creator per universe.

To sort of tie all this together, most of us - as far as we know - can agree that it is a lot to disagree about even within such mundane concepts as the number of sticks and the number of universes. It was as if we are all getting the short end of the stick as they say. If you think that these muses are strange, consider them as poems, one after another, joined together at their hips as it were. It has been postulated that the universe as we know it, has been carved out of a piece of wood, taken from a hockey stick. That seems at least as plausible as other creation myths such as the one that speaks of the long end of a stick. Never mind, if you don't like the universe you live in, move to another.

Blocks

A WRITER SUFFERED unfortunate incidents. First, there was a writer's block; nothing could be written. Next came a reader's block; nothing could be read.

A mathematician friend thought he had found a solution. He remembered the phrase: "I am not not happy" which necessarily means that "I am happy". A negation of a negation cancels each other. Applied to the writer's predicament, "block block" should cancel each other. Hence, the mathematician went on his way to inform the writer that he had no blockage.

Unfortunately, before the mathematician could reach the writer with the good news, the writer suffered a third block. This was a general block; nothing could be done or undone, seen or unseen, heard and unheard, and so on.

The mathematician now had to ponder the new "block block block" situation that logically should be equivalent to "block". In other words, the writer should now be able to pick the block to suffer from, the mathematician concluded.

The writer could not really comprehend the message from the mathematician, suffering as he did from a general block. The mathematician suggested that if the writer could, somehow, get a fourth block, everything would be as before.

The writer decided, somehow, to whack his head with a piece

of two-by-four, in other words a wooden block. Thus, the writer relieved himself from all his blocks and he lived happily ever after. The writer took the precaution of always carrying with him a sturdy piece of wood. The only lasting effect from his ordeal were a clear mind and the ability to speak softly.

Moral: If you must speak softly, carry a big stick.

Note: Not in any way inspired by Theodore Roosevelt's advice: "Speak softly, but carry a big stick."

A Business Paradox

SUPPOSE A CORPORATION, at intervals and over time, had a program of buying up its own shares. Part of the reason for this was to raise the share prices; (who likes to have $1 or $2 shares when you can have $20 shares, say). Another reason is to impress the financial analysts; it certainly gives the impression that the upper-level management has the utmost confidence in the corporation's future and that would entice the analysts and the average investor to buy its shares which further raises the share price. It is a win-win situation for everybody. In the fullness of time, the day arrived when the corporation had bought back all its shares. Put another way, the corporation now owned itself. The morning after the day that the corporation owned itself one hundred percent, all the employees showed up as well as the upper management and the board of directors. Everybody wanted to know what the corporation was up to. As a courtesy to the corporation, the offices of the president and the chairman of the board had been vacated and combined into one really big office with as many secretaries as possible. After this self-less effort, everything came to a standstill. What instructions would emanate from the big office? How would any instructions be distributed? To whom? How could you ask the corporation for a raise? Who would you ask for permission to take a day off?

Despite all the unanswered questions, nothing happened the

morning after that memorable day. Not getting any instructions to the contrary, most of the employees took the usual lunch break; some adding a few minutes just to test the reaction of the corporation. In the afternoon, many began to miss the benevolent dictator, the CEO who received incentive pay for making everybody else miserable.

The first day had passed and the corporation which owned itself still existed even though very little had emanated from the big office. The little bits and pieces that emanated were probably due to a secretary or two trying to have something to do. The corporation which owned itself still had not found its own voice. The general feeling was that the corporation had to do something with respect to the Securities and Exchange Commission or SEC. That agency required that anybody owning more than five percent of a corporation must so declare. In this case, the corporation which owned itself would have to report one hundred percent. What would the SEC say? Could the agency grasp the paradox of a corporation owning itself?

After days of uncertainty, the corporation which owned itself added other days of uncertainty except for the one or two secretaries who apparently had made some connection with the corporation somehow. The paradox of a corporation owning itself began to get national attention. Out of the blue as they say, came news that due to this national attention, individuals had ransacked their families' storage trunks to find a few stock certificates here and there, issued before the SEC even existed. Imagine being that old. On the other hand, the corporation did no longer own itself completely. The corporation which almost owned itself decided, all by itself, that it would sell itself to the public. There emanated from the Big Office what would be the most creative, the most visionary, the most sensible, the most generous, the most unselfish decision in the recent annals of the corporate world.

The Butler Did It

THE LION, THE King of Beasts, had been taught to walk on his hind legs and to use his front legs and paws as well as any human used his arms and hands. The Lion was dressed in a butler's suit and he served the guests with finesse and aplomb. He carved the roast, never spilled a drop of sauce, served the wine and gave the ladies his special attention.

His butler impersonation was the highlight of the circus' performance. The lion tamer was sitting at the head of the table, his wife at the other end and assorted circus employees and volunteers were sitting at the two other sides. The lion tamer kept his whip discreetly in his lap, hidden by the tablecloth. His silvery pistol was made in the shape of a spoon and placed among the silverware at his plate. But Simba the Butler was always the perfect gentleman; he had never given a single guest a single scratch.

This evening, the Lion, the King of Beasts, did not feel his best. His lower back was aching, his paws were hurting, and the butler's suit felt tighter than ever. The last dish to be served was blueberry pie. As the Lion was about to cut the pie into eight pieces before serving, he happened to glance at his tamer and noticed his self-satisfied, even arrogant expression.

So, the Lion did what every self-respecting butler would do under the circumstances. He took the pie and threw it into the face of the lion tamer.

Even the lion tamer had to admit that it was a good idea. Never had their performance been more appreciated by the audience.

Moral: Smirk And Ye Shall Be Smirked.
(T.T.; 1977)

The Butterfly Effect

PREDICTABILITY: DOES THE flap of a butterfly's wings in Brazil set off a tornado in Texas? Title of a paper by Edward N. Lorenz given to the American Association for the Advancement of Science, Washington DC, 29 December 1979.

Ever since I became aware of the butterfly effect, I have been reluctant to flap my arms. Comparing my magnitude to a butterfly's magnitude, it is almost mandatory for me to move as little as possible lest some windblown disasters wreak their havoc on the other side of the globe, more or less.

Not so my friend Ishmael. He couldn't care less, even less than less. After all, as he put it, as long as nothing happens in his environs everything is OK. Why should he care if others get blown away far, far away? Besides, it is probably just a matter of chance anyway. Being unpredictable, there are ways to live with it or there are ways to live without it. Being skeptical, I tended to agree with him even as I disagreed with him.

Ishmael told me a story about his maternal grandfather. Ishmael always tells me a story of this maternal grandfather whenever he gets stuck with some uncertainty. The story, more or less, is this: Grandpa got interested in ants. One day he followed an ant as it hurried about doing its chores as best it could. His ant was marching with about half of the ants in the colony (it was assumed), the other half was marching in the opposite direction. Of course, there were contacts now and then between the two columns mostly checking that the ants had the proper credentials. Any non-colony ants were promptly assassinated. All of a sudden, Grandpa's ant and its associates disappeared into a hole in the ground. Grandpa carefully removed some soil hoping to discover what happened underground. All that Grandpa could find was a U-turn; that is, his ant and the others made a U-turn and emerged from the hole in the ground and marched in a direction opposite to their previous direction. Grandpa watched his ant as it kept on going, eventually disappearing into another hole in the ground. Soil was removed and another U-turn was discovered. That was the story. As I had noticed over the years, Ishmael's stories, inherited from his maternal grandfather, always dealt with ants. His stories inherited from his paternal grandfather, on the other hand, were about bees and honey.

Now I felt that I should make a contribution to the treasure trove of my friend Ishmael's stories. I remembered that two of my grandparents had a short but colorful history. As soon as they were married, both very young, they both disappeared. I never understood how my grandparents could have disappeared while at the same time my parents, years later, were able to produce me; it seemed like a missing-link situation to me. So I asked my mother, how come all this? She answered very vaguely that a tornado in Texas had something to do with it. She told me even more vaguely that the family could trace its lineage to Pedro, the first emperor of Brazil.

Some of these events, of course, are better imagined that scrutinized. Why should ants build structures underground which allow them to make U-turns? Yet, humankind is doing that every day of the year. What connections are there between tornados in Texas, butterfly wings in Brazil and the march of ants between two holes in the ground? While not obvious, the connections are there for those who can imagine the connections.

Communal Living

I had a house with many rooms, but I was alone.

I met the girl of my dreams. Then we were two.

The girl of my dreams met the man of her dreams. Then we were three.

We needed a housekeeper. Then we were four.

The husband of the housekeeper had no place to live. Then we were five.

A young pregnant girl had been thrown out of her parents' home. Then we were six.

The boy friend of the pregnant girl wanted to be near her. Then we were seven.

The housing inspector for the city wanted something to inspect. Then we were eight.

Having an inspector on the premises, I hired a carpenter. Then we were nine.

The inspector took an interest in the housekeeper. Then we were still nine.

The housekeeper wanted help so I hired a cook. Then we were ten.

The cook preferred to cook for the girl of my dreams. Then we were still ten.

The carpenter built the largest room of the house; he wanted the housekeeper to move in with him. Then we were still ten.

A middle-aged professor from the nearby university wanted to research communal living. Then we were eleven.

Assuming that stuff is cheaper by the dozen, I hired an accountant. Then we were twelve.

The City told the housing inspector to stop inspecting the house. Then we were eleven.

The man of my girl's dreams decided to move next door where it was not so crowded. Then we were ten.

The accountant questioned the expenses of the carpenter; the carpenter got annoyed and hired on as a carpenter next door. Then we were nine.

The middle-aged professor decided to move next door where there were more females to study. Then we were eight.

The boy friend of the pregnant girl moved out; he could not persuade the girl that they should make better use of her pregnancy. Then we were seven.

The accountant lost interest when he sensed that a declining number of persons meant declining numbers. Then we were six.

The housekeeper's husband saw better opportunities elsewhere. Then we were five.

The four remaining guests felt that communal living was OK as long as the work was done by somebody else.

And now I have this enormous house all by myself. Once again I am alone. But, all I have to do is to clean up the house and invite the next influx.

> **Moral:** See "The Tragedy of the Commons" by Garrett Hardin, Science, Dec. 13, 1968.

> < ...*From the archives* ...>

Crime And Embarrassment

DAD, WHY ARE you not in prison? How can you answer a question like that from a little boy? True, I carry suitcases full of legal tender, bring them home for safekeeping and now and then take out a bill or two for groceries. We, my wife, that little boy and I, live in very modest quarters, not more than two bedrooms at best. Our car is more than five years old and is rather beat up. We hardly ever travel except when I have to make errands to straighten out some family business deals. It is called keeping a low profile, meaning that in my line of work you should never stand out in any way. Ideally, you should be so ordinary that nobody would suspect you of anything. No wonder that this kind of life is pretty boring for the wife and the kid so the two of them look at television a lot. I try to convince them that all that cash in all those suitcases in the closets will one day be ours, more or less, if we behave ourselves for the next twenty years or so when I am due for mandatory retirement.

But, back to the kid's question "How come you are not in prison, Dad?" Questions like that are asked in many families because television and even movies try to teach the new generation that crime does not pay. At the end of any television crime show, all the crooks are arrested and sent to prison and they are never heard from again. My associates and I are amused. The cops, in real life, hardly ever catch anybody. In my opinion, those who call themselves members of law enforcement spend their time looking at television crime shows in the evening just to feel good until the next morning when they have to go to work and to confront real life.

Let me give you some real-life cases picked at random from my own experience. Consider the case of the petting rabbits. We train each rabbit to run after Brinks armored trucks. When the truck stops and the two guys emerge, they cannot resist petting the rabbit whose fur is saturated with a nerve-gas potion. The guards promptly pass out and all we have to do is to take the sacks of cash and who knows what else. As is obvious, two of us wear Brinks uniforms and in the rush of everyday life nobody notices anything unusually, not even the presence of a rabbit. We drive away from the crime scene at a speed that the rabbit can handle. At the end of the affair, we throw the rabbit a few carrots for work well done. While the rabbit is preoccupied, we spray it with a nerve-gas antidote. Good running rabbits are hard to find these days and their training is vigorous, but it is worth the effort. The Brinks guys eventually come out for their coma. They are too embarrassed to mention the rabbit. Law enforcement officials scratch their heads and assign the case to a cold file somewhere.

Next, consider the case of the hollow tree trunks. You don't kidnap the President; you kidnap those who guard him, that is, the agents of the Secret Service. The basic flaw in the strategy of guarding the President is that nobody guards the agents. Not so long ago, we had a President who loved the rustic life. He bought himself a ranch at a few thousand feet elevation. The President loved chopping wood, splitting rails and building fences. The ranch was almost surrounded by a National Forest where some logging was allowed. There were stands of age-old growth, trees that had survived a succession of forest fires. The result was trees with hollow trunks were rather common but that was only obvious after a tree was harvested. The family hired an arborist to lend his expertise in selecting the hollow trees we were interested in. The arborist and his associates had no trouble blending into the logging business helped by a rather generous fee, of course. All we were interested in, as far as the Secret service was concerned, was timber and taking an occasional candid photo of the President.

The Secret Service agents were, for the most part, bored. Watching the chief executive swinging his ax has limited appeal after a while. In their off hours, the agents, male and female, took hikes in the National Forest to relax with themselves or with a proper mate. One day, our team nabbed two agents and put them in aluminum canisters which were then fit into the hollows of two harvested trees. Why aluminum? The arborist wouldn't tell us. Anyway, the canisters were well equipped so that hardly any survival skills were necessary. We mixed those two logs in with the other logs, passed inspection by the National Forest rangers and we were on our merry way. Please note that you don't kidnap just one agent. If only one was missing, it would probably be shrugged off as a disgruntled agent heading for Canada, there to write his memoirs. But, if two or more agents disappeared at the same time, then even the Secret Service begins to wonder and then to wonder some more.

We dropped off the two agents in their canisters at some pre-selected site and then in various ways asked for a generous ransom. With no fuss, the Federals paid up. The millions that we collected were probably marked or their serial numbers recorded or both. To be on the safe side, we sold our millions for half the face value to another family who was willing to take that small risk. If law enforcement ever solved the case, they would never dare to bring it to court. If we were brought to trial, how could they possibly go public with the Secret Service agents assigned to guard the President who had been held in hollow tree trunks for ransom? They would be laughed off the map, so to speak. They couldn't possibly withstand the embarrassment. So they settled.

You don't rob banks; that's for amateurs. You rob those who rob banks. How do you know who robs banks? -- By observation, mostly. You begin by getting to know some part of the city. In time, you will notice some guys drifting from bank to bank, pretending to do some bank business. In a rational society, you go to a commercial bank and a savings-and-loan once in a while. Those who visit two or more banks in a single day for many weeks are potential targets. If the suckers have the nerve, they will strike sooner or later.

While the amateurs are in the planning stages, we just relax and soon they will be doing their business with a bank in your area of surveillance. The papers, the newscasts, the men and women of the public will scream bloody murder and demand the arrest of these despicable creatures who are stealing their money. Be patient, wait until the robbers have accumulated a worth-while kitty. To illustrate, our family has the amateurs under observation to figure out the opportune time to strike. Sooner or later, they will call out for pizzas. We rob the delivery person, using a gaseous substance that will put him or her under for a while and sprinkle the pizzas with generous amounts of stuff certified to keep the digesters sleeping for a day or two. One of us put on a delivery uniform, ring the bell and we are all set. Law enforcement has plenty of time to catch the robbers with the information from the delivery person. The amateurs go to prison and we get the cash. An alternate way to get the cash is to rent an apartment next to the amateurs' hideout. While they are out scouting for their next opportunity, we kick a hole in the apartments' common wall. To finish the job, we obviously take their accumulated loot. All we lost was a month's rent for the apartment and living expenses.

Back to the theme again; in the-hole-in-wall method, the amateurs have no recourse. They cannot complain to the police nor can they complain to any of the families since they operate outside the structure of the anti-law enforcement. The hole-in-the-wall method should embarrass them enough to quit their thieving ways and leave crime to the professionals. Our families don't worry; there are always new recruits working their way up the organization ladders where they get rigorous training in all aspects of the business. Amateurs are not tolerated.

As I approach mandatory retirement after 20 years of service, there is one caper I would dearly like to organize, namely some embarrassing incidents for those film and television producers who insist that crime doesn't pay. Somehow, I will promote scripts that are so good that all the producers will clamor for them and will willingly pay millions for them. All you have to do is to start rumors by paying a number of people who have the gift of gab. As the rumors spread, the scripts are auctioned off at higher and higher prices. The higher the numbers get, the higher gets the next number. The producers pay us millions and as the scripts go into production, the paper they are printed on disintegrates originals as well as copies. The scripts are reduced to dustpans of cellulose. Nobody has actually read any of the scripts since reading is delegated to assistants who in turn delegate the reading to their assistants until there are no assistants left to read anything. Since nobody has actually read anything, there is no memory of what was in the scripts. If you were a producer, wouldn't you be embarrassed if all your costly scripts turned to dust? You would, but they wouldn't. An alternate scenario would be that all the paper used in the entertainment industry by the truckload would simply crumble into dust, sort of like the films preserved on acetate nitrate. That would really be embarrassing. But, how would you do it? Be patient, I'm working on it.

So son, we have come a long way from the time you were a little boy asking me: "Why aren't you in prison, Dad?" when we were still living in that crummy cold-water flat. As you can see, all the waiting for better times has now paid off big. As you know, reading these notes jotted down in my own private code, these incidents from my almost 20 years in the business will show you that crime does pay. You will do very well as long as you can embarrass enough people. Keep that e-word in mind when you take my place in the family.

Also, always take advantage of the unexpected. You wouldn't embarrass me unexpectedly, would you?

P.S.: Son, feel free to use any or all the capers I have outlined here as well as those that I have transmitted to you orally over the years. Why don't you go into show business? With all these never-done-before ideas of mine, add yours and you will never cease to embarrass people and to profit from it.

Dark And Bright

LITERARY CRITICS HAVE agreed that the worst first sentence of a novel in the modern era is: "It was a dark and stormy night". Compare this sentence to: "It was a bright and sunny day". This sentence has not met any ridicule from the critics; maybe they are just unaware of it, or maybe critics don't concern themselves with any lighthearted stuff.

A publisher who published doom-and-gloom novels persuaded himself that a sunny and upbeat novel might sell even more copies than his usual gloomy stuff. His publishing house announced a literary competition; open to all, for the best novel. The basic requirement was that the sentence: "It was a bright and sunny day", had to be the first sentence of the submitted novel. Also, the rest of it should reflect the upbeat and sunny feeling of that first sentence.

Time passed and novels began to trickle in. The publisher took a random sample and checked the first few sentences and sometimes the last sentence or two. Many authors began with: "It was a bright and sunny day, but it was followed by a dark and stormy night". Most of the novels checked in the first batch, followed the ruts in the usual gloom-and-doom tradition after the first sentence.

Somewhat discouraged, the publisher waited a few weeks before he took a second sample from the incoming novel stream. The beginnings of these reflected an effort to be more lighthearted, but by the fifth or sixth sentence they slipped back into the mainstream. A typical scene at that stage was: "He cut her throat. She was surprised. She slipped on a pool of her own blood. She fell and was fatally wounded when the stiletto heels of her shoes pierced her heart. Outside, it was a bright and sunny day."

By now, even more discouraged, the publisher waited several weeks before he dipped his hands into the novel stream again for a third sample. He thought that love-making activities of a young, beautiful couple would bring a bright and sunny feeling to the narrative. The closest to this ideal he could find was this paragraph: "Barely able to walk, barely able to erect himself and something else too, he staggered toward the bed with something sweet in it. As he reached the bed, he grabbed that sweet something and embraced a lumpy featherbed." The publisher, perhaps recognizing his own physical condition, became consumed with rage. "There will be no sex scenes featuring the elderly in my books", he screamed.

He began to falter in his drive toward the bright and the sunny. Maybe gloom-and-doom stories had a point after all, he thought. If bright and sunny stuff seemed to be no different from the gloom-and-doom stuff, what was the point in pretending that there were two genres in literature when there is really only one?

The publisher decided to give the novel competition one last chance. He picked up the very last submitted one from the slush pile and read the last paragraph: "At the conclusion of this bright and sunny day, Halvar Mars and Marthas Mars decided to continue living together as husband and wife for the next few weeks". "Who the hell are Halvar and Marthas Mars?" thought the publisher. "I give up!"

Moral: In high-quality literature, bright is dark and sunny is stormy.

Note: First used by Edward Bulwer-Lytton (1803-1873) in his novel "Paul Clifford" (1830).

(an interruption)

Dialogues

A: I hit my head.

B: Did you walk into a low beam?

A: No, I didn't have the time to wait for a beam, so I hit my head with a hammer.

C: When you say "time and time again", what do you mean?

D: What do *you* mean? Do you mean concurrently or consecutively?

C: No, I mean the average of the two.

E: I shot myself in the foot.

F: Why did you do that?

E: Because it was there.

G: Is it true that an old hen is younger than a middle-aged dog?

H: Why do you want to know?

G: Because, if I can't answer an easy question, how can I answer anything?

I: He's all screwed up.

J: Why do you say that?

I: Because he's so normal.

K: Who is the actress who played the lead in Disney's "Cinderella?"

L: I'm sorry to inform you that after the picture was completed she was erased.

K: How was I supposed to know that?

M: Suppose you get a question you can't answer?

N: Ask what the answer is; that's why they asked the question.

M: In other words, if you can't answer then invent the question?

Digging Up, Digging Down

THE OTHER DAY I had to go to my uncle's place to baby-sit his aunt. My overnight stay included sleeping on a bed in a small room, so small that there was hardly any room for a bed. Yet, I never slept as well anywhere else, including my own bed in my own room. I speculated a lot on why that should be. I told my family, my theory was, that it was because my legs were closer to the walls in that smallish room.

The whole family seemed to get upset by that speculation. "Why can't you do something useful?" they asked. For instance, they wanted me to dig up the backyard instead of reading books as was my wont. About the digging, I told them, that before I could do that I had to read a book on how to dig up a backyard. Besides, didn't they really mean digging down? While I read that book, I could not dig obviously. I further pointed out that I also had to read a book that explained how to read a book properly. Out of curiosity, I also wanted to read a book that explained how a book was created, or manufactured, if you will. Digging the backyard either up or down or both would require a lot of mental preparation.

The members of my family thought otherwise. Most of them maintained that the only preparation I needed was to put my hands on a spade of suitable sturdiness and then start digging. To me, this obsession of theirs that I should dig up or down in the backyard was rather strange. It was at least equally strange compared to the fact that

I slept so well at my uncle's place while babysitting his aunt just because my legs were responding so well to the closeness of walls.

The family members could not understand why I spent so many nights at my uncle's place just to babysit his aunt. I told them that I felt I owed that to him as well as to her. Both had been very nice to me. For example, they had never asked me to dig up their backyards and the reason for that was, it was no point to it, since I was babysitting my uncle's aunt. In other words, I was too busy to dig something up or down just because it might be important to somebody else.

These somebody elses have always, or at least usually, caused me a lot of trouble as long as I can remember. Do that and do this and then do this and do that. At times, it is very hard to distinguish between these somebody elses and members of my family. Just about the only difference between those two groups is that the somebody elses do not ask me to dig in their backyards. Also, they don't seem to mind either that I read books. Recently, I read a book on family relations that seemed to say that a member of a family should do what the other family members want that single person to do, all in the name of harmony. I would tend to agree with that except that I should not be required to dig up or down in anybody's backyard; leave that to somebody else.

Life, if not hard, is at least confusing. No matter how many times I baby sit my uncle's aunt, it never seems to be enough; there never seems to be a retirement in my future. Similarly, after a certain number of backyard diggings one should be able to retire from that. I don't even know if I would like to be retired; it would be so different from what I have gotten used to. If I were to retire I would tell my family members, please don't bother me anymore with any of your hare-brained schemes. I am not going to dig up or down anything anymore. And that is final.

Moral: Some things are meant to be confusing.

Dropping Babies

BEING A POLITICIAN poses many hazards. One of them is how to handle babies. Parents like to take pictures of their babies in the arms of a politician; who knows; one of them may win the election and be the next president of the United States. There is some short-term immortality associated with that. And the babes in arms can point to, sometime in the future, the pictures of the event in their photo album as their claim to fame.

Nevertheless, holding babies is one of the hazards. Men by nature are awkward handling babies and so far only men have been elected presidents even after women got the right to vote in 1920. Until recently, no candidate for the presidency had ever dropped a baby, at least according to official records. Early in the current election season, however, one candidate did drop a baby; the baby landed on some soft turf and suffered no apparent damage. Even so, that candidate was no longer deemed fit to be president by the voters of his party in the very early primaries. The other party, of course, could hardly hide their glee in having eliminated a formidable opponent that early in the game. Alas, according to an old proverb, "pride goes before a fall".

The glee of the opposition party did not last very long. One day, twins were deposited in the arms of their leading candidate and, incredibly, the politician dropped them both. As way of explanation, the candidate maintained that he had been spooked by some operatives of the other party. Unofficially, it was caused by a bunch of young, strutting females shouldering themselves into the picture-taking proceedings, thus reducing the candidate's attention to the twins. This time the babies landed on a hardwood floor, it was reported, and there was some concern that they had been seriously hurt. A medical team of the candidate's party maintained that the babies had not been hurt in any way, the principal reason being that the spot of the hardwood floor where they fell was carpeted. A medical team of the opposition party maintained that the twins had suffered severe internal injuries. Anyway, the leading candidate who had dropped the twins lost the next primaries and would not become president.

The primary season came to an end. The final phase of the presidential election campaign began, but the two parties were still arguing about the baby droppings. The single-baby party maintained that dropping two babies was much worse than dropping just one baby. The two-baby party insisted that a drop is a drop is a drop and besides the twins weren't hurt at all as was evident from several pictures of the two at play somewhere. Despite all the arguing, the two parties agreed that since holding babies was an integral part of the electioneering process, it could not be banished. Instead, caution had to be paid to avoid any spooking of the candidates. Wherever the politicians appeared henceforward, there were no holding of babies unless they were standing on cushions surrounded by elderly women who had been certified as mothers.

Both parties got a nasty surprise when a third-party candidate appeared, threatening the election of candidates of either of the two parties. Operatives of the two principal parties got together to scheme something out. Suppose, it was suggested, that they could locate a set of triplets, somehow get them into the arms of the candidate, then somehow spooking the third-party candidate into dropping them. Indeed, all this came to pass and the triplet candidate was eliminated. Henceforth, no more babies were dropped.

Moral: Elections may be won or lost by falling babies.

Early Bird Got His Worm

EARLY BIRD WAS born quite prematurely, but he got over it. No wonder, then, that he was never anything but "Early" to his family and his contemporaries. He grew up in a conventional way in a conventional family with conventional ideas. The family's energies were devoted to business and family members were expected to devote themselves to its businesses and to increase the family's wealth which was substantial.

Early, however, grew up to detest business and to love worms of all kinds. To him, any worm was a good worm. Early also grew up to detest birds; these pathetic remnants of the dinosaur age, these killers of worms, these despoilers of statues, these flighty wanderers ignoring earthly concerns, these dead ends of evolution. To him, all birds were fit to be eradicated. Worms, in contrast, were simple, noble creatures; these plowers of earth, these faithful servants, these founding species of evolution. His family, naturally, was horrified at the prospect of one of its members getting into the worm business. Some attributed Early's peculiar interest to be the obvious effects on him of his very premature birth. Early's mother, of course, did not agree since the family tended to blame her because of her irregular hours, her strenuous exercises, and her minimal appetite, all contributing to her too slender body. The opinion of some was that if Early as a fetus had been growing in more comfortable surroundings and had not been surrounded by hard muscles when soft layers of fat would have been more beneficial, he would have turned out differently. Later in life, Early held the opposite view; by being born prematurely he had been given a head start in getting into the worm business.

Family members wondered, how can you have business dealings with worms? Early, however, knew that they were trying to make him look foolish, phrasing their question as if worms were deaf and dumb. Through kindergarten, grammar school, high school, college, and graduate study, he was devoted to his worm research. Early's ambition was to genetically create species of worms that would put ordinary worms to shame, in a metaphorical sense. Ordinary worms would always have his deepest respect.

Early, by now Dr. Bird, had many new types of worms in mind. The obvious first step was a class of worms that could be introduced into human veins and arteries so that they could eat away and hence clean out all kinds of deposits, plaques and whatnot. Some of his fellow researchers suggested that the worms themselves would be obstacles to proper blood flow. Besides, what worms eat and digest would then have to be excreted. Early's retort was that any worm debris would be blood soluble. Later, Early announced that he had developed breeds of intelligent worms so small that the blood flows would hardly notice their presence. Dr. Bird further envisioned the creation of other types of worms for other purposes, such as cleaning out debris in brains and repairing spinal cords.

Dr. Bird received patents for all his genetically engineered worms and wealth was pouring in. His family now realized that Early's premature birth had been a blessing; the wealth poured in several months earlier than otherwise would have been possible.

As one capstone of his incredible life, work, and worm research, Dr. Early was awarded a Nobel Price. Even more glorious was the Golden Worm Award from the Invertebrate Society.

Moral: We are all worms - evolutionary speaking

The Echo Diet

A FELLOW BY the name of Echo had an enormous bulk and a weight of many hundred pounds. If you had assigned a hundred pounds to each finger on one hand, you would have to add some fingers from the other hand to arrive at an estimate of his weight. His weight depressed him so much that he decided to commit suicide. His mind may have resided in a lot of blubber, but it was keen. If he were to commit suicide, he would device a method that was so original and so unconventional that it would be his legacy to the ages.

Echo was partially inspired by prison movies where the condemned are confined in cages and under constant surveillance waiting for their walk to the death chamber. Those cages have vertical steel bars imbedded in reinforced concrete on the floor and the ceiling. They have a narrow door with a solid padlock. Another inspiration was the gorilla cages at most zoos. So, Echo gathered together all the necessary materials and carried them all by himself to some god-forsaken patch of land beyond most traces of civilization. He constructed his prison cell, slammed its door shut, turned the key in the padlock and threw that key as far away from his cage as he could. There was no hope of ever retrieving it.

Days and nights went by. Echo half-remembered an estimate that human beings would die within ten days if they were denied both food and water. If only water was available, they would die after about thirty days. These thoughts of water and food led Echo to observe that during the night, dew condensed on the steel bars of his cage. He could lick that dew off the bars and indeed he did. Night and day, some food arrived on the wings and the feet of insects, providing frequent snacks. As Echo became more and more adept at survival, the day of his execution kept receding into the future.

This dew-and-insect diet, plus the gradual withdrawal of fat from his blubber, gave him enough nourishment to keep on living. As he kept on living, he got thinner and thinner, shedding hundreds of pounds. Echo, even with his keen mind, had not anticipated such an outcome. One day, he realized that he was thin enough to squeeze himself sideways through the gap between two adjacent steel bars. The temptation to do so became too great to resist. Echo decided to go back to civilization and devise a more original, unconventional and fool-proof method of committing suicide. On the other hand he thought a little bit later, now that he was slim enough to escape from a gorilla's cage, then maybe he was onto something with his dew-and-insect diet. He would promote his Echo Diet Plan. He still had his cage, good as new, on some patch of godforsaken land almost beyond civilization. Echo decided to rent out his cage, then throw away the key. All the renter had to do was to wait to reach a weight of about a hundred to two hundred pounds or so, depending on the spacing between the steel bars. Then they could squeeze themselves out of the cage and walk back to civilization. The Echo Diet Plan became so popular that he built steel cages in all fifty states and rented them out - for a hefty fee, of course.

Moral: Don't despair; there is a diet for everybody ...almost.

Random Thoughts On Educational Administrators

WHILE MOST TEACH, some administrate. An administrator is, by education, a teacher but he or she does not want to teach. True, most of them have to start at the bottom - in their view - as teachers, but they don't want to teach. These species are easy to recognize. They are eager to serve on any committee that comes along or they create their own committees. The subjects and the substance to be dealt with are irrelevant. In addition to committees, a special assignment is a big building block. You get to touch, at times, those who are above you; you want to know their names and foibles and you want them to remember your name but not your foibles - only your strength of character and your enthusiasm and willingness to agree with anything coming down from above.

Eventually, one of the eager beavers gets to be the assistant to an assistant in the mid administration structure. Finally, you are relieved of the repetitive chore of doing any teaching. As you gradually rise in the administration you still have to deal with teachers, but now you can explain to them how to teach. All this explaining leads to an ever greater and greater proficiency in the art of teaching teachers; of course, to teach teachers is not easy; they are set in their ways and they seem to resent advice from non-teachers even from those in the educational administration structure. If you don't have structure, what have you? Further, it is irrefutable that those who administrate would not have achieved their position in the administrative hierarchy if they had not been excellent teachers.

When teachers fail, as they often do, an administrator has to step in to address student concerns. Students, of course, are the mothers' milk of education (to paraphrase Jesse Unruh). The more students, the more funding you get from the state. The educational administration structure needs money. How many teachers realize this?

Electrons, The Conservation Thereof

CIVILIZATION IS EXPERIENCING the very tail end of the Age of Oil; as we know, the world is running out of oil. At the same time, we are now at the beginning of the Age of the Electron and already we are at a point where we may be running out of electrons. There are only so many electrons in the universe and when they are all used up there are no more. A similar situation occurs with respect to photons. Fortunately, the Sun can provide the necessary photons for a few more years. Obviously, we must begin to plan ahead.

But, back to our primary concern, the imminent shortage of electrons; consider computers, they are a constant drain of valuable electrons. Consider telephones, consider farming, consider just about any device used in our manufacturing sectors. Who knows how many electrons are used up just to produce the average-size car, not to speak of the average-size locomotive? Even smaller items such as candy bars, nail and shoe polish and baby shoes take their toll on the electron supply.

So, what can the average person, or anybody else for that matter, do to avoid this threatening shortage of electrons? The average person and everybody else can shut down their computers, stomp on their calculators, rip out their telephones and report to the authorities any unnecessary use of electrons. At least that is one way.

While the situation may seem hopeless, we don't have to despair. All we have to do is to practice electron conservation. Paradoxically as it may sound, we can run our computers and all other electronic devices with devices that scoop up all the used electrons and re-energize them. The idea is similar to ideas employed in the emission controls of the exhausts of personal cars; gasoline is put in at one end and water vapor comes out at the other end. In a computer, say, hydrogen is put in at one end and only electrons come out at the other end. (Note that the hydrogen atom has only one electron, the absolute minimum.) Those electrons at the other end are trapped in suitably designed bags, stored and put away for future use. It is obvious that if we all practiced electron conservation, mankind may yet avoid another crisis of its own making. The trouble is that "all" will not participate in the conservation efforts. Man is inherently selfish and those who have gathered and stored enough electrons for their own use may simply ignore any appeals to share their bounty with the rest of us.

Moral: Electrons, photons, quanta of any sort, must be shared or we are all doomed.

The First Law

LOST IN THE mist of time is how the first law, written or unwritten, came to pass. Men were probably considered, even then, as the stronger sex - in a physical sense. Therefore, it is reasonable to assume that men declared that men could have as many wives as they wished. A follow-up law would be that women had to obey their husbands - no matter what. Since even in the mist of time, biology would be the same then as today which meant that births were evenly divided between males and females. In other words, if a man had four wives, say, that meant that three men would be without a wife. Or, to consider an extreme case, suppose a man had hundred wives that would mean that 99 men would be without women. Biology being then as it is today, that meant extreme sexual deprivation for a lot of males. So, if there was a first law, there had to be second law saying, in essence, that a group of deprived men could share one wife. Consequently, if there were a first and second law, there must be a third law spelling out the procedures that a group of men must follow when sharing one wife.

It is easy to imagine that a woman in such a situation would complain. That would lead to a fourth law setting up a sort of arbitration board. Even in the mist of time there must have been some measure of fairness. To take an extreme case of 100 men sharing one wife, it was obvious that something had to be done even if women had no say in the matter. So, there must be a fifth law specifying who and how many men would arbitrate disputes in such cases. But should men having more than one wife be allowed to serve on the arbitration board? So, again, if there was a fifth law there would have to be a sixth law settling the dilemma. It is fair to assume that the many deprived men, being necessarily in the majority, would restrict non-deprived men to serve in an advisory capacity only.

It is also fair to assume that those serving in an advisory capacity in turn would take some advice. While, of course, women had to keep quiet in public, at home, at night, in bed, and so on, they would certainly give their husbands many earfuls. As the mist of those misty times slowly receded, there had to be a seventh law regulating how women could give advice, publicly or privately. For instance, they could not give any financial advice to anybody. They could not give advice on what we today may call birth control. Men, obviously, were afraid that if there were not enough females born, who would do the work? So again, if there were a seventh law, there would have to be an eighth law saying in effect that women should mind their own business.

In our enlightened times, with the mist of time completely cleared and brushed aside, laws continue to be passed, night and day, because if there is one law, there has to be a second law, if there is a second law, there has to be third law, and so on forever. But by now, there are laws saying in effect that women can do whatever they damn well want to do. It's enough to drive real men to tears. And it all happened because in that faraway misty past, men were not smart enough to strictly enforce that first law that gave birth to all the others.

Moral: What would men do without women?
(And/Or vice versa?)

Fissionball

CASEY, THE GREATEST slugger of them all, was more than a baseball player and a home- run champion. He was an institution and an icon. But, even institutions and icons fall apart sooner or later. Take the curious case of Casey in the World Series some seasons ago. One afternoon it came to pass that Casey hit the ball with all his might and the ball began its flight into the stands where a fan caught it. The fan discovered that he had only half a ball in his hand. It further happened that the other half of the ball was caught by an infielder of the opposing team. As Casey was leisurely running around the bases for his home run, he was tagged by the other half of the baseball before he could reach third base. The questions that arose, then, were twofold. Had Casey scored a home run or only half a home run? Further, was half a baseball sufficient to tag somebody out of the game? It seemed that these questions had no answers, at least not answers that were supported by any sort of logic.

So, instead of trying to decide the undecidable, all attention was concentrated on the split baseball. It was soon discovered that the interior of the ball had been cut roughly in half. This cut had been disguised by the standard cover, that is horse leather, which had been scored on the inside to ensure that the ball assembly would split when hit by Casey's bat. The question now was who was in the World Series and would benefit from all this confusion? Or, was it just a prank by a fan trying the spice up the game a little bit? Were any gambling interests involved? How about an employee on the assembly line in a baseball factory? The questions were endless, not a pleasing prospect.

It was decided to go back to the fact that a baseball had been split into roughly two halves. What would be the implications for other sports? Suppose that a football in the game of American football had been pulled on by two players from opposing teams and the football was ripped into two parts. Each piece of the football was carried to the proper end zone and hence both teams scored a touchdown- or would it be half a touchdown for each team? It is obvious that in any sport featuring balls, there is always the possibility of split balls being created; the problems of split balls are not confined to just one or two sports. All we have to do is to consider tennis, golf, basketball, handball, softball and, last but not least, rugby.

In general, balls are everywhere from our sun, to our Earth, to our sister planets and so on. In the universe there are balls and more balls everywhere. Let us take an inward journey all the way down to the atoms. Each atom is like our solar system, the electrons playing the role of the planets and the nucleus acting as the electrons' sun. Simplified, of course, but not too much off the mark, until about around 1938/1939, the atom was considered indivisible until Lisa Meitner and Otto Hahn showed that fission of uranium was possible. When bombarded with neutrons, a uranium atom could be split into two fragments with the excess mass converted into energy. This led to Einstein's letter to president Roosevelt where he suggested that sustained nuclear fission might be possible thus creating bombs of unprecedented power. The Manhattan project followed. In August 1945, after nuclear bombs had destroyed Hiroshima and Nagasaki, World War II ended.

One conclusion that one can draw from these notes is that if a ball in play in any sport should split into two or more fragments; that is significant only at the moment when it happens. Afterwards, it is insignificant, something to laugh at. When an unexpected event in science occurs, such as the fission of uranium, it may be something to fear forever. As a figure of speech, Casey batting a ball to pieces could be said to analogous to a stream of neutrons splitting the uranium atom into fragments.

Anyway and eventually, Casey admitted that the split ball was his idea, done for his own amusement and for the befuddlement of the fans. He had wanted to prove to himself that he was more than a legendary baseball player. He had also wanted to give the public a demonstration of nuclear fission and all the confusion and misery that went with it. Yet, in the history of baseball the incident will probably be recorded as malicious mischief. It is hard to believe that Casey meant what he tried to say. Baseball as levity? Baseball as a metaphor for life? But, baseball is just an entertainment, isn't it?

An Afterthought: Maybe the heading of this piece should be: *"Fissionballs or How To Draw Conclusions From Meager Data"*.

The 20ᵗʰ Floor

A PERSON FELL from the 20ᵗʰ floor and survived the fall with only minor bruises. Naturally, this event was met with suspicion and skepticism. Some suggested that it was a decimal error; the person had really fallen from the second floor. Others used the experimental method. Dogs, and even cats, were thrown to their fates from every floor from the 20ᵗʰ down to the second. No cats or dogs survived even a second-floor drop.

Yet others relied on faith. Martyrs from every known faith jumped from the 20ᵗʰ floor certain in their belief that they would survive the fall. Each martyr hoped to give a public demonstration of the superiority of the one and only true faith. None did. At ground level, support personnel tried to substitute their squashed martyrs with live persons, but the attempts were so crude that they were quickly disallowed.

After all this activity, suspicions and skepticism were strengthened. Could any independent witness verify that a person had indeed fallen from the 20ᵗʰ floor? Where was this alleged jumper now? Surely any person surviving such a fall would claim responsibility, be famous, and make a lot of money from a second fall from the 20ᵗʰ floor.

Eventually, so much confusion had accumulated that no one

was any longer comfortable with discussing, or even believing in the pros and cons of the event. What remained of the controversy were some dead dogs, cats, and martyrs.

Moral: Not everything that happens happened.

Food Demonstration

DR. I. N. Humane was visiting a fellow benevolent ruler who believed as he did, that while a regime should be loving, it must also require discipline. One day, Dr. Humane got an urgent dispatch from his regime's Head Disciplinarian that there was a run on apples by the citizens. A year's normal supply was stripped from the stores in days and apple cores were discarded everywhere, contrary to all rules and regulations. Dr. Humane hurried home to have urgent consultations with his advisors. One of them ventured that perhaps it was a sign of incipient disturbances, keeping in mind that old saying "An apple a day keeps the doctor away", he said.

The Good Doctor kept that in mind while trying to control his fury while also decreeing that all apples were to be confiscated and incinerated, all apple trees to be cut down, and no more wasting of foreign exchange on apple imports. Love and peace flourished again until another of his advisors noted another matter of concern. The citizens were buying potatoes in huge amounts, seriously depleting potato reserves. It was ventured that potatoes were just replacing apples in the national diet. Someone, as lovingly as possible, suggested that maybe, just maybe, some citizens were thinking of the Irish Potato Famine. It was silly of course, but maybe some maladjusted minds wanted to prepare for a famine. Absolute nonsense, of course, because everyone knew that everybody was well fed. The

Good Doctor, however, declared that all potatoes were to be withdrawn from the market places pending further study of the issue.

The Good Doctor and his advisors began to ponder if other food demonstrations were possible. A far-out proposal was sheep, as in "a wolf in sheep's clothing." Intensive investigations sought to determine how many sheep the nation had a few weeks ago versus the present number. A small decline was detected. The Good Doctor decreed that all sheep had to be kept under surveillance at all times. That was the top priority for all the agents of the departments of Love, Guidance and Detection of Unhappiness.

Unrest, as the Good Doctor saw it, was persuasive, but the citizens saw it as statistical flukes - at least that was what everyone told the Love Counselors. As time went on, further food demonstrations were detected. Most foods left the market places, menus were more and more restricted - many had to live on pancake mix and spinach. The Good Doctor was shocked, absolutely shocked, that his advisors could have overlooked Popeye the Sailor Man, he of strength through spinach, strength used to smash his opponents. The Good Doctor realized that his loving regime, very regrettably, had come to the beginning of the end thanks to all his incompetent so-called advisors. He decided to withdraw his deferred pension in the form of convertible foreign exchange held by the Love Treasury, funds that were no longer of any use to anybody since apples were no longer imported. He would visit benevolent heads of state who shared his views of love with guidance and to get advice regarding his investments.

Moral: Food is the ultimate weapon.

For The Love Of Mike

LIFE ISN'T EASY, but romantic love is even worse. Once I knew someone who knew someone who was in love with a girl. This girlfriend was a sweet thing who did sweet things, so everything seemed to be headed in the right direction. Being an honorable man, the second someone wanted to marry that girl. At regular intervals, he asked her to consider his proposal of marriage. The girlfriend always answered in a way that was sweet and caring, but still the words meant "No". One reason was the seasons. In the summer it was too hot. In the winter it was too cold. In the fall the weather was too uncertain. In the spring the weather was even more uncertain. Another reason was the capricious nature of love. She maintained that if they got married, there would probably come a time when she or he or both of them no longer felt that acceleration of exhilaration, the source of all true love. Yet another reason was her love of Mike.

The first someone (as above) didn't quite understand what "love of Mike" meant. It didn't seem to mean that the sweet thing was in love with some other guy, one that she would be more inclined to marry- no matter what the season might be. Not at all, the second someone (as above) insisted to the first someone. That phrase was just a phrase that drifted around in the universe, a sort of filler that one could grasp and put in here and there as needed. It didn't really matter what love of Mike might mean or not mean.

Back to the "I", who knew that someone was in love with his girlfriend whom he wanted to marry. Despite the problems with the four seasons, the girlfriend was persuaded to at least take a vacation together which would not require any adjustments relative to the seasons. So, the two of them went out into the world to receive sweet things and to give sweet things, sweet gifts between the two of them.

It took some adjustments to travel. They wanted to travel happily or at least be in a satisfied mode. That meant selecting the proper places with regard to seasonal altitudes (in general, as the altitude increases, the average daily temperature decreases) as well as paying attention to latitudes and longitudes. Finally, it meant to have some contact with their home bases. That was an unfortunate mistake. One day, the girlfriend got a call that made her so frantic that she lost all interest in sharing sweet things with anybody. She had to go home. Why? She wanted the second someone to know. Because Mike needs me, was her answer. Mike had been run over by a car, but he eventually recovered. After the recovery, the second someone again took up his quest, suggesting that everything ought to be the way it was before. No, the girlfriend insisted, I have to spend more time with my cat.

Naturally, I was furious at the two someones who had tricked me into believing that their two-layered tale would have something interesting to tell me or anybody else. If they had told me at the very beginning that Mike was a cat, I wouldn't have bothered to pay attention to anything as insignificant as a cat named Mike. But that, unfortunately, is the state of what is called modern literature. This multiple-layered approach, combined with multiple-twisted turns, is to make us all so confused that we don't notice that at the end of the tale all that is left is a cat. Even a simple love story has to be made complicated.

(Suggested by a R. Miller story)

Forth And Back

HE FELT DISEMBODIED. Winds carried him aloft to the bluest skies, he swam the widest oceans and he passed through any earthly obstacle. As he walked through a granite mountain, he saw a tunnel and took this easy path. Far in the distance were lights, becoming brighter and brighter. He heard voices sounding like his parents, grandparents, other departed family members. The voices wanted him to come, to be with them, to rejoice together.

He turned his back to the lights and the familiar voices. Angry, the mountain spit him out, rocks tore at his body, and he was embodied again. He sensed that his body was incomplete, as if a leg or an arm was missing. As he awoke, she was there - as always. This emerald, this loving spirit, this joy, this other Eve, this woman, his wife.

Moral: A good wife means a good life.

(With some apologies to Shakespeare's Richard II.)

Four Twenty Two

THE SPIRIT, APPROACHING its 15 billionth year of being, absentmindedly left its microphone open while dictating its decisions. Somewhere in the universe, on an insignificant planet orbiting an insignificant star in an insignificant galaxy, a being of feeble mind but of acute hearing, noticed the Voice. The being heard that it was its turn to demise; it was scheduled for 4:22. The being didn't quite catch the day or whether it was AM or PM. Anyway, the being asked a watchmaker to make it a digital time piece which omitted 4:22; i.e. after 4:21 came 4:23. This device was easily made and the being carried it with it at all times. It expected that it now could live forever. However, that didn't happen. The being demised at 4:22 anyway is some unknown method of time keeping.

> **Moral:** No one can fool the Spirit. Besides, local time is not universe time.

Fractions (or how many?)

I ASKED HIM: "Are you OK?" "No," he said. "Why not?" I asked. I wanted to know. "Things were going so well and yet things are not going well" was his answer. I asked him what he meant by that. "Everybody was so happy," he said, "and now they are not so happy". I tried to cheer him up; that way, at least he would be happy. "Tell me something pleasant," he told me. That was easy enough. I told him how many statues there were of him at last count. That seemed to make him happy for a minute or two, but then he was back to his gloom-and-doom mood again. And so it went for a long evening. I told him all the positive things I could think of and then some. I tried to instill him with a positive attitude, but whenever I told him something positive, he answered with something negative. No, he didn't want to watch another parade. No, he didn't want to un- veil another statue, particularly those where he was sitting on top of a horse; for one thing, all the horses were always bigger than he was. Once a sculptor did make the horse smaller than him; he could still hear the snickering behind his back. No, he didn't want to view another parade. There were too many of his non-birthday parades already. All those tanks rumbled by the reviewing stand, then drove around a few city blocks, and then rumbled by the reviewing stand again, spewing out Diesel fumes. No, he didn't want to wave or sa- lute to the same soldiers passing by so many times each year that he was certain he could recognize all of them if he ever got the compulsion to walk the streets of the capital. No, he didn't want to marry, or even summon, another pretty girl. He felt that girls these days didn't have the ardor or stamina that girls possessed in the years gone by, including his wives and daughters.

I had known him for a long time; we grew up in the same desert village. I could never really call him my friend, but his friends acted as if he was, so they were very nice to me. As he rose, slowly but surely, to great power he kept summoning me now and then to his various palaces. He seemed to need someone who he could trust completely even though he could never trust anybody completely.

As that evening wore on, I had exhausted my supply of positive questions and he his negative answers, when he suddenly said:"I worry about our population", apropos nothing. From previous evenings, I knew that he sensed that he had to confront a basic paradox of statesmanship: No matter how justified, necessary, and desirable, a society can't lock up the whole population. Some had to do the work, some had to produce the food stuff, some had to distribute the stuff, some had to maintain the roads of distribution, some had to do the political work and, certainly, not some but many had to serve in the Army, the Air Force, the Navy, and the Border Guard.

It disturbed him that sitting where he sat that he faced an impossible situation: the best he could do was to try to estimate the proper fractions of the populations that should be in the prisons and the work camps. Also, a substantial number of guards had to watch those populations; somehow it seemed improper to let the prisoners watch themselves. He had to admit, even to himself, that no matter how justified the incarcerations might be, a part of society had to remain at large.

Thinking back to the days when he was on his path of ascension, he sensed that things were much simpler then. All you had to do was to rough up some men, women, and kids and the rest would be sensible enough to join the cause. From among those who signed up, there were always some that in turn would rough up men, women, and kids to persuade others to join the cause. The whole process was almost automatic until seemingly everybody had joined the cause. It was revolution by chain reaction. At times, of course, it was necessary to execute a few here and there just to concentrate the minds of those who had tendencies toward opposition.

As I listened and listened to him that evening, he kept grappling with the basic question: What was the proper fraction between the whole population being imprisoned and none being imprisoned? Both extremes were obviously impossible. He asked me to propose a reasonable fraction. I avoided that trap by joking that back in our village school; even the teachers couldn't do fractions. I gathered that as the evening kept wearing on that the fraction he had in mind was about one half, that is one half of the population inside and the other half on the outside. My opinion, which I kept to myself, was that the two one-half fractions were equally implausible.

When the evening finally came to an end, I went back to my apartment in the sub-palace that he insisted I use; desisted I did not. During the next weeks, I detected a subtle shift in official policy carefully hidden in the official press. In time, the new policy would bring down the fraction from one half to one third. My boyhood friend, though, had miscalculated but not in the sense of the one-half fraction. If you subtract one third from one half you get one sixth. One sixth may seem like a modest fraction of the whole, but when released in a fairly short time, it could overwhelm the existing structure of society. And that is what happened. The change was too sudden and the dissension of my boyhood friend began. He had calculated the fractions correctly, just as we had done in that faraway place in time and place in that village school. This time, however, the calculating did him no good.

The end came very quickly. I lost my rooms in that sub-palace and he lost his palaces. Then the palaces disappeared and my friend disappeared. Some thought he had disappeared into the nether world, others maintained that he had disappeared into the everlasting sands. My personal opinion is that one day he did the irrational, to me at least, and took a walk through the streets of the capital to receive his customary ovations. I don't think he got very far before he disappeared, into fractions too small to be recognized by anybody.

Moral: Computations with fractions are never easy

Gold Teeth

MY FIRST REACTION on that fateful morning was that something was not quite right. And sure enough, it wasn't. All my gold teeth were missing. My first thought was how could anybody do something like that to somebody else? My second thought was, why hadn't I felt something? Third, fourth and other thoughts followed, one after the other. You don't lose gold teeth without you noticing it. My dentist had spent countless hours putting them in and I still keep all his billings as souvenirs. It is, of course, possible that the dentist had removed them so that he could make some extra money. Suppose that he had put me completely under, but even then I would have remembered stepping into his office. The conclusion seems to be that my dentist had nothing to do with it.

Being a now-and-then student of recent American history, I clearly recall the year 1492 and the years thereafter. Even though the *conquistadores* came to find spices, they also kept their eyes open for gold. Some Indians here and there were put to useful work such as gold mining and gold panning. Gold was rare at that time and it still is. Due to their advanced weaponry, after some years, the remainders of the Indians were defeated and even more of them were put to useful work, particularly in the gold business.

Consider again, then, what happens when a more advanced

civilization, at least with respect to weaponry, meets a society that, relatively, is still in one of the stone ages. Suppose there are other civilizations which are far superior to Earth's civilizations out there toward infinity. Suppose there is a planet with lots of intelligent creatures where everything is up to date, however, no matter how up to date they are, gold is so rare that they can't get enough of it. Following the pattern of the year 1492 and the years thereafter, all they have to do is to go to Earth, put all of us to work in the gold business, and then return in triumph to their home base with so much gold that it is hardly worth anything anymore. Even in space there are unintended consequences.

But, back to my missing gold teeth; a civilization much superior to ours could easily put us all to sleep for while. After the space voyagers have taken whatever they want to take from us, they apply retroactively their erase-memory machines. That way, when they leave, nobody is any wiser as to what really happened. (Somehow, they must have missed me; always the forgotten) One has to agree that that is a very neat *modus operandi* when combined with the spirit of 1492.

I asked my dentist how much it would cost to replace my stolen gold teeth. He mentioned a figure I knew I couldn't afford - supply and demand again. What was the point anyway? As soon as they were put in, who knows, they might get stolen again. And if yet another set was put in, it too might be stolen. This theft business could go on *ad infinitum* as other civilizations wanted a share of Earth's gold supply. So, I didn't replace my missing gold teeth. As I traveled around in my own civilization, any time any of my brethren opened their mouths I could see right away that each had many teeth missing.

The principal lesson that I learned was that we better speed up our technology and catch up with all those civilizations out there in space. It is time to fight back and not be patsies or we will get robbed of everything we hold dear. It is time to fight and rob back. It is time to be more civilized.

Disclosure: These remarks were inspired - in part - by the film "Forgotten" (2004)

A Grain Of Salt

ONCE UPON A time, there was a man who proclaimed that he could leave his fingerprints on grains of salt. The commentators at that time advised their followers to take that claim with a grain of salt. As time went by, there were other proclamations that said if the grains of salt were large enough, such as a ten-pound or even a one-pound grain, putting one's fingerprints on those grains could be easily done. Imaging, then, a downward search where the grains of salt became ever smaller, there would come a point where an imprint of a fingerprint would be impossible. As the downward search reached the smallest atom, it was no longer possible to maintain that fingerprints could be imprinted. The atoms bore the imprint of God not Man.

A Love Story: Halvar

CONSIDER HALVAR MARS. He is the president of a university describing itself as striving for excellence. Consider his age of 70 years. The day after his 70th birthday he had to retire - said the Board anyway. Halvar Mars said: "No!" The Board pointed out to him that a successor had already been appointed and that he, Mars, had to vacate his office no later than the day after his 70th birthday. Mars refused to vacate his office. He had to concede that technically he may be retired but on the other hand, even more technically, that didn't mean that he couldn't stay in his office and thus still be president with all the powers of that office. Besides, his secretary was not scheduled to retire, so how come he had to?

Thus the Board and Halvar Mars were at an impasse. At home, however, there was no impasse. Mars' wife, Marthas Mars, said that since he was retired he should stay home, not stay in his office all day and keep his secretary busy. Mars said: "No!" Marthas, however, had a totalitarian streak, or whatever it was, in her character. Marthas said: "Yes!" Halvar Mars realized that it was hard to have an impasse with Marthas. She had a peculiar ability to intimidate him. Whatever the ability consisted of, she could modify his attitude, his behavior, and even his thoughts on occasion. So, Halvar Mars modified himself to say: "Why?" "Because it is the right thing to do", said Marthas.

Halvar Mars thought back on their long life together. Even

before they were married, Marthas had this ability to somehow in-timidate him, not in an obvious ways; it was there like water, air, earth, and fire. That they were going to be married just seemed to him something foreordained, something that was obviously going to happen, no matter what else fate might have had in mind.

Halvar Mars loved Marthas and he knew that she loved him. That she did love him had always puzzled him to some degree. Why should she love him with the world full of better, kinder, smarter, more handsome, more virile, more attractive, more considerate men of all ages? But, what was the use of wondering; with Marthas what-ever happened just happened no matter what.

Halvar Mars had reached his "Why?" stage and felt he was in retreat from his "No!" stage. So he asked Marthas: "What should I do?" "Retire" said Marthas, she always spoke to the point.

So, the day after the day of his 70th birthday, he went to his office, gathered up his things and plants, said good-by to his secretary, and left the campus. He had to restrain himself from not going up in the campus tower and cry out to the world: "No!, No!, No!".

Moral: What is most incomprehensible about love is that it is incomprehensible.

(A back story suggested by the 1981 novel "Eldorado" by an unknown author.)

Published In Harpers Magazine

March 1975

EXHORTATIONS ABOUT BEING useful, unselfish and a Good Samaritan generally come from the wrong sources and are aimed in the wrong direction. Thus I give you Thorsen's law of exhortation's: exhortations to perform or engage in basic and vital societal services are most fervently made by those who have no intentions of performing or engaging in those services themselves.

The President of the United States and the presidents of our corporations jet around the country urging the conservation of resources and energy.

Members of the President's Cabinet and the president's corporate cabinets are driven in their limousines to meetings where the crisis of scarcity is discussed. Conservation appeals are issued after each meeting.

Assistants to the officers of the Cabinet and the corporate cabinets are sent to symposia in Hawaii or the Virgin Islands to keep the outlying districts informed about the latest crisis and to discover conservation ideas that can be passed down to the lower echelons.

And so on down the ladder of our society. Among those who occupy the lower rungs of the ladder, it is understood that, if you have to ask how much something costs, you can't afford it. So you do without.

We can now formulate Thorsen's law of consumption: The more one consumes, the more he feels an obligation to urge those below him on the ladder of affluence to consume less.

A corollary to this law is: one man's necessities are another man's waste.

Really sincere appeals to reduce consumption and waste can only come from those who consume the least, say, from those living below the poverty level as defined by Federal statisticians. Are there any individuals or groups among the poor who are public-spirited enough to buy the necessary time and space in the media to educate society about the wastefulness of waste? I doubt it.

We are forced to admit the truth of Thorsen's law on attitude toward waste: each person aspires to be as wasteful as those above him on the ladder of affluence.

Clearly, the only viable long-range solution to the problem of waste is to forget it ever existed.

By: Thomas Thorsen

Having Fun, Being Happy

THE ROOM WAS about as I had expected it to be. It was furnished with a large desk, a high-back chair behind it, a couple of other chairs, shelves filled with books in conservative bindings and, of course, the couch.

The first time I laid down on its leathery skin, I felt a little uneasy. I thought I could feel a little of the body heat that the last person had left behind.

"Why did you come to see me?" he asked. "Because," I said, "I want to feel more relaxed about having fun, being happy."

"How do you feel now?"

I tried to put it into words, but they were, as always, inadequate. "It seems sort of sinful" I said, "having fun, being happy."

"Why?" he asked.

"So many things need to be done. There really isn't time to do anything else but getting things done."

"Why not?" he asked.

"No matter what you do, there is always something else that's more important to do."

"Give me an example," he said.

"I remember my mother standing in the door, crying, almost begging me not to read those books. Smut, she called them, but they weren't. I should study so that I would get good grades and get into a good college. Or at least, she said, I should get out and get some fresh air. But on Sundays, I liked to sit in my room reading. So I began to put the novels, the short stories, the plays and the essays in the plain brown covers we used for school books. When she peeked into my room, she thought I was studying and she tip-toed away, saying nothing. I was having fun, being happy.

"That's all?" he asked.

"I felt insecure about having fun, being happy," I said.

Then I told him about other things that made me feel insecure.

On the second day, I stood out on the sidewalk for a while, trying to guess behind which window the couch was. I took the elevator up to his floor, getting a pleasant sensation from its high speed. I read the sign about the maximum capacity and the place where the complete certificate was on file.

His receptionist was still young, still beautiful and I think she enjoyed that. His patient came out, but she was not young and she was not beautiful. I don't think she enjoyed that. When I was lying on the couch, I felt the warmth she had left behind.

"Today," he said, "why don't you tell me about an experience, or a feeling, you've had recently?"

"I'm a little afraid, a little uneasy about having fun, being happy. Sometimes, I get the feeling that it's better to do nothing than to do something. Others may not understand what I'm doing. Or why I'm doing it."

"When I sit at my desk doing my work, I feel relaxed," I continued. "When I sit at my desk writing, I feel uneasy. Others may find out what I'm doing. If they looked over my shoulder, they could read what I'm writing, but it is very unorganized and very incomplete. I rewrite several times, trying to reduce the imperfections. When my wife comes into the room, I hide the sheets."

"Why do you write?" he asked.

"Because I like it" I said. "But I don't like the uneasiness, the feeling that I can get caught doing it. I often ask myself: Why don't you do something useful instead?"

"What do you write about?" he asked.

"When I first started to write, I tried to write fragments of an autobiography. But I couldn't take it seriously. So, I wrote about other things that amused me in their small way, where facts were not important."

"Tell me about some of the things that amuse you, that you write about," he said.

"One story is about the anxieties of an important executive in an automotive company. He discovers that the ornamental design displaying the name of one of their models has a misspelling. They have to recall hundreds of thousands of cars to correct the spelling."

And I told him other stories.

On the third day, I walked around in the lobby before I took the elevator to his floor. As I entered the waiting room, the reception-ist was on the phone, talking and laughing softly, saying words that meant anything you wanted them to mean.

"Today," he said, "why don't you tell me about your family?"

"I have a great family," I said. "We get along fine, my kids and I; my wife and I. I watch the kids grow up and they watch me getting older and I wonder if they are going to grow up to be like me or like somebody else."

"When I come home at night, I look at them. Sometimes they talk to me. Sometimes I talk to them. I wonder if they are happy having me as a parent. I wonder if they are having fun, being happy, or if they are just pretending."

"They go to bed. Later my wife goes to bed, and then I rest. I turn on all the lights and sit in a chair doing nothing. Once in a while, I take a pad on my lap and write. I feel embarrassed sitting there and writing. I should be sleeping."

"About two years ago, the family was out of town. I had the lights on all night and I slept on the couch in the living room. When they came back, I felt secure again. I felt good sleeping in the bed room, next to my wife."

"Yesterday," he said, "you told me about some of the stories you have written. Tell me another story."

"Another story is about a safari in East Africa. They are hunting prides of lions that have turned vegetarian. These lions must be destroyed since they threaten the ecological balance."

And I kept on talking.

On the fourth day, I bought a rose in the lobby. I put it in a trash can before I reached the waiting room. She said a few friendly words to me.

"Why do you feel insecure about having fun and being happy?" he asked.

"Somebody may be looking and they may not like what they see."

"Why should that bother you?" he asked.

"I don't know," I said. "You tell me."

"Tell me about your childhood," he said.

"As a little boy, I was licked in the face by a cow. Years later, I was licked in the face by a girl. That's what I remember best, being licked."

I told him other things about my childhood. I told him about my parents.

"Do you think you're a good parent?" he asked.

"Not particularly," I said. "I don't seem to be able to have fun, be happy with the kids. Not completely anyway. There's something holding me back. Part of me stands in a corner, or behind a corner, sort of, watching what the rest of me is doing."

"The kids scream a lot. They run around yelling. I can't scream or yell in a convincing manner. I feel insecure when I scream. And I don't like yelling and screaming. It upsets me. I like it quiet."

I talked about what the kids do.

"Have you ever written a story about kids?"

"No," I said. "Never; I don't think I've even tried."

"Maybe you could make up a little story right now?"

I closed my eyes and thought about it for few minutes. Then I told him: "A little boy sees a little girl far, far away. He wants to play with her, so he runs and runs toward her. When he gets close to her, he sees that she is a big girl, almost as big as his mother. She asks him: Are you lost? No, he says, and runs back to the point from where she looks like a little girl again."

I didn't know what the story meant. Maybe he did.

On the fifth day, I bought a rose in the lobby, but when I entered her waiting room, she was not there. I put the rose on her desk.

"Why do you want to feel more relaxed about having fun, being happy?" he asked.

"I want to enjoy having fun, being happy," I said. "Maybe I could be more productive, accomplish more."

"What do you plan to accomplish?" he asked.

"There is always work, doing it, planning it, thinking about it."

"Do you enjoy your work?" he asked.

"I feel secure when I work. I like feeling secure."

"Anything you can tell me about your work?" he asked.

I told him about a recurring dream that I have. "There's an urgent message on my desk in the morning. I must come to the President's office immediately. I use the elevator, but it doesn't stop before it reaches street level. It opens directly to the sidewalk and I'm swept away in a constant stream of people. I get carried away, block by block. Finally, I manage to get on a bus. It drives off in the wrong direction. It stops far out in the country. The driver and the passengers get out and disappear. I find railroad tracks and I follow them back to town. It takes me all night. I arrive at work at the usual time. On my desk, there is an urgent message. I must come to the President's office immediately. The same sequence of events repeats itself, again and again."

As I left that day, I couldn't see the rose anywhere on her desk or in the waiting room.

On the sixth day, when I entered the waiting room, the receptionist was talking on the phone, saying words that meant anything you wanted them to mean.

"Do you enjoy your life?" he asked.

"Most of the time," I said, "but I feel confused when I'm having fun, being happy."

"How would you describe your attitude toward life?" he asked.

"I have a reasonable attitude toward life," I said. "I'm sensible about life."

"What do you mean by reasonable and sensible?"

"I don't expect any more than I get."

I wondered if he liked that answer. Maybe another answer would have been better. During a subway ride once, I heard somebody say: "There's always light at the end of the tunnel." A companion answered: "Except at night." I liked that answer.

Then I told him about another story I had written, about a middle-aged man taking a bath. He forgot to close the drain. Water was pouring into the tub, but it only reached a depth of a few inches while he took his bath. As he got out of the tub, he noticed that the tub was draining. For the rest of his life, he would always remember how stupid he had been not to realize that the drain was open. The thousands of times he had remembered to close the drain before taking his bath, he never remembered.

He probably thought that it was a silly story, so I didn't tell him another.

On the seventh day, I stood on the sidewalk looking up at the columns of glass windows as they stretched and stretched higher and higher; the last frames seemed to pierce the sky. But on that day, I decided to turn back and go home. After all, what good would it do?

Having fun, being happy isn't that important.

Besides, there is no building, there is no lobby, there is no elevator, there is no receptionist still young and still beautiful, and he never talked to me. I had made it all up in my head, having fun, being happy as I did it.

(From 1974)

By Thomas Thorsen

The Highs And The Lows
Or The Word Carriers

ANYBODY CAN COMMIT to memory a play by Shakespeare or any one of the books and testaments of the Bible. In contrast, it takes years of training and dedication to be able to commit to memory a single word and then to carry it in one's head from periods of seconds, of minutes, of hours, of days, of weeks or longer as required to the exclusion of all other words and without any contamination by those words.

The first paragraph, then, explains and summarizes why anybody, and myself in particular, would want to be a word carrier. I care about the purity of words and in the defense of those words against any contamination by other words. I became a certified word carrier after having gone through rigorous training programs where I obtained a bachelor's and master's degrees in word carrying. Then I served an internship at a word transport company. Basically, the internship consisted of additional training of being able never to be distracted by word hecklers, be they amateurs or professionals. No matter how intensely one was heckled, an intern was expected never to let the maintenance of the purity of words to be compromised in any way.

After the completion of my internship, I was fortunate in being hired as a word carrier for the prestigious company of Highs & Lows, a limited liability firm. As could be expected, this company occupied a stately building where the offices of the Highs were located at the penthouse level while the Lows worked in a deep basement. When a command was issued by the Highs to the Lows, the transmission of it could not leave any word trail as well as any other trail. Of course, this is where the word carriers were the invaluable communications links. No codes could be used; any methods of mass communication as well as written and oral instructions were not to be trusted.

So, the commands were delivered, one word at the time, by word carriers oscillating between the penthouse and the basement. The easy part was carrying a word from penthouse level to basement level. We were allowed to use the "down" elevator; it was comfortable and absolutely soundproof; there were no distractions at all. On the other hand, when going up with an empty head there were distractions galore. First of all, we were only allowed to use the "up" stairs. Somehow, those stairs were very uncomfortable; every step was of varying heights. Some sections of the stairs were steeper than others. And of course, just walking upstairs to the Highs under the constant pull of gravity required most of your attention. In addition to that, the going-upstairs people were letting off steam of varying degrees after the strain of carrying a word down to the Lows. It was almost like going back to heckling school during one's internship.

After some time of employment, my attitude became a little more relaxed; even word carrying- strenuous as it was - could be done in a more relaxed manner. I began to interact with some of my going-up colleagues by a smile or a nod of the head or a wave of the hand and even an occasional "Hi". Being a male, after all, implies for most of us an interest in females. I noticed a young woman; she seemed very nice, looked good and the trips up the "up" staircase did not seem to bother her at all. That, of course, signaled a strong constitution which is good. Actually, I had met her before; she had been one of the hecklers during my internship. I wouldn't say that she had been vicious, but her heckling had made a mark on me. Of course, bygone must be bygones especially among word carriers. One's professional life and one's private life must be strictly separated.

Occasionally, a High would come down to check on the Lows. There was, of course, no direct questioning. Quite often, a High would ask: "Are you happy?" which meant more often than not "Are you finished?" On the other hand, depending on the way or manner that "happy" was said, it could mean other things. If spoken in a whisper, it seemed to imply "This is extremely important". If spoken very slowly and menacing, it could mean: "Get to work and do what you were told to do". If spoken very hesitantly and with a slight stammer, it probably meant: "We the Highs are concerned that you the Lows are not equal to the task". The whole point of the word "happy", then, was to emphasize an oral culture so that there would be no paper trail and no other trails. Even if someone among us carried a recording device, the word "happy" would be meaningless because there was no way to know in what context the word was used.

But, I am straying and very much so. I want to get back to the telling of my private life. In particular, I want to get back to that female with a prior life as heckler of me and others. There was not supposed to be any fraternization among the word carriers. Nevertheless, despite all oaths taken, all ethics courses endured, all professional attitudes dear to me, I convinced myself that I should get that heckling girl into a bar. She must have similar feeling about oaths, ethics, and professional behavior, but she went into that bar with me anyway.

We tried to leave our professional lives aside for a while, but it was not easy. The old ways certainly persist. I ordered straight whiskeys for the two of us. Having consumed them, I asked her: "What is your favorite word?" She answered: "Beer", obviously kidding me. Anyway, she turned out to be an accomplished drinker. No matter how many straight whiskeys I sent her way, her favorite word that evening remained "Beer". We kept meeting each other at other bars, but no matter what the alcohol content of the drinks was, whatever her favorite word was at the beginning on any particular evening, that remained her favorite word all evening. I began to detect a pattern in her choice of favorite words. Consider this sequence: "White", "Ring", "Flowers", "Bride", "Soon", and so on. Those words could mean many things depending on the sequence in which they were arranged. Anyway, I stopped drinking anything with alcohol in it and so did she. I discovered one evening that one of my favorite words was "Love". At another evening, my favorite word was "We". That same evening, her favorite word was "Do". We put our two favorite words together and got "Do We" and "We Do". That is, first the question and then the answer. The phrase "We Do" was a sort of plural of the traditional "I Do".

One day, a High came down from his perch and asked us: "Are you happy?" He said "happy" in such a way that it meant "what are you two up to". We didn't tell him, but we were fired anyway. We didn't give up on the word-carrier business. We began our own company, "We Do" we called it. Rather than letting our word carriers limit themselves to one word at the time, our firm let them carry two words in their heads at the time as suggested by our trademarked phrase "We Do". The Highs & Lows Company could not compete with us. We were obviously twice as efficient as our former employer that only allowed one word per round trip. At the same time, we did not fool ourselves. Sooner or later there would be three-word companies, then four-word companies, and so on. The time would come, eventually, when one might as well commit to memory a play by Shakespeare or any of the books and testaments of the Bible. While efficient, it would no longer be possible to maintain the purity of the words.

Hope's Eternal Spring

SUPPOSE YOU DON'T feel so good. Suppose you live in Southern California. You should begin to drive north as soon as possible. Take the Interstate 5 freeway, follow it for a while, and then take a connector road to Pacific Coast Highway, also called California 1. Still driving north, you arrive at the area called Big Sur or the "Big South". Here, California 1 is a two-lane road clinging precipitously to steep hillsides that seem to grow out of the blue of the Pacific reaching for the blue of the sky. At some point on the road, there is a faded sign that announces "Hope's" together with an arrow pointing uphill. It is perhaps possible, with a powerful four-by-four all-terrain vehicle, to drive the disintegrating road up to Hope's, but few have tried and fewer yet have succeeded.

Eventually, you arrive at Hope's, short for Hope's Eternal Springs. Since hardly anybody visits Hope, he will be pleased to see you. Hope is very slim which he attributes to a lack of food and water. If he wants food and water, he has to get downhill to California 1, walk to the nearest cluster of houses, walk back to the sign, and somehow climb up the hill to his place. This effort requires as many calories as there are calories in the food he can carry. And water, Hope says, is so heavy. You take a good piss and you have gotten rid of at least one pound right there. So, a food-and-water trip probably shows a calorie deficit. The water in the springs, says Hope, tastes foul and smells foul; it is only fit to spit in to avoid using a more accurate description.

Yet, the springs are the reasons why people somehow manage to crawl up the hillsides to Hope's. The general theory is that the more foul smelling and foul tasting the water is, the greater are the health benefits thereof. The springs drip. The accumulations of drips are put into oversized wine barrels. You can rent a barrel for the daylight hours for a very steep price, but the water pilgrims keep coming anyway. To cut down on this rental expense, some barrel renters sublet their barrels to others for an hour or two. Hope doesn't mind as long as he gets his full daylight-hours fee.

That is Hope's attitude even though it brought him big trouble once. A sub-renter didn't get out of the barrel when his time was up. Renter and sub-renter had a quarrel, push came to show, the guy and the barrel got knocked over, and they rolled together down the steep hillsides, crossed California 1, and wound up in the Pacific where they were no longer viable. Law enforcement personnel suspected foul play since through their binoculars they could trace, in reverse, the barrel's path down the steep hillsides. They naturally wanted to talk to Hope, but were never able to move themselves up those steep hills due to their lack of exercise and determination. Hope put himself on reduced rations of food and spring water until the crisis blew over.

Despite all his troubles, Hope had a sunny outlook on fate and life, in part due to his beautiful view of the Pacific. Besides, the springs kept dripping and the barrels kept filling up, drawing water pilgrims from Southern California. That was then. Now, years later, the best-laid plans of mice and men, including Hope, disappeared one day when a severe earthquake shook the Big Sur area and the springs stopped dripping. After that, once in a while,

I visited Hope to cheer him up a little bit. Not that he needed any cheering up. He expects another earthquake any time and then the springs will be dripping again.

Moral: Hope springs eternal. (At least according to Alexander Pope in 1733.)

House Umbrellas

THE OTHER DAY, I went to a home-improvement sales presentation on house umbrellas after receiving a special invitation to that event. As the topic suggests, just as there are personal umbrellas there are also house umbrellas. These umbrellas are larger and more sophisticated and are suitable for houses of practically any size as I learned. They are devices for preserving wealth. It is no longer necessary to replace a leaky roof nor is it any longer necessary to have your home air-conditioned. In short, house umbrellas keep water out as easy as they keep heat out.

On the day when I attended the sales presentation, there were many doubters and they were not shy about expressing their doubts to the people who ran the meeting. One doubt was: suppose the house umbrella leaked or that it could be torn to pieces by natural forces? This doubt was met with disdain. House umbrellas do not leak nor can they be torn to pieces. Next question; it was back to the wind question again. The presenters pointed out that all these questions were dealt with in the booklet handed out at the beginning of the meeting. A simple solution to the wind problem is to let the house umbrella, in the shape of a propeller, be connected to a drive shaft which in turn will turn a generator which in turn will provide electric power sufficient for just about any-size house.

Somebody had the nerve to ask what warranties were associated with the purchase and installation of house umbrellas. Briefly, the answer was that there was no need for warranties since house umbrellas were installed for free. As to any warranties on the house umbrellas themselves, they were the best in the business. Another question was: how long have you been in the house-umbrellas business? The answer was: A long time. But as the presenters said, to be more specific, we were all invited to view a house umbrella in action the next day.

The next day, we met at the demonstration house which had a fully installed house umbrella. It looked pretty good, sort of like a beach umbrella over a sand castle except, of course, on a much grander scale. And grand it was, this marvel of human ingenuity as the presentation people put it. For our benefit, they had workmen, using axes, punching holes in the roof to insure that it was truly leaking absent a house umbrella. The presenters had a rain-imitation machine spraying water from all conceivable angles. There were no signs of house leakage anywhere. Other workmen installed a wind machine that blew hurricanes in any direction. The house umbrella rotated and the whole house lit up. It was such a persuasive demonstration that even the doubters among us bought the whole house-umbrella package. All we had to do now was to wait for the free installation.

We, the pioneers, waited and waited but no matter how long we waited nothing happened regarding the free installations. As a group, we finally decided to open the heavy cartons containing the whole house-umbrella assembly. What we found inside was some average-size rocks, a personal-sized umbrella, and a metal rod that according to the assembly instructions was intended as the drive shaft of the house-umbrella power unit which would generate the electricity to light up our houses. We, the pioneers, were all set to go.

If Only

IN THE U.S., women gained universal suffrage by the 19th amendment passed in 1920. Many women - probably more than many - are still not satisfied. After centuries, even millennia, of male dominance and suppression, shouldn't there be a day of reckoning for the males of the species for all those atrocities against the civil rights of women? Today, metaphorically speaking, that reckoning is at hand. Based on the census, there are more women than men in the U.S. (and if not, that is just another example of the perfidious nature of men) implying that the number of female voters exceed that of male voters. Hence, if only women voted in unison, then all kinds of changes could be made. According to the U.S. Constitution, one method of amending it is to hold conventions in several states and if approved by two-thirds of those conventions, the amendment passes. Hence, if only all women voters participated in the process, whatever the women wanted would become part of the constitution. The obvious first item of these conventions would be to pass an amendment that would deny all men all voting rights from the local up to the federal level. Other appropriate amendments would follow. What could be more fair, considering all those centuries - or more - of male dominance and suppression?

What would be the practical effects of this women-only constitution? Henceforth, all U.S. presidents would be women, all governors of the states would be women, all members of Congress would be women, all members of the state legislatures would be women, all members of county boards and all city councils would be women. All law enforcement agencies would be staffed by women. The list is almost endless, all the way down to the smallest unit of society, the family.

What can men as a class hope for in the women-only infrastructures, be it private or public? They would all have to accept their subordinate role. If they didn't, female units of the proper law enforcement agencies would take care of them. What would be the effects of the reversal of roles have on family life? That is simple enough, consider what the family structure was before and then take the mirror image of it. From various polls, it was concluded that many men - or somewhat less than many - thought that the just passed amendments had always been part of the U.S. constitution.

So, even if some men here and there were annoyed, men in general did not protest the post-amendments era too much. There was a certain glee among the male citizens that women now had to support the family while at the same time being stuck with the travails of childbearing. Male citizens had more time playing golf and other sports. Guess who did the shopping, the cooking, the cleaning, the washing and all the other fun things they had avoided before. Men took solace in that human biology could not be changed by any amendment; there were still activities where they were required biologically, at least up to a point. They had to recognize, however, that modern science had found ways to get around that requirement too.

By and large, women and men were not at war. At a lower level of combat, there were groups of men convinced that if only a male Susan B. Anthony would emerge, then the U.S. would come to its senses and once again be a beacon to the world.

Moral: If only death was abolished, we would all live longer.

The Impossible

A MAN OF means loved money, games, and competitions. One day in the late fall, he arranged an ocean fishing derby with a prize of several million dollars. The participation fees were substantial; in the aggregate they would add up to several million dollars more than the prize. The rules of the competition were: 1. To catch a fish. 2. Tag the fish with a certified derby tag. 3. Release the tagged fish into the ocean. 4. The next day, within five hours from noon, if a competitor catches the tagged fish he or she earns the prize.

As anticipated, a great many paid the participation fee, neglecting to consider the impossible odds. Remarkably, one contestant did catch the fish that she or he had tagged and released. The promoter who had hoped to make millions to add to his millions, instead, had to part with most of his millions. Afterwards, the promoter had a gnawing suspicion that he had been made a fool of.

Moral: Even the impossible is possible.

Questions: Can a fish be taught to return to its trainer despite the pain of the hook?

Or, perhaps a scuba diver was an accomplice?

Improvements

FIVE THOUSAND AND some hundred years ago, the First Couple was pushed out the Exit. They faced a world they had no knowledge of. They did not know how to grow food, how to make clothing, how to build shelter, how to find their way in the new world.

During those five thousand and some hundreds of years, the descendants of the First Couple invented agriculture, how to clothe their bodies, how to build structures and roads and ships, how to navigate the oceans, how to accumulate a body of knowledge that could hint at the nature of life and the universe. After those years, if you were fortunate by birth and ability, you could live a life of pursuing happiness while enjoying amenities not available in the Garden of Eden.

Moral: The past gives the future hope.

Addendum

During those five thousand and some hundreds of years, the descendants also learned how to kill their fellow beings with an ever-increasing efficiency.

Moral: Not all improvements are improvements.

The Inventor

SCIENCE HAS DECLARED that there are about 85 different ways to tie knots commonly used in Western civilization. By trial and error, an inventor set out to construct a machine that would be able to tie all the known knots. He was an adherent to the Edisonian edict that an invention is "one percent inspiration and 99 percent perspiration". The inventor tried out his invention on window-display dummies and the knots were perfect and even beautiful. As the next step, he tried out the machine on himself. Unfortunately, the dummies had idealized dimensions befitting their display function, including very small neck sizes. However, the inventor's neck measurements were on the sturdy side, a minor discrepancy one would think. Contrary to his expectation, the first machine-tied knot on a human subject choked the inventor to death.

Moral: He should have invented a shoelace-tying machine instead.

(A mathematician has calculated that there are 40,000 distinct ways to lace up a shoe with two rows of eyelets each according to Petroski, American Scientist, May/June '03)

It Was Hard

RECENTLY, SOME RESEARCHERS cloned a prehistoric man who had lived about fifty thousand years ago. They had found some DNA on his bones that had been unearthed at an archeological site. And soon enough, a surrogate mother gave birth to the fifty-thousand-year old man. After a decent interval to allow him to grow up into a young adult, the researchers began to ask him about life in those prehistoric times. After all, eyewitness accounts of life in prehistoric time were hard to come by.

In session after sessions, the young man did his best to recall how daily life was in those faraway times. It was hard, said the witness. About the only tools available was a rock or two which by luck had something of a sharp edge on them. It was hard to catch any animals for food so the best thing was to wait for them to die and then eat the carrion. In season, there were edible nuts and berries in the fields and forests. It was hard not to starve in the off-seasons. It was hard to hunt and forage so often. It was hard to live in a place with terrible heat followed by terrible cold, something that for some reason seemed to repeat itself forever. It was hard to keep warm when it was cold and it was hard to keep cool when it was hot.

The researchers went along with this it-was-hard stuff for a while. For one thing, they wanted the witness to tell them about community life, its structure, about its leaders and followers, about rest and recreation, about family life, child and elder care and what else which might be of interest to those living in the modern era. The witness told them that there wasn't anything like that. You were on your own and if you couldn't handle that, you disappeared. Anything about love and marriage, asked the researchers. The witness said no, as far as he could remember there were no love and certainly no marriage. As he had grown up in our era, he had some inkling of what love and marriage meant, but in the old days it meant very little. Then, you took whatever you wanted if you had the strength and if you didn't have that you went without. Besides, as he understood our marriage ritual, that ritual had something to do with religion, as least some of the time. Sure, in the old times that he tried to recall, there was some sort of religion with worshipping, if you had the time, of some rocks and trees and things like that.

This led the witness to another side branch of his recollections. It was hard to get to anywhere else, said the witness, because we didn't know where that anywhere else might be or how to find our way back again. If you dared to go to anywhere else in the old times, you had to be prepared for the worst. Different tribes, if you could call them that, worshipped different rocks and trees and so on, and since you didn't know what to worship and what not to worship, they were only too happy to note your blasphemy and then use a rock and a hard place. They would put together a substantial meal from your remains.

The researchers wanted to know about relationships between men and women. That is easy, said the witness, the women were so strong and independent that the only relationship you could have with a woman was if the woman wanted it. Beyond that if you tried to take the initiative you were, on the average, doomed. The witness, having observed the present-day custom in this regard, was pleased that men seemed to be on their way to independence.

The witness' memory provided some random bits and pieces

now and then. For example, in those early times most things didn't have any names, and that was hard. If you wanted to bring attention to any of these things, you had to point. This was very inconvenient because if you pointed to something in the distance, with all that background, nobody really knew whether you meant a tree or a bird or some enemies hiding in the grass or bushes. At times, some tried to communicate with each other by a collection of grunts, gestures, jumping up and down, or just shaking their heads up and down or back and forth or sideways. The witness never understood anything of this. That was not just inconvenient; it was a hard way to live.

At times, the witness made some remarks on living in the present versus the faraway past. He was annoyed at some things, in particular his foster parents. They seemed to expect that he should, as they put it, behave himself. What did they mean by that? It partly meant he should pay attention to what they called time; that is looking at all these clocks everywhere. It was a time to sleep, it was a time to get up, there was a time to eat, there was a time go to school, there was a time to study, there was a time to do your own thing, which was hardly any time at all. Then, there was a time to get to bed. The next day, the same routine had to be followed all over again.

The witness had a difficult time adjusting to the behavior of young girls. They were strutting around like they owned the universe, but they seldom inflicted physical harm on the young men even when those men misbehaved. A common defense mechanism of the men, the witness noted, was running away whenever women appeared. But, just like in the old days, running away didn't do much good because the women ran faster and were stronger. The same can be said of women of the present time, except that now they use different and more subtle tactics. In fact, said the witness, the tactics were so subtle that he hadn't deciphered them yet.

When the researchers had run out of questions, the witness questioned them about his bones; could he have a look at them?

Flabbergasted, they told him that that was not possible. We can't take the risk that you might contaminate such important relics. At least, the witness persisted; show me where my bones were dug up? Again, he was told that that was impossible, the place was top secret and if the secrecy was let out, their competing researchers would commit any kind of sacrilege to get at his bones. The young fifty-thousand-year old man didn't quite understand their concern. He thought that the least they could do in return for his services was to show him his bones and his burial place. In fact, he was pleased that he had been buried. It had never occurred to him that anybody would bother to do that. Perhaps he had misjudged some of his contemporaries at that far-away time. It was easy, of course, to make misjudgments.

Division By Factors Of Ten

A JOURNEY OF a thousand miles begins with a single step. (Ancient Chinese proverb)

I have always wanted to make a journey of a thousand miles, so I began with a single step. It required some effort, but I succeeded in completing it. I took a second step and I was near exhaustion. Next, I took a third step. Only with an utmost force of will did I manage to complete it. Then I discovered that my steps had been taken in the wrong direction. So, all my efforts had been for naught; I was even further away from my goal than I had been before.

For my second attempt, I decided to reduce my journey's goal to a hundred miles and to orient myself in the proper direction. Due to the exercise I had obtained during my first attempt to follow the Chinese proverb, I was able to take the first three steps without too much difficulty. During my fourth step, though, I nearly stumbled on a pebble on my path and that slowed me down. I was able to detour the pebble during my fifth and sixth step. The effort exhausted me and I had to abandon the hundred-mile goal.

After a period of rest and after checking on the direction that my feet were pointed in, I decided to make a third attempt toward a goal of a ten-mile journey. Now with the stamina built up during my previous attempts, I could easily complete the first sixth steps. During the seventh step, the slope of the road increased which slowed me down to some degree. While in my eighth step, the slope of the road increased further so that I slid backwards to where I had been at the end of the seventh step. Seeing no point in taking steps nine and ten only to slide back to somewhere within the seventh step, I decided to reconsider the intent of my journey.

After a period of extended rest while maintaining mental activity, such as plotting the best course ahead and considering the obstacles in the path of a one-mile journey, I set out toward my goal again. This time, the first steps were taken quite easily even after climbing the steep slope associated with a bypass of the eighth step. This bypass had been planned by me as a further challenge to my journeying. Everything went well until the twelfth step when it began to rain. There were menacing clouds above my path; they would probably gather together to create lightning and thunder. Regrettably, the inclement weather forced me to abandon my one-mile goal. One mile, of course, is such a modest distance anyway so there could be no doubt that if the weather had been better; I could easily have completed the journey. It is always satisfying to know that one can reach one's goal no matter what the obstacles may be.

Moral: To reach one's goals, the goals must be realistic.

A Life After Death

AFTER WHAT LATER seemed like a long sleep without dreams, I woke up. It was cold. I sensed that I was lying on a hard slab, covered with only a thin white sheet. I wrapped the sheet around me and tried to shake off the cold. Around me there were other slabs covered with white sheets and some that seemed to cover other creatures. It dawned upon me that I was in a place that I had always dreaded. My first coherent thought was to cry for help, but I changed my mind. Those who had put me here would probably not be very cooperative faced with the loss of a profitable item.

I found my way out of the slab room and carefully sneaked out of the building. It seemed to be about midnight judging from the position of the moon, if that is possible. Next, I thought I could walk down to the Medical Center and get all this straightened out. Further thought led to the conclusion that the personnel there would be very embarrassed if one of their misdiagnosed clients walked in the door; that could cause all kinds of havoc and I wasn't up to it. The safest alternative seemed to be to walk back to my house which was within a reasonable distance even in my condition. So, dressed only in that thin white sheet, I carefully made my way home. Having reached it, I knocked discreetly on the front door. I heard some shuffling of feet but no other reaction. I didn't blame them. Had it been me, I would never have opened a door to any stranger at an hour or two after midnight. I went around to the garage and lay down in the family car, one of those cars that you can put down the rear seats to create a cargo space. I gathered as many pieces of cloth and towels I could find. With that white sheet and the other stuff, I was sufficiently comfortable to fall asleep.

When I woke up, the car was in motion but stopping here and there, probably at stop signs and traffic lights. Whoever was driving would probably cause an accident if I announced my presence. On the other hand, I was getting hungry and thirsty and that was a good sign. Anyway, I did not want to cause any accident. I would bide my time until the car was back in the garage.

After the return of the car and when everything seemed quiet, I got out of the car, opened a bottle of water and took some dried fruit stored in one of the cabinets. I put on some old work clothes. Being now fairly presentable and no longer hungry or thirsty, I pondered my next step. Still, my sudden appearance would almost certainly cause havoc or something even worse. Saved by the bell, so to speak, I heard a phone ringing followed by general commotion. Just to be sure, I hid in the clothes cabinet. And soon enough, the whole family packed themselves into the car and took off.

In their hurry, they forgot to lock the doors so I had a look at the house. Everything was as I remembered it. The phone rang; it was a clerk at the Medical Center reminding me of my appointment at the Cardiology Department the next day. To sort of getting back to the routines of daily life, I called the family's dentist to get an appointment a few days hence. Then I called an investigative reporter at the local paper. He said he would look into it in a few days if he could find the time. That way, the clerk, the dentist and the investigative reporter could sort of reveal the fact of my non-demise. The family would learn to accept that I was still around and that I had not been stolen off that cold slab.

When I heard the car coming back I hid in the working-clothes cabinet. They were crying, swearing, and using the word "sue" quite often. They made quite a racket. The rest of the day was not eventful as one could expect, at least from my place in the garage. I was toying with the idea of putting a sign on the door of my cabinet saying "Look in the cabinet!" but of course I didn't. The spectacle I was involved in had a certain amusement value by being that proverbial skeleton in the closet. However, sanitation was beginning to be a problem. While not incontinent, I was not a complete teetotaler either. After dark, I dug some pits here and there in the far corners of the property. Sleeping sitting up in my cabinet was not too comfortable either. I longed for stretching out in a bed and a cleansing in a bathtub. I was getting impatient with the appointment person at the Medical Center, with my dentist for not reminding me of my appointment and with the investigative reporter for not investigating fast enough. Not once did the family take a peep inside the work-clothes cabinet. I was beginning to seriously consider a "look-in-the-cabinet" sign again.

Anyway, cabinet or no cabinet, I was obviously in the throes of several dilemmas. If I came back, the family could still sue but the final settlement would be much greater if I stayed missing. The slab people would certainly settle for a sum of some magnitude. On the other hand, if I went on living, I needed money and other resources. You might say, I would need a bigger cabinet. Then again, the investigative reporter should be able to make a bundle by his concocting such a tale. Or, if I wrote a piece titled "Living to Tell the Tale" it should easily make millions.

Days and nights went by and I was still living in the cabinet. After the next convulsion emptied the house again, I went into the house and picked up an assortment of clothes and credit cards and left. I was reconciled to my fate of being a wandering non-person, at least for a while. As luck would have it, I ran into a neighbor who had been out of town for a while. I told him my tale and it was easy to see that he could barely constrain himself from laughing. As they say, I have always depended on the kindness of neighbors. Now I depended on to him to keep on laughing when he told my tale to my family.

Anyway, damn the laughing neighbor. He wasn't the type that could laugh very convincingly. Still, considering the appointment clerk at the Medical Center, the slab people, my dentist, the investigative reporter, the credit-card people, and who knows who else, they would gradually convince my family that I was around somewhere so there was no need to run around being upset. We should all get together some time.

From my point of view, I would be OK. Since you can die only once, I could not die a second time. I have always wondered how the world might be some hundred years from now, or some thousand years - or whatever number of years. Now I didn't have to wonder anymore; I would be there in person and see it for myself. True, my life insurance company might sue me for breach of contract, what with my several lifetime annuities making payments to me forever. You are not supposed to live forever. The pension people would also be unhappy about them paying out lifetime pension payments with no end in sight. More importantly, though, I would be happy.

Listening To Wine

PRESENT-DAY EVALUATIONS OF wines are done by taste. The connoisseur swirls the wine in a glass, smells its aroma, takes a tiny sip to taste it and then spits it out. The next step is to choose any number of fancy words from the wine connoisseur's vocabulary, arrange those words in an artful sequence, note the wine's vintage and finally say a few words about the origin of the grapes, usually a vineyard in some province in the South of France. In conclusion, the connoisseur will comment on his or hers deep friendship with the owners of the estate who can trace the lineage of men and grapes back several centuries. In summary, much ado signifying nothing, to borrow a couple of phrases.

The proper way, though, to evaluate a wine is by listening to it. Put a wine in a glass and really listen to it. The proper procedure is to bend over, turn your head until the ear area is horizontal, then put the ear over the opening of the glass and listen to what the wine has to say. It can be awkward, of course, to go through these maneuvers. That is why so-called wine connoisseurs refuse to use this method even though they all should know better by now. They are, obviously, afraid of making fools of themselves should they spill some wine. For the beginner it might be best to mix some gelatin into the wine, to create something like Jell-O where the wine surface can be vertical. It is then possible to put an ear in the wine glass without bending down and turning your head.

Of course, all of us are familiar with seashell noise. Put a seashell to your ear and you hear a faint sound as if the oceans were slowly inhaling and exhaling. There is a similar sound when you put your ear over a wine-glass opening. This sound, or noise, must be subtracted before listening to the wine. Another background disturbance is a shattering noise sent back from the future, signifying the ultimate fate of all glass.

So, having learned to ignore the seashell effect and the glass-shattering effect, one can truly begin to listen to the wine in earnest. If after the two subtractions there is no wine noise, the wine is no good. If there is too much wine noise, the wine is no good. One must consider the whole wine-noise spectrum and thus take into account both the amplitude and the frequency of the wine noise. Most seem to prefer a wine with large amplitudes and high frequencies. On the other hand, there are those who are partial to small amplitudes and low frequencies. For some reason, not quite understood at this stage of wine research, the noblest wines have ultra-low amplitudes coupled with very high frequencies. Wines with those characteristics are almost invariably from California. Wines with the opposite characteristics are usually from a region of France and imply low-quality wines. Needless to say, not many Frenchmen listen to French wines.

As a final suggestion in this transition period from tasting to listening of wines, one should be of good cheer and stout heart and not be afraid of the multitudes of naysayers. As a final thought, consider a comment made by Karen Blixen where she pointed out that the human body will turn the noblest wine into urine. This dilemma can now be avoided by simply listening to the wine; there is no need to swallow it. This leads to another dilemma. If one can enjoy wine simply by listening to it, why would anybody bother to grow grapes and make wine in the first place? Except for some spillage of wine now and then, there would be no market for it. Dilemmas indeed.

Moral: *"Aller Anfang ist schwer"* to quote some wine growers in the Rhine area.

Magic Realism

GABRIAL GARCIA MARQUEZ, the Colombian Nobel laureate in literature, is known as the farther of "magic realism". His novel "One Hundred Years of Solitude" is an example of this genre. Consider this paraphrase of pages 242 and 243 of the American edition:

"Fernanda wanted to fold her sheets in the garden and asked the women in the house for help, among them Remedios the Beauty. She was very pale and she was asked if she was feeling well. The Beauty answered: "I never felt better". As she had finished saying that, Fernanda felt a delicate pull of the sheets that took them out of her hands and opened them wide. Remedios the Beauty began to rise. The women watched her waving good-by in the midst of the flapping sheets that rose with her. The sheets seemed lost forever when Remedios passed the upper atmosphere and entered another realm. Fernanda, burning with envy, came to accept the miracle, but for a long time afterwards she prayed to God to please send her back her new sheets".

The Man In The Living Room

ONE DAY I came home and there was a man in the living room. Naturally, I said to my wife: "There's a man in the living room". My wife checked and she said: "There is no man in the living room". And that's the way it all began. Whenever I was in the living room, the man was there. As soon as my wife entered, he was gone. An aphorism, generally attributed to Leonardo da Vinci, says: "A thing that moves acquires as much space as it loses". A possible interpretation of this aphorism is that one can be *doing* in one place while *being* in another place. In other words, the man in the living room was just *being* there while at the same time *doing* something somewhere else.

The question arose was the man in the living room *doing* or was he *being?* So I asked him some questions such as "What are you thinking *now?*" at one extreme to the other extreme "Did you use a sledge hammer *yesterday?*" He didn't seem to understand the first question, but he said "No" to the second question. If I interpreted these answers correctly, yesterday he was *being* while today he was *doing*. So I asked him what he was doing. As far as I could see, he didn't do anything. Yet the man in the living room said he was doing something. Could he be thinking? I wondered.

With my usual patience, I hang around for a while to witness what he was going to do. Finally, he went to the book case and removed a book. I knew the book was Opus *9*. I was very familiar with the contents of that book. It had a sweep and grandeur that you seldom see in print these days. The book was a collection of fables, short and long stories, poems and rhymes and aphorisms taken from various sources such as the notebooks of Leonardo da Vinci. If nothing else, the man in the living room had excellent literary taste and I always appreciate that in a human being.

The whole thing reminded me of Harvey, that six-foot tall rabbit, except of course that the man in the living room was not a rabbit. Anyway, the man couldn't stop reading. After Opus 9, he read Opus 8 and all the opuses down to Opus 1. Not to disappoint him with Opus 0, I called my wife and as soon as she showed up, the man disappeared and all the opuses were back in the book case.

By the way, there is a Norwegian word "vardøger" which means "Premonitory sound or sight of a person shortly before he arrives." As an example, my cousin #3 arrives from work at exactly 5 PM. At 4:45 PM, you hear the key being inserted in the front-door lock, the door opens, he walks straight to the bathroom and then flushes. Nobody pays any attention to the 4:45 PM noises; it is just his vardøger announcing that he is on schedule and that he will be home at 5 PM as usual.

So much for all the uncertainties inflicted on us by the man in the living room.

The Man Who Had No Shadow

SOMETIMES YOU ARE up against something you don't want to be up against. Take the case of the man who had no shadow. How is that possible? And even if it was possible, how could it be? Or, basically, how could he do it?

To begin with the basics, where there are no lights there are no shadows. Suppose, for example, that a person is deep down in a mine of some sort and there are no lights whatsoever and the person doesn't carry any matches. Man or beast trapped in such a predicament can see no shadows. Cave explorers exploring caves without lights have recently become a popular sport. Doing cave exploring only is too tame an adventure for today's adventurers. But cave exploring without lights is notoriously difficult to verify to the satisfaction of the organization that keeps track of worldwide cave records. I have been a record verifier of in-the-dark sports for many seasons and I can report that a verifier can't verify anything unless he or she cheats a little and that is just to get back to the cave opening. You have to strike a match now and then to find your way back.

Caves, then, are not the places to do basic research. A man of means realized that fact and he constructed a massive complex around a room that was completely sound insulated and completely light insulated. It was suggested, maliciously, that the man used his means to get into the record books that had eluded him when he used natural caves. The man of means put himself into that light insulated room. The first year of not casting shadows passed, another year followed and eventually the old record of not casting shadows was surpassed. At that point, a verifier had to be appointed and due to my experience with caves, I was chosen. That I had verified records before by striking a match now and then was not mentioned because nobody but me knew about it.

I was led into the elaborate testing complex and I reached an inner sanctum where I was left alone with the man without a shadow. I said hello and he said hello. Then I tried to get the feel of the room by feeling my way around the walls. The man and I conversed now and then just to verify that he was there. He was there but where? I got to know the locations of several pieces of furniture. I was not sure if I ever got close enough to touch the test object. Once in a while when I was groping my way around by touching the outsides of pieces of furniture, I thought that I also touched the outside of a man sitting down.

As we got to know each other better, he and I talked and talked and talked again. He asked me if his girlfriend was OK. I gave him a message from her that she had asked me to transmit to him saying that she was OK. She had also asked me to give him a second message concerning the exercises he ought to be doing in anticipation of that exciting day of his release. Her muscles were OK as I had verified myself several times.

As we kept talking, the man without a shadow at one point told me that the purpose of banning any light was to set an example for mankind; it was not important to him to set a new record in his chosen field of interest. What was important was the struggle, not whether you win or lose. I finally had enough of the dark and the absence of shadows. From my days of cave verifying, I had a few matches left. Since I was getting worried about getting out from this peculiar room, I struck a match. Lo and behold except me there wasn't anybody in the room. The ceiling, so high it was out of reach, was full of all kinds of electronic gear. I stepped on the match as fast as I could, hoping to put it out before any of those sensors noticed it. As I said to myself, it is better to crush a match than to light the darkness. Somehow, I found my way back to the world outside and verified that indeed the man without a shadow was alive and well and that he looked forward to his release. I hoped that would not be too soon because of the well-distributed muscles of his girlfriend. On the other hand, considering all that electronic stuff in the ceiling, maybe she was busy already.

A Postscript

The man of means got out of that dark room to face a new record of not having a shadow. The event took place on a heavily foggy and cloudy day followed by others days of the same weather. To myself, I wondered what he would do when sunny days returned. As always, sunny days did return and I witnessed his scheme to further extend his record. He was surrounded by at least half a dozen bodyguards much taller and wider than he was. Shadows were cast but his shadow was nowhere to be seen. Using the bodyguards' shadows to cover his own did not seem quite fair even though there was nothing in the rules that forbid it. Most of us felt that he was cheating, even though we hadn't anticipated this bodyguard scenario. Rules being rules, the man of means kept accumulating days after days and eventually years after years to add to his record of not having cast a shadow. It appeared that nothing could stop him from his elastic use of the rules.

One day, the impossible happened to make the man of means' records meaningless. From among the masses there arose a man, of ordinary stature, that did not have a shadow under any circumstances whatsoever. The man of means tried various evasive measures to nullify this threat to his up to now unblemished record. It was rumored that the man of means had made an arrangement with the man without a shadow to merge their two bodies into one body. It didn't work. The shadow of the man of means did not disappear no matter what they tried.

The public got tired of all these manipulations and felt that whether anybody had a shadow or not wasn't that important. Based on the public's sentiment, all records that had to do with shadow casting were considered null and void. By this time, the man of means had no means left.

Massage
(Or: The Two And The One)

THE BELL AT the front door rang and I opened it - the door, of course. Two men in their probable thirties stood there and they also carried between them what seemed to be a collapsed table. One of them said we are here from your Health Maintenance Organization and it is time for your annual massage. I had never had anything like that, but I invited them in anyway. Then I called my HMO and asked about this supposedly annual massage. The spokeswoman said there was no such thing. On the other hand, she said, if there are two masseurs with a collapsed table at your place, why don't you take advantage of getting a free massage?

I asked the two how long the massage would take. They estimated an hour plus. I felt that was too long for not doing something useful, so I said I had to get a paper first. At the bookstore, I was about to lay my hands on a copy of El Pais, a Madrid-based daily, when a little old lady in regular shoes grabbed the last copy. So, instead I had to be satisfied with a two-week old copy of Die Welt.

When I and the paper got home again an hour or two later, the two of them were still there. There was also a third person present, a sort of middle-aged woman who apparently had come from the HMO to check up on the other two. She implied that she was a masseuse. This lady took charge of the whole massage thing. She unpacked something, sort of like a dinner plate with various stuff on it. It was mostly some small brown grains, reminding me of raw brown sugar. Also, sprinkled here and there were some very small white spheres that didn't remind me of anything.

The middle-aged lady said that before I could have the massage, I had to ingest the stuff on the plate. Being by now flabbergasted, I said that I never heard of such a preliminary to a massage. The two and the one assured me that it was a very common practice. Since it was so common I was willing to ingest the stuff with water. They told me that water was unacceptable. How about milk? I suggested. No, that was also unacceptable. Then the two and the one of them went into a sort of huddle, very similar to American football practice. They did not seem to be able to agree on the next play, water or no water, milk or no milk, something else or not something else.

I interrupted their huddle to ask if the stuff on the plate had been taken all at once or if it was possible to divide it into two portions, or three portions, or whatever. The two and the one could not agree on the number of portions either. By now, all these preliminaries had taken so much time that there was no time left for my annual massage. The two and the one could not agree on whether to quit or not either. Finally, I went to bed and told the two and the one to agree on something not later than next morning.

I woke up in the morning and the two and the one were gone leaving not a single trace of themselves. The dead bolt on the front door was engaged. After this observation, the phone rang and it was the lady at the HMO I had questioned the day before. She wanted to know if I was satisfied with my annual massage.

Moral: A dream is a dream is a dream.

Mayhem

I WAS SENTENCED to 60 lashes. When the day came for that judgment to be executed, I grabbed the whip from the guy with the hood and whipped him with 30 lashes. After all, he was only following orders. It certainly raised my local prestige to be the lasher rather than a lashee. After our breakfast together, I gave the guy in the hood a few pats on his back to show that I bore him no ill will. He almost fainted, he was still too sore to bear a pat. Before we broke up, I took his hood; I wanted it as a souvenir to help me remember that morning. I was surprised, though, to notice that the guy wasn't a guy at all, but that is probably irrelevant. What really matters is to take pride in one's work. And so the first quarter of the day came to an end.

Lunch is a sort of the break-even point of the day. The heavies are not as heavy as in the morning and their afternoon crews are just getting up and almost running. The only question they cared about was: in what direction? I carried no basic weapons except my legs and that probably settled their direction. Not being one to accept submission, I told one of the wrecking crews that they better change their direction or I was going to unleash myself. I favor my left leg; it looks innocent enough at rest and at first glance, but appearances are not everything. Anyway, I gave my right leg the day off that afternoon and then I went on my path of destruction. As a warm-up exercise, my left leg began breaking and crushing bones. The wrecking crew retaliated, but their efforts were pathetic. Not only did they stop to take care of the wounds inflicted by my left foot, they made no efforts to walk on broken legs or putting their eyes back in their sockets. Being a man of a peaceful nature, I did not take undue advantage of the crybaby's misfortune. And the second quarter of the day came to an end.

Dinner time gives time for reflection and a pause in the strife for existence. Of course, behind the facades of peaceful exteriors, there are rumblings and hissing and growling for those who care to listen. It is like sitting in front a theater curtain where behind it the bloody plays of Shakespeare are rehearsed. Suddenly, one hole after another is punched in the curtain. The devils and their disciples pour through the holes and attack our precious existence. This is going to be a two-legs, two-arms and one-head battle against the forces of evil. The devils' disciples are the most vulnerable, having human form. So, annihilate the disciples. The most effective method is to grab the disciples by their two legs and treat them to the pleasures of the Olympic track and field event of hammer throwing which borrows the movements of whirling dervishes. Then, mow down anything connected to arms and legs and use pointed-headed heads for edging. Any normal heads can be used as battering rams; then onto the devils; those without human forms. A little bit of napalm here and that will loosen them up. Oh, how I love the smell of burnt devils in the evening! Why use violence to curb violence? Because it works. Now, let the devils clean up the mess. The third quarter of the day came to an end.

Time for the evening meal and a night-cap as well as reflection. Maybe, in the long run, arms and legs and heads are insufficient weapons in the fight against evil. But, not to worry, our precious selves have accumulated knowledge of metals and chemicals and atomic detonations. Anyway, the fourth quarter of the day has come to an end, but what a lovely day it has been. Finally, it is time for bed and dreams. My wife will be watching over me and wake me up as necessary.

Mechanical Engineering

TAXI DRIVER SMITH arrived at the central taxi depot at his appointed hour. He was assigned Car 58; not too bad but not too good either. Car 58 was about average considering engine stalling and accident proneness; some cars collide with other cars more often than others. Smith thought that it was a matter of the car's temperament. Some cars look more trustworthy than others and hence picked up more passengers. Car 58 did not have an aura of trustworthiness in Smith's opinion.

Anyway, Smith drove out of the depot and within two blocks he was hailed by a male pedestrian. The pick-up wanted to go to some place in Upper Manhattan. Driving along, Smith used the rear-view mirror to keep an eye on his passenger. He seemed nice enough, but even crooks look nice these days. Then, between one glance and the next, the passenger had disappeared. Smith stopped the car and sure enough the back seat compartment was empty. Yet, you cannot disappear from a car going 45 miles an hour. He drove back to the depot and demanded another taxi, explaining what had happened. The depot staff laughed out loud, but they assigned him Car 68 and parked Car 58 in the back of the depot just to keep from laughing at the sight of it.

Next week, Car 58 with a different driver, also had a passenger who disappeared. The laughter subdued as a New York Times reporter picked up the scent of a story. Another week and another passenger disappeared from Car 58. Finally, the New York Times conducted a deep probe, found the missing passengers who all maintained that they had been driven to their destinations. They had no recollections of having disappeared even though the deep probe documented that these fares had used several hours to reach their destinations within Manhattan.

The New York Times printed all that was fit to print about the result of its deep probe. The national and international press reprinted the Times' study. The deep probe had deep consequences. Husbands began to disappear for several hours before appearing again. Wives began to disappear for several hours before appearing again. Children ditto, politician's ditto, priests ditto, evangelist's ditto, senator's ditto; you could think of any ditto and it was dittoed.

Society began to shake at its foundations. The Moral fibers of society were stretched and then stretched some more. What were the explanations of these disappearances? Were there any religious reasons? Was there any extraterrestrial interference? Were these happenings instances of mischief and foul play?

As the national crisis grew so did the proposals to eliminate it. Even some mechanical engineers began to show an interest in the problem. A group of them got together and purchased Car 58 from the taxi company for pennies; it would have nothing to do with that car anymore. The engineers dismantled Car 58 and found a space underneath the back- seat cushion, just large enough for a grown person to crawl into and out of. The engineers contacted those fares of Car 58 and got their confessions. The New York Times did not see fit to print any of them. The rest of the country slowly accepted the obvious. Husbands and wives no longer disappeared and reappeared, nor did anybody else.

Moral: Even the obvious is not obvious.

Mini-Fables

Notes For Mini-Fables
(... with tongues in cheeks ...)

A Bushy Tale

THE HARE AND the fox had lunch together and talked about what had happened to them since yesterday. The hare observed that the fox didn't look very good. The fox admitted that he probably didn't. As he put it, "I swallowed my tail and it got stuck in my throat," "So, how did you taste?" asked the hare. The fox ignored the question.

Moral: Some questions are unanswerable.

On Drains

WHEN NOAH'S ARK was filled to the brim with pairs of males and females, it began to rain. It was as if Heaven had opened all its windows and soon the Earth was covered with water. After all the sinners had drowned, God decided to let the Earth be restored to its pristine state. And indeed, the Earth recovered because there was a drain somewhere that God could use at his discretion.

Moral: Why didn't God use his other discretions?

Light Years

AN ASTRONOMER AND his team at the University of California at Berkeley announced their discovery of an orbiting star called 55 Cancri. It is about 41 light-years from Earth and has five planets, one of them being an Earth-like planet that could harbor life. The astronomers sent that planet an electronic inquiry asking if the inhabitants were interested in communicating with Earth. After 2x41 light-years the answer came back and it was "No!"

Moral: What did they expect?

("they" would have to be grandparents, great-grandparents, great-great-grandparents et cetera depending on the rules of employment and tenure at that time as well as available health care and adequate nutrition.)

Mini-Fables II

Advice

MISTER X WENT to see his doctor. He told him: "When I walk backwards, I get dizzy". The doctor gave Mister X a thorough physical examination and many medical tests. When the test results were in, they met again. The doctor seemed to be in deep thought; he nodded his head and shook his head as doctors are prone to do. Finally, the doctor's advice to Mister X was: "Don't walk backwards". Mister X followed the advice. Henceforth, he would always walk forward and he was never dizzy again.

Moral: The practice of medicine is an art, not a science.

Relativity

A HARE AND a tortoise walked in opposite directions along a highway. When they met, they nodded to each other as old acquaintances do, and then continued on their journeys. Both could look back and claim that he or she had out-distanced the other.

Moral: On the highway of life, deceiving oneself is easy.

Excellence

AN ARDENT FAN of the boomerang practiced and practiced to become the best boomerang thrower there ever was. One day, he made a perfect throw and the boomerang came back to hit his head with such force that he died.

Moral: Excellence comes at a price.

Molehills

NOT SO LONG ago, the word went out to men and women everywhere to live their lives to the fullest. "Do your own thing", "Realize your dreams", "Dare to live your life" were some of the slogans. These slogans were meant, of course, to lift the spirits of men and women, to encourage them to dream their dreams, but nothing more was intended.

Suddenly, an irrational frenzy swept the land. Men and women everywhere lifted their eyes from their tasks at hand and dreamed of faraway horizons. They went out to conquer the unconquerable, climb the unclimbable, reach for the unreachable. No one cared to tend the fields or harvest the crops, to work in factories or offices, sit in sulkies behind trotting horses or watch them race. No one cared to work at any of their common needs. Soon there was no one to enforce the laws, protect the weak, or heal the sick. No one cared to do the chores.

Fields were abandoned and soon they were taken over by moles and gophers. Orchards were ruined by neglect and insects. Pestilence and famine scourged the land. War was avoided only because men were too weak to fight and women were too weak to argue.

Men and women realized they had to come to their senses. A new slogan was broadcast to men and women everywhere: "Give us men and women to match the molehills!"

Moral: When Necessity beckons, Glory must wait.

Molehills II

Part I: (Paraphrasing: Encyclopaedia Britannica). The common mole is a small burrowing mammal, soft-furred, with minute eyes, and broad and strong forelimbs adapted for digging. It is about six inches long with a tail of one inch. The body is robust and cylindrical, and, owing to the forward position of the front limbs, the head appears to rest between the shoulders. The forelimbs are short and muscular, terminating in broad shovel-shaped feet. The hind legs are long and narrow and the toes have slender claws. The food of the mole consists of earthworms, in pursuit of which it forms underground excavations. The sexes come together about March and the young- generally from four to six in number- are brought forth in about six weeks.

Part II: (There is a mole in my garden.) For weeks now, we have been plagued by not less than one mole. It is a very cute one, at least the one which sticks its head up at the entrance to its underground empire and then surveys the world around it to see what is happening. After a while it retreats to his tunnels and puts an earthen plug at the entrance to keep the world at bay. I have personally observed this behavior by standing very still, pretending to be an apricot tree. I have also personally tried to kill it, but it is still digging despite the fact that my mental powers are exceeding its mental powers. It is now a battle against the elements and the elements are winning. It is time to get to bed and perchance to dream as Shakespeare might have put it.

Part III: (There is a mole in my head.) There is a very big something in my garden. Looking at the thing through the kitchen sliding door which is made of glass, it seems to resemble a little old lady in a very shabby, perhaps dirty outfit; it is hard to tell. Or, the thing could resemble a very small old man. It is hard to see what might be happening since the thing showed me it's back only. I asked my wife about all this and she saw the same that I saw. Meanwhile, the creature continued just sitting there except using its hands to rearrange the gravel within its reach. Let me add that it was sitting on the ground in a sort of lotus position. The two of us seemed to think that sitting that way while moving some gravel now and then was within tolerable limits. Considering that in our garden everything is in its place and nowhere else, this was a major concession on our part. Besides, what is the work ethic of a creature that just sits there, hardly moving its hands and arms, if at all? And then, hard to believe, the creature suddenly disappeared. After some time, I ventured to open the glass sliding door and went outside. Checking on the place where the creature had sat, all I could see was that all this moving of gravel had resulted in a two-dimensional outline of a common mole. The scale, of course, was hardly one-to-one since the length of a mature mole is six inches while the length of the pictorial mole was about six feet. No wonder that my wife and I felt a tinge of fright now that we saw what we were up against, a six-foot long common mole, certainly not a very common mole. I sent my wife inside, fearful that she would be taken hostage. If that happened, what could I do to save myself? So, with considerable lack of courage, I began to look around. And then suddenly, the ground all over our place began to heave and roll like waves on a wind-tossed ocean. It didn't take much reflection to realize that a six-foot mole at a depth of another six feet was hunting for who knows how many feet-long earthworms, its only source of nourishment. My wife and I agreed that disturbing the very earth on which we were treading on was beyond the reasonable limits of nature. It was time to get into action. I got a big shovel and began to dig for moles or earthworms or both. Innocent as I was, I was ready to do battle with the forces of nature; I had set myself up against odds that I didn't like. My idea, as far as I could tell myself, was that if I could get the creature exposed to daylight again, it would capitulate and make itself disappear. This attitude on my part, of course, was based on several of the myths that mankind has saddled itself with in the course of evolution.

It didn't take long before I made contact with the creature. And that is the last thing that I remember. My head, specifically that part of my skull just above my right eye, hit something blunt, something hard, and something unusual because a flash went off in my head as if a photographer's flashbulb had gone off in my head. Not only that, I was utterly confused and very dizzy. After this gap in my memory was filled in, I was still confused and only slightly less dizzy. And that is what I remember after all these events besides worrying about the eyesight of my right eye. As it turned out, after a few days I had nothing to worry about anymore because no more flashbulbs went off in my head.

Part IV: (There are no more moles.) As usual, the whole family went out to lunch together, just like any other Sunday. I had something above my right eye that looked like a skin mole, but nobody noticed it so I pretended I didn't notice it either. The family, of course, knew about all this nonsense about six-inch as well as six-foot moles. But all the members of the family were utterly oblivious to what had happened because it was such a common-day occurrence after all; it was just a source of merriment. All this leads to the conclusion that what is so strange about the activities of moles, the mechanics of dreaming and having lunch with the family? It all melts together in a smooth and continuous narrative so seemingly seamless, so absolutely convincing to all the participants involved that it is hardly worth the effort to bother with any of the details, let alone any close examination of the facts. Any objections fade into the smallest of molehills.

(or, mother said so)

The Mother

LIFE AND DEATH are so intertwined and yet they are not properly organized for the efficient functioning of society. Why not have a breeding season, say a month each year, so that births would occur within a very predictable nine months later. Everybody would know what to do and when to do it, plus or minus half a month. Any births occurring outside this time frame would be deemed to have cheated and would be eliminated. You cannot create order out of disorder. Since deaths follow a more erratic pattern, it would be hard to find something akin to the nine-month period for births. Consequently, a pattern has to be created such as once a month some of us would have to be eliminated based on the true data from the Statistical Bureau. In summary, those who were expected to give birth would give birth and those who were expected to die would die, thus creating order out of disorder, a benefit for all.

The Dear Family headed the Statistical Bureau and had made everything plain and simple and everybody would benefit from plainness and simplicity. Regrettably, you can't run a statistical bureau without running into the unexpected now and then. (For the record, the narrative of this revelation is told by an omnipotent entity who knows the past, present and future and who cannot always distinguish between them.) Consider what happened or didn't happen the other day, a few days after the month's elimination event.

The Most Senior Member of the Dear Family, approved, as always, that month's numbers - but with one exception. The Member noticed the name of someone who had been a dear friend of his in his childhood and the Member deemed that this male citizen should be excused for the time being because he wanted to have a chat with him about the good old days. This order from the Member sent a chill into the hearts of the Bureau bureaucrats. That month they had advanced the date of the elimination process for a few days to get a longer weekend. Now, this childhood friend of the Most Senior Member had already been departed. What could the bureaucrats do? Members of the Family did not consider an innocent mistake innocent. It occurred to a bureaucrat here and there that all they had to do was to come up with a substitute from next month's elimination event. They found a very willing substitute who possessed the necessary qualifications: height, weight, date of birth, disabilities, affiliations, participating in patriotic events, follower of rules and regulations and other items kept track of by the Statistical Bureau. They taught the substitute to imitate the voice of the departed. It was a perfect match.

After this foreplay, the substitute was deemed to be ready to be ushered into the presence of the Most Senior Member. The Member was so pleased with the substitute that he decided to postpone the departure of his childhood friend until further notice. All the substitute had to do was to listen and to nod his head now and then. Finally, the Most Senior Member asked the question that had gotten stuck somehow in his mind, the mind that was the friend of all goodness and the enemy of all non-goodness. He asked:" Why did you call me a jerk at the breakfast table in the house of my mother? It was at 10 A.M. on my 13th birthday which, as I recall, fell on a Friday."

The substitute quit nodding, but he could not recall that his briefers at the Statistical Bureau had ever mentioned that the Member had had a mother. So the substitute answered with what was the only thing he could say: "I didn't. Your mother said so."

Night Watch

SAMUEL SWOWELL WAS a lexicographer or as Samuel Johnson (1709-1784) put it "a harmless drudge". Still, Mr. Swowell had accomplished a lot before and after he became the night watch man at the Oxford Universal Dictionary (OUD) published by a company in Great Britain. The company insisted on being helpful to anybody night or day. Hence, the company was open for business 24 hours a day, seven days a week ready to attack any word problems that members of the public brought forth in person, by phone or other electronic devices.

Samuel Swowell did not mind the night shift. Hardly anybody bothered to struggle with words when they ought to be sleeping or at least being in bed. Every hour or two, someone would call to ask about the meanings and other particulars of words that kept them from falling asleep. Swowell prided himself to be a sort of emergency-room doctor for words. He had a copy of the OUD in front of him and if he couldn't find a word or its particulars, he would wing it making up reasonable-sounding erudite mini-lectures that would satisfy anybody half asleep or more.

Then one night his life would change as he later realized. A young woman (he hoped) asked him the meaning of the word *defenestration*. That was easy; Swowell opened the OUD and read to her "the action of throwing out of a window". She thanked him and the next night she wanted to know what sort of windows the definition had in mind. Was it rectangular, circular, triangular or some other shape? She wanted to know that if something that was thrown was too big for the window opening, then what? Swowell's erudite mini-lectures were of no use either, nor was the OUD.

The next night she called again and wanted to know if there was a word that meant "the action of throwing out of a door"? The young woman also wanted to know if there were words which could describe any of these throwings taking place on a Sunday, say. What is the point of a dictionary being universal if it isn't universal? Swowell tried to point out to her that words, as we know them, are not all inclusive; there are times when we have to fill in the meanings ourselves.

Her nightly calls by now were driving Swowell closer and closer to the edge - and he was afraid of the precipice ahead. So, he invited himself to visit her at her apartment, on the seventh floor on a Sunday. It occurred to him that this was an excellent place to get some practice in throwing things through openings. Alas, the windows were made of thick auto-type reinforced laminated glass. The doors were as solid and intricate as bank-vaults. Even if you managed to throw something through those doors, all you would accomplish was get into the next room or the hallway. There was an elevator, but for some peculiar reason, the elevators to the seventh floor did not operate on Sundays. Swowell, therefore, concluded that he would ask the powers to be at the OUD to be transferred to a position on the first floor of the company's headquarters. But, at OUD such requests had to be literate, full of allusions, impeccable logic, proper use of punctuation, homonyms, use of archaic language and show other signs of intellectual activity. So what, all that Swowell had to do was to think back to all the mini-lectures he had given to the girl on the seventh floor. Now, if he only could, somehow, induce that girl to keep on calling, but not from any location higher than the first floor. If he could do that, it would not matter if he was defenestrated.

> **Moral:** The love of words and the love of a woman both have the same source of persistence.

Noah's Helpers

ACCORDING TO THE Bible, Noah was a righteous man, blameless in his generation in contrast to the wickedness and corruption of the rest of the human race. Before God sent the flood to cover the earth and destroy all humankind, He warned Noah and instructed him to build the ark in order to save his family and specimens of every kind of animal. (Oxford Dictionary Of Allusions)

The Noah family consisted of Noah, his wife and their three sons with their wives, in all eight members. The ark was to be 133 meters in length with proportionate width and height. It was impossible for the Noah family to construct an ark of that magnitude all by themselves. They needed a crew of shipwrights and assistants. They had to have teams of oxen and wagons to transport the needed materials. The family had to employ teams of hunters to gather up pairs of male and female animals from the known world and to herd them to the location of the ark. All these men, women and children had to be fed, had to have basic accommodations and had to be paid; the animals had to be taken care of. The Noah family, then, needed organizers and clerks. That is where I came in. I was to supervise the logistics of the whole endeavor and to report directly to Noah. The pay was good, Noah and family seemed to be nice people and although the purpose of the whole project seemed obscure, it could lead to a nice recommendation for future assignments and employers.

In retrospect, of course, I should have been suspicious of the whole endeavor just by the location of the project. You would think that a ship would have to be built at the water's edge and not on the inland site that Noah had chosen. Further suspicions should have been alerted by the magnitude of the project. Noah, as far as I could determine, had no experience in building anything. He was rather awkward with his hands and he had little practical knowledge. When the shipwrights asked for directions and details, Noah could give them that until sometime in the early afternoon. After that, he usually ran out of ideas and he told everybody to come back in the morning, this in spite of the apparent urgency of the project. The next morning, he was filled up again with ideas as if he had received new instructions and insights overnight. It was obvious that Noah and his family had deep faith; after the afternoon recess, they prayed frequently and at great length. Once in a while I overheard snippets of their prayers; these snippets seemed to concern themselves more with construction details than with faith and divine guidance. What was really hard to understand was the rounding up and the herding of breeding pairs of all animals known to man. What possible purpose could that serve? I put all these suspicions together and I had to conclude that the whole ship-building project was a matter of life, death, and the pursuit of human perfection.

From that point on, as I continued to do my clerking for Noah, I also did what I had to do to insure my own survival. Why did I not warn my friends and colleagues on the project? That is a good question with only evasive answers. On one level, I was just doing what the Noah family intended to do to us. On the next level, how was I to know the scope of the deadly havoc that awaited us, which was beyond my comprehension? And, if I had told the others, would they have believed me? I think not.

I began to write down everything that I could about Noah's ark project. The day came when the ark was completed and only finishing touches remained. As the touches were done, I hid a few sheets of my manuscript underneath each touch where nobody would check anymore. That done, I survived to tell this tale by disguising myself as an animal about my size. I will not dignify that animal by naming it; suffice to say that I had to eliminate one animal so that after the deluge that animal species would become extinct in the new world.

The forty-day flood began and all of Noah's helpers perished within the first hour of the first day. To me, that seemed a rather cold-hearted deed by a righteous man. But, Noah could always claim that all that he had done was to follow orders.

As the ark became stuck on Mount Ararat, I collected all the pages of my manuscript and sneaked away in all the confusion in my disguise as an animal. Later, I joined other survivors, mostly fishermen and other mariners who had survived the deluge in their boats and by catching fishes in the sea.

I am aware that Noah's recollections are different from mine. His recollections were published and they are still being read today. I don't understand why my manuscript about the same events shouldn't merit the same prominence. Maybe it was due to the fact that I had not omitted all the unpleasant details.

Moral: Life, liberty, and the pursuit of happiness *trump* Death, deceit, and the pursuit of vengeance.

The Non-Existing Man

THE OTHER DAY, I received an invitation to the birthday party of a man who did not exist. Being one of the pillars of my community, I did not accept the invitation without consultations with my advisors. They all agreed that I should go. So, on the day of the winter solstice, in a hall of enormous proportions, I attended the birthday party of the man who did not exist. In many speeches, short and long, the non-existing man was hailed as a visionary, one whose thoughts and actions had made humanity come to terms with its humanity. Through the ages, his words and deeds had a profound influence on civilization as we know it.

On the whole, I thought that the birthday celebration of the man who did not exist was inspiring and comforting. No one - that I knew - could object to his presence even in absentia. I was of the opinion myself that had I not existed, I too would have been a beacon for all of humanity to follow. But, as soon as you are born, you begin to sin.

After the celebration of the man who did not exist, I was interviewed by members of the press to give my views of the proceedings just concluded. Contrary to my expectations, the first question concerned the apprehension of some that the celebration did not extend itself to a woman who had not existed. After some finessing on this point, I was able to convince the press corps that whether we celebrated a man or a woman that did not exist was not important. Both are human beings and what the world needs now is love sweet love - to quote somebody. What humanity does not need is more bickering and strife; peace and quiet are more important.

What surprised me a great deal was that when we, the celebrants, had worked our way through the press corps, we were confronted with a large crowd of demonstrators outside the hall. Some carried signs complaining that we had not celebrated the birthday of the man who did not exist with sufficient passion and sincerity. Others carried signs lamenting that this birthday celebration of the man who did not exist was way in excess of what was proper. Some signs went so far as to denounce any celebrations whatsoever of the man who did not exist. Since all these arguments were reduced to a few words on placards of inadequate size, you had to guess at their proper interpretation. There seemed to be a wide resentment of the status quo. How about all of us, many placards asked, we who exist today, as well as those who existed in the past as well as those who will exist in the future, don't we deserve birthday celebrations too? Why are we less important than those who do not exist?

The placards argued back and forth without coming to any conclusions. Even I, a pillar of my community, had to admit that those who denied the importance of any non-existing human being had a point. After all, I would not hire anybody who did not exist and who, therefore, could not do any useful work, be it manual or intellectual. On the other hand, when you are a leader in the community, you have to provide an example that the populace is willing to follow. So, if we celebrate the birthday of the man who did not exist, it is because we need to have a perfect person to guide and comfort us.

Moral: Whether a Man did or did not exist, is beside the point.

Notes On Aliens

THE USUAL STUFF about aliens coming to Earth and wreaking havoc is not what will happen. Since they came to us first rather than us coming to them, the aliens must be much more advanced and so-phisticated in technology and science, including biology. Earthlings will not be exterminated by the use of force. We will simply be elimi-nated, slowly but surely, by applied contraception. The aliens will change the atmosphere slightly by adding to it a gaseous contracep-tion compound which will make all humans on Earth sterile. Since the maximum verified age of humans is about 130 years, at the end of that period there will not be any homo sapiens left. So, all that is required by the aliens is to show a little patience and the Earth will be theirs in about 130 years.

A seemingly logical defense against a contraception attack is to attack with an anti-contraception attack. All that that will ac-complish is to make the aliens impatient and make them consider extermination by conventional means. Or, if cooler heads within the alien community prevail, they will simply invent an anti-anti-contraception method and so on ad infinitum. All that this fever-ish activity will accomplish is to pollute the atmosphere. The only longtime solution to the contraception problem is to reach some kind of accommodation with the aliens. If they want the Earth, let them have it. But while saying so, remind the aliens that Earth is not worth waiting for. Why not try some other planet not quite as insignificant and not so far out of the way? Your alien brothers and sisters are probably laughing at you behind your back - and snickering too - for having bothered to colonize Earth. Nobody likes to be laughed at - even aliens. They will probably pack up their things and be on their way to a more sophisticated planet, one which is worthy of their presence.

How do you recognize an alien? As far as human beings are concerned, the aliens look like human beings. They blend perfectly into any natural or physical setting and into any ethnic or cultural background. Yet they are - in a way - easily detectable because they never seem to die. There is no record of any alien found dead anywhere on Earth. While mankind gradually dies off due to the aliens' gaseous contraception method, the aliens prosper and produce their offspring, although no one has ever seen their offspring, there must be offspring somewhere.

By the way, the aliens' gaseous contraception method easily explains why the dinosaurs died out. It happened because some tribe of aliens did not like dinosaurs. One can, of course, speculate endlessly about this and that. As an example, consider this question: that gaseous contraception compound might still be in the Earth's atmosphere, how do you get rid of it?

Nut Business

YOU MAY HAVE noticed that the preparation of various ethnic dishes require pine nuts. What you probably don't know is how devastating this requirement can be for those who have to gather the pine nuts. There are no pine-nut plantations; all nuts must be harvested in the wild. That means that harvesting must be done either in the far North or at very high elevations elsewhere. High elevations mean rugged mountains where pine trees are struggling to survive and also it means that pine-nut harvesters can hardly eke out a living. Far North or high up mean terrible climatic conditions which is the first of many difficulties that faces the very few people who have to live in those areas. There are just a few villages here and there with a few hundred inhabitants each. What may be called cities, are so far apart that there is hardly any communication between them, in the sense of people-to-people contact. Pine-nut harvesters are condemned to live isolated lives, deprived of cultural stimulation and human contacts. Remarkably, some pine-nut harvesters are married and, even more remarkably, some of the families have kids.

The pine-nut harvesters must provide for their families. Compare the difficulties faced by these providers in the far North or high up versus the ease to provide for them if they only had lived close to the equator and close to sea level. This observation leads us to enumerate some of the physical hardships endured by the typical pine-cone harvester during a typical work day. First he has to get out of bed, then light the stove, put on warm clothing, say good-by and trudge into the wilderness. It is almost a requirement that the harvesters must be male. If he is lucky enough, he finds lots of pine cones on the ground covered by snow. These cones are so bulky that he cannot possibly carry them with him. Out come the special tools required for the extraction of the pine nuts. It is hard work, it is dangerous work; the cones do not give up their nuts easily. Suppose that there are no cones on the ground, but there are lots of cones way up on the pine trees. The harvester climbs up the pine trees one by one, suffering scratches everywhere. Getting down the pine trees is even more dangerous. The most efficient way to get down is to slide down. While loggers speak of widow makers when cutting down trees, pine-nut harvesters speak of wipe-out makers. If you don't slide down a pine tree trunk properly, anything extruding from the male body may be sheared off. As already mentioned, not all pine-harvesters have kids.

By now it is around noon; it is time for a short rest. Ernest Hemingway begins his novel, *For Whom the Bell Tolls*, with this description of a pine-nut harvester resting at midday: "He lay flat on the brown, pine-needled floor of the forest, his chin on his folded arms and high overhead the wind blew in the tops of the pine trees." Hemingway may not have gotten the season correctly (no snow), but he certainly got the mood at midday correctly.

After that short rest, the pine cones get harder and harder to find. In order to support his family, as a last desperate step, this pine-nut harvester heads for the local "Big Chute" where pine trees are abundant and pine cones even more so. However, any cone harvested comes at a steep price. The "Chute" is so steep that if you misplace a foot, you will probably slide down the "Chute" for hundreds, maybe thousands of feet while rocks, roots and trees destroy your clothing and eat away at your flesh. But, lots of pine cones will follow you downhill, so for some pine-nut harvesters the risk seems worth taking.

At the end of the day, this typical pine-nut harvester has a few nuts in his pouch, probably not sufficient to put food on the table for his family. Occasionally, the pine-nut wholesaler shows up and gives him a pittance for all his labor; a prime example that the living-wage movement should be concerned with. Anyway, if you ask a pine-nut harvester if his life is worth living, he mumbles something. That is taken to mean that things could have been worse; suppose he had to collect sesame seeds for a living. Some of the harvesters will tell you privately that they dream of Southern climes and collecting coconuts from swaying palm trees.

So, next time you enjoy a meal where pine nuts are an ingredient, give thought to the hardships that the pine-nut harvesters had to endure to provide it. Better yet, boycott pine nuts. If there was no demand, there would be no need to have pine-nut harvesters. Being freed from their strenuous life, they would move South and closer to sea level, there to switch to picking coconuts. If certain ethnic groups don't heed this boycott call, maybe more attention should be focused on these groups.

Moral: Be a socially conscious diner without prejudice.

An Ode To Here

WE BUMPED INTO each other more than we met each other. I was headed in a North to South direction while he was following an East to West direction. We exchanged the usual pleasantries, each of us, in voice, blaming ourselves for the bumpy way we had met while, in thought, we were very much irritated at the other's carelessness. On this particular point, of course, I was just guessing; I'm not a mind reader. What happened next and thereafter, though, are just plain facts. All of a sudden he asked me: "Are you here?" Of course I was here unless I was invisible or he had no vision. Sometimes, it is difficult to know what to answer, so I didn't answer. His next question was: "Are you there?" "Where is there?" I asked. "Not here," he answered. Obviously, there are only two places where you can be, here and there. As we continued to ask and answer inscrutable questions and answers, I finally got the idea that he was talking about California. He mentioned the Pacific several times. The Pacific, he said, has such a mellifluous sound; the mere mention of it has such a soothing effect on everybody. Even the meaning of Pacific gives you a peaceful feeling.

Strange, I thought, here we are in California, *the here*, considering *the there* that everybody else is consigned to. So, the question arose, between the two of us, suppose you are somewhere else but you want to be here, what is the best way to get here? My companion- having talked to him for a while, seemed to be entitled to this courtesy by now – said, that the best way to get from there to here is along an East-West direction. You begin by climbing the Sierra Nevada Mountains, then take a leisurely hike down its foothills on the other side, then cross the Central Valley - that breadbasket for us all - and after crossing the minor mountains of the coastal range, you finally reach the Pacific; this place of places, this place of peace, of gentle waves, of far-away horizons, this threshold to the rest of the world.

I gave my companion my idea of the best way to enter here. Cross the state border in the North then continue along a general South direction. Walk through the redwoods, cross the rivers, reach the San Francisco bay, continue through the Central Valley, get to the Los Angeles plain and finally transverse the deserts only to be stopped by an international border; then you have truly traced the spine of California.

True, my companion and I may have crossed a few hills too many, gotten lost in metaphors and entangled in contradictions. But, here we were at the crossroads of the world nearly out of words and gestures. I asked my companion: "Where are you going next?" "Far, far, away" he said, "to a place where no one has ever heard of California."Once I find such a place, I know that I have reached my destiny. Then and only then will I cross the Pacific, wade ashore somewhere on the California coast, touch the land with my feet and hands, knowing that at that moment, of all the moments of my life, there will never be another as wondrous".

While I understood my companion's sentiment, I couldn't help wondering why you would go anywhere when you are here already.

Moral: If there was no *there*, then it would be no *here* either.

Off To The Races

LEOPOLD HE CALLED himself. Leopold also called himself the king of horse racing or Leopold King for short. True enough, he owned several racetracks and he had substantial fractional ownerships of many more. These racetracks were upscale indeed; no county-fair racetracks were of any interest to him.

But Leopold sensed a subtle change of attitudes among the horse racing fans. The fans' enthusiasm of yesteryear was gradually diminishing. Leopold thought he knew why and the why was, that greyhound racing was getting more and more popular. Imagine, stupid dogs chasing mechanical rabbits that they would never catch. To compete with this greyhound phenomenon, Leopold introduced various innovations at his racetracks. He had saddles turned half a revolution so that the jockeys faced the tails of the horses. Another innovation was the two-man saddle so that one jockey was the lead jockey while the other was designated as the co-jockey. Neither the rear-facing jockeys nor the tandem-jockeys aroused the interest of the public for more than a few weeks. It was recognized that Leopold's innovations were very crude attempts at low-brow humor that were unworthy of the sport of kings.

Inspired by greyhound racing, Leopold decided to get rid of jockeys altogether; these diminutive creatures earning prices and fees beyond the ridiculous while at the same time, on the average, steadily gaining in weight that was steadily slowing down the horses. The only problem was; how do you train horses to behave like greyhounds? It had always puzzled Leopold why horses could be made to race in the first place. They had, it seemed, no incentive to do so, in contrast to greyhounds that at least had the incentive to try to catch rabbits. Similarly, if one wanted to have horses-only races, what incentive would there be for the horses to race? At one of his experimental racetracks, Leopold tried many things, but none of them worked with any sort of predictability. As an example, when the horses were at the starting gates and the gates opened, the horses just stood there. After a while, a few might venture a few feet, just enough to socialize with other horses. To get the horses going, Leopold and his crew tried various noises such as rock and roll music and other boom-boom noises, but the horses were still idling at the gates. They even tried firing off cannons, but it didn't work.

After further experimentation, Leopold realized that he had to bring jockeys back into the sport. Instead of mechanical rabbits as in greyhound racing, Leopold replaced the rabbits with wooden life-size cut-outs of retired jockeys. These jockeys' job was to get into one-on-one relationships with the horses to gain their trust and affection.

Horse racing came back from its slump and Leopold could again call himself the king of horse racing. Public confidence in the gambling aspect of the sport of kings was based on the sure and certain knowledge that horses were not smart enough to fix a race. Horses of any age do not understand what fixing means or how to do to it even if they had the ability to understand the term. It was a sort of two degrees of separation situation insuring unpredictability, fair play and fair odds. But, there will always be a few naysayers no matter how perfect a system is. Some suggested that anybody with a syringe filled with the proper ingredients could easily fix a race. Also, how about the jockeys thrown out of work by the new innovations? Would they be immune to temptation?

Moral: There is never a thing that is a sure thing.

The Oleander Syndrome

OLEANDER, AS HE was called, knew that he was born with several severe birth defects. His right leg was where his left leg was supposed to be. His left leg was where his right leg was supposed to be. Similarly, other body parts such as arms, ears, eyes, lungs, kidneys, and what not were not where they were supposed to be. It was as if everything had been transposed.

Consequently, as soon as he began to talk and was able to write bits and pieces, he applied for several disability pensions, one for each for his birth defects. The disability bureaucrats gave his applications their proper scrutiny. After repeated investigations, the Disability Board allowed one pension for the mix-up of Oleander's two legs. Members of the Board noted that as far as they could see, the relative positions of the big toes were as standard as one could wish. On the other hand, this was a subjective observation. Since Mr. Oleander was the one who had to live with his disability, he had to be the ultimate authority on his own defects such as his difficulty in walking.

The interchange of the right and left eyes caused Mr. Oleander's vision to be so dim that he could hardly see. The interchange of the right and left kidneys required dialysis treatments. The Disability Board granted Mr. Oleander a disability pension for each these birth defects and also most of the other defects.

Mr. Oleander gained the attention of the medical community as well as the general public. Some voices from the public suggested that with the current state of medical science where, for example, a defective heart could be replaced with a better one; it was even possible to replace the whole heart-lung assembly. Therefore, why couldn't Mr. Oleander agree to surgery that would get all his body parts in their correct positions? Compared to the cost to the public treasury of Mr. Oleander's multiple disability pensions, the multiple surgeries would pay for itself in the long run. Mr. Oleander doubted that this was the proper way to proceed. What was important was to correct his and his children genetic makeup, not just to correct the mechanical aspects of their bodies as it were. That would hardly benefit anybody, long term or short term.

And so it was that nothing was done, long term or short term. Mr. Oleander was satisfied by being called a walking miracle even if he didn't do much walking. His children, also born with similar birth defects, got multiple disabilities pensions too.

Soon, there were others who were diagnosed with the Oleander syndrome. The medical establishment eventually concluded that the syndrome was caused by an insidious virus. There was no known cure for these multiple diseases and it spread rapidly throughout the nation and then to all the continents. The nation and the world could no longer afford to pay any disability supports.

It was concluded that since the Oleander disease would in time affect everybody, it was deemed further that the Oleander syndrome would be considered the normal condition and hence no disability support was any longer necessary. Mr. Oleander and his offspring were not convinced.

On Bushes And Birds

AS NURSERIES GO, it was a modest affair. The Walther and Vonder Vogelweide Nursery were in the business of selling bushes of sizes from inches tall up to the heights of small trees. Walther's task was to grow the bushes while Vonder was in charge of enhancing the value of these bushes by shaping them into fanciful shapes such as dogs, or ducks or cats, or birds, or horses; any shape limited only by Vonder's imagination and the suggestions from their customers. As time went by, Walther and Vonder noticed that the most popular creations of Vonder's were simple bushes, of average height, so shaped that two birds seemed to be perched on different branches. The birds seemed almost lifelike; even a slight breeze made their wings flutter.

Walther was pleased by the sales volume of the two-birds-in-a-bush creations. Yet, he was also jealous of Vonder's ability to create them. True, he raised the bushes that were required for her work; obviously, if there were no bushes there would be no fluttering birds. In fits of resentment and jealousy, he caught himself more than once being tempted to trim a bird from one of his wife's masterpieces. One day he did; the bird in his hand was a heavy burden. He was ashamed of himself; if nothing else because his deed meant a substantial monetary loss. The value of a one-bird bush was far less than a two-bird bush.

Vonder pretended not to notice her husband's discontent. She took the further step of changing her bush designs. She sculptured bushes that obviously were life-size versions of her husband; they became the best-selling items of the Vogelweide Nursery. Walther was now so pleased that he no longer felt any resentment for being the grower of the bushes.

The significance of Vonder's life-size portraits of her husband was not lost on the community. Wives and girlfriends would order bushes shaped to look like their husbands and/or boyfriends; women know what every man wants. As an added incentive, Vonder would guaranty, in writing, that she would re-trim, as required, any bush as long as she lived. Also, any bush portrait would show a likeness that was based on what it had been a decade or so ago. Upon divorce, remarriage or change of boyfriend, Vonder would re-trim the bushes to reflect the new relationships - for a modest fee.

Moral: A bird in the hand is not worth two in the bushes. (As of August 15, 2004)

Serendipity: On the eve of August 31, 2004, I was reading "A History of Norwegian Literature" (Edited by H. Naess, University of Nebraska Press, 1993.) In the section devoted to the Norwegian poet Herman Wildenvey (1886-1959), there is this quote from one of his poems:

"Let the bird in your hand fly away in a rush.

Then open your heart and stretch out your hand,

For those better birds, the two in the bush."

On The Periphery

MY PERIPHERAL VISION frightens me. I hold my head steady and in the peripheral region between seeing and not seeing, there are all those devils and monsters nibbling away at my being, trying to destroy my mind and to poison my body. I turn my head and all those devils and monsters, of all sizes and all colors, scurry around to find new hiding places where they can hide while devising new techniques for my destruction.

Consider the other day. My head was turned straight forward and the various colonies of creatures seemed to have taken the day off and were resting in the crevices of my mind waiting for an opportunity to strike again. So what happens? A little fellow, I had to assume, came into my peripheral view being very nonchalant about the whole thing and did not seem to have a care in the world, or shall we say in my world. By the wisdom accumulated by me over the ages, the most dreadful thing that can happen is when peripheral creatures try to ingrate themselves with you. Something is up their sleeves; you better watch out. I applied the standard maneuver first, that is I turned my head abruptly. That didn't seem to bother him; he was still there hamming it up just as before and still very much alone. He must have something up his sleeve.

Then this devil opened a door, a rectangular door with the

colors of the blackest black and the whitest white, depending on how you looked at it. It was an opening to the abyss, I surmised. What else could it be? If I had had any sense at all, I would have kept turning my head and hope that he would disappear. But I knew I couldn't do it; how often do you have the chance to look into the abyss, the void of all voids? Besides, if I dismissed the present crew of one, there was no guarantee that another crew would be any better.

The next step was to establish some practical way of making contact with that nonchalant creature that just stood there next to the door he had opened. The first obvious step was to make myself small enough to squeeze through the door to the abyss and then move on. So I moved on and whatever size I was required to have at any particular time was the size I had. The nonchalant fellow was my guide and he asked me what I wanted to see. My first wish was Hades, that place of all places so dear to mankind. Next, due to my ethnicity, I asked to see Valhalla the place where my ancestors spent their days in battle and then relaxed in their off hours resurrecting their fellow warriors and sharpening the edges of their weapons to prepare themselves for another day of wholesome slaughter. Of the more modern sections of the abyss, I dropped by the headquarters of various study groups - one messiah per group - each of them devoted to explain to the other groups why their founding messiahs were wrong. There was one and only one divine being and only one divine text and non-believers would all be pushed into the abyss never to be heard from again. I asked the nonchalant fellow how come this belief was possible considering all the activity I was witnessing. The fellow said that this place was a sort of pre-abyss gathering to see if some agreements could be worked out.

I shook my head and the whole pre-abyss set-up disappeared,

even the nonchalant fellow was no longer within my peripheral viewing area. It was an interesting experience, though. On the other hand, maybe I shouldn't try to show mankind the true and certain path to salvation. As long as there are no agreements among the factions at the pre-abyss gathering place, it would probably not be possible.

Once On Shore

DUE TO A number of unforeseen, unusual, unreasonable, unpredictable, and unlikely circumstances, I found myself stranded on a small island somewhere in the vast expanse of the Pacific. The island had a few coconut palms. With some hastily prepared stone and wood tools I could survive on coconut meat and coconut milk indefinitely. This predicament I had to endure for a long time. It was not a life I had envisioned for myself. I was destined for a greater calling.

In my prior civilized life, I had often heard of the power of prayer. So, I prayed to Him and told Him that I would really appreciate some help in getting off the island; a small boat would certainly help. True enough, the next morning a small boat washed ashore. "Is that sufficient?" asked the Voice. I noticed that the boat had no oars and no sail. So I prayed again, asking for two oars and one sail. The next morning, the three items drifted onto the island. Again, the Voice asked me if those items met with my approval. I said that I approved; I even said thank you. I prayed for the third time where I asked the Voice for safe passage back to civilization. The next morning, I was sailing the small boat, helped by a gentle but firm wind while steering it with the help of one oar. It occurred to me that the second oar was really surplus, but I kept it anyway for mostly sentimental reasons. When I got hungry, fish jumped into the boat. When I was thirsty, a shower took care of that. Occasionally, the Voice asked if

I was OK. I assured the Voice that, under the circumstances, I was doing as well as could be expected.

After what seemed like weeks or months, I was back to the continent whence I came. Big consternation. During my long absence, I had been declared dead and my estate had been divided among the members of my family and even some of my friends. Since I was legally dead, I had no legal standing in court to challenge the living and to make my estate whole again. Yet, as everybody could see for themselves, I was physically alive. Big dilemma.

For me, that dilemma was solved by a combination of volcanic eruptions, lava flows, and typhoons. All official records in my locality were wiped out, including death certificates as well as other paper manifestations of civilization. Otherwise, civilization itself did not seem to have suffered. I could again be considered to be among the living and I wasted no time in gathering the pieces of my estate around me.

Life went on as it should. Once again, I was the lord of the manor, so to speak. After months, maybe years, the Voice spoke to me and asked: "Shouldn't I get some of the credit?" The Voice added something inscrutable when He said: "Have you heard of the common saying "Once on shore, we pray no more". I didn't want to listen to such talk so I ignored the whole incident. Why does the Voice speak in such a befuddled manner?

Suddenly, one day, due to unforeseen, unusual, unreasonable, unpredictable, and unlikely circumstances, I was again on that small island somewhere in the vast expanse of the Pacific. It was back to a steady diet of coconut meat and coconut milk. I concluded that it was time to pray again. There was no answer ever. I wrote this stuff and dug it down in a safe place, marked with a (rock) cairn. One day, maybe, someone will find it, read it, and consider the unfairness of it all.

Moral: Hell has no fury like a Deity scorned.

Outdoors-Indoors

DURING AN OFFICIAL outdoor event during the first term of his office, where I was present, the President slipped on a banana peel and fell into the arms of his female vice president. What had been rumored was now escalated into fact. Why? Because it was no longer possible to slip on a banana peel due to the fact that now all bananas were genetically modified not to have any peels. So the question arose how had this particular banana peel slipped through all the safeguards built into the various check points erected by the federal authorities. It was suggested by some that the definition of what was a banana was imperfect and hence the source of all the confusion. Once the President had gotten up and had untangled himself from the vice president, he was furious because his wife was furious and the vice president was furious because her husband was furious and the rest of the establishment was furious because everybody else was furious.

Despite all the fury, the President was elected to a second term. One of the first decisions he made after being sworn in was to decree that henceforth all outdoor federal events would be held indoors. At the beginning, this decree made common sense to the populace. As time wore on, however, there arose a suspicion that gradually developed into an opinion and then to a near fact that the President had dealt himself a straight flush. It was based on the rumor that the

President and his vice president were seen to have ascended together the stairs up to the living quarters of the White House. Since this was probably true, it sort of followed that as they entered the north bedroom, the President slipped because of a fold in a Persian rug fronting a bed. He fell into the arms of his two-term vice president who had slipped on the same fold next to the same bed just before the President did. It was a good thing that these nearly simultaneous events happened to take place indoors and not outdoors with so many witnesses present.

According to tradition, the vice president was elected as the new president. Now, of course, her husband was the target of malicious gossip rumors. He was just sitting there having not much to do except getting up in the morning, eating three meals a day and looking at the evening news which was mostly about his wife. And then to bed, usually without his wife; she was busy, busy; too busy to be busy with him. From a distance, that sort of life for him seemed sad and it was sad until he got the idea of contacting his wife's predecessor. He sneaked out of the White House and took a public transit conveyance to the former president's residence. It was, of course, closely guarded by the Secret Service and who knows what else and who else. With the help of a local garbage person, he managed to pass a note to the former president. It didn't take long before he came practically running out of the compound; he was starving for attention and couldn't think of enough words of thanks that somebody wanted to know about his legacy. What the husband had in mind, of course, was to ask him how he had managed to fall into the arms of women even in public without suffering any consequences. He said that you had to have a gimmick such as banana peels or Persian rugs. You arrange a contrived mishap, and since almost everybody does not want to witness the president making a fool of herself or himself in public, you are shielded by the aura of the presidency. Do what you want and you will still be president. —The husband of the

President took the advice and he did whatever he wanted to do. His gimmick had something to do with raw eggs, slipping on ice (seasonally), fake blood and other spectacle helpers. Eventually, he too would become president.

A Pebble Game

A GULL FROM a faraway place came down from the sky in a graceful glide to a feet-down landing on a pebble beach. On his webbed feet he waddled up to the gull closest to him. "Let's play a game," he said, "I lose, you win, how about it?" "Sounds good," answered the other gull, "what sort of game do we play?" "I throw a pebble into the surf. If you find it, I'll feed you for a day.

The gull from the faraway place threw a pebble into the surf. The other gull tried to find it, but it was lost among all the other pebbles. "Too bad" said the gull who had invented the game. "You owe me a day's feeding. Now you throw a pebble." The other gull threw a pebble into the surf and the gull from faraway found it almost at once. The other gull was impressed. "Remarkable" it said. "How in the world did you do that?" "You owe me another day's feeding," said the gull from far away.

The gull who had invented the game always found the pebble. The other gull never found the right one. They played the game until the gull from faraway had won several weeks worth of feeding. Finally, it said: "Now get busy, I'm hungry". As the other gull went to gather food, the pebble-game-inventor thought; "Even gulls are gullible."

Moral: Dishonesty could be a good provider, maybe

The Perfect Society

HERE AND THERE were the beginnings of a perfect society. The bits and pieces of such a society came together and hence into existence. All went well for a while. The first inkling of trouble began when too many from the outside this perfect society wanted to join it. But a basic tenet of the perfect society held that it should not have too many inhabitants. On the other hand, closing the borders to the perfect society, requiring border guards and support personnel, contradicted everything it stood for. Those looking in on the perfect society from the outside, deplored that they could not be part of it. Even more remarkable, members of the perfect society began to lodge a complaint here and there. Some citizens, just a few of course, sensed that while they were all perfect, some seemed to be more perfect than others.

Another complaint, barely audible, was that a perfect society would be impossible to improve upon and hence the only possible evolution of society would be toward an imperfect society. Questions arose from the fact that in a perfect society, whole categories of professions and institutions would be obsolete. There would, for example, be no need for lawyers, law enforcement personnel, military organizations, the courts, congressional, state, and local elections. What would all these people do for a living? Also, even in a perfect society citizens will die now and then. Replacements had to be chosen by some procedure. Should it be by appointment? That would imply that some citizens had to decide. But who should decide? To some, this smacked of elections. Besides, how should minimum qualifications be agreed upon? It occurred to some that nepotism could arise even in a perfect society.

The impossibility of avoiding death was the Achilles heel of the perfect society. Since all citizens wanted to delay the inevitable, that seemed to require doctors and nurses, and lots of them. So again a dilemma arose because you just couldn't take an unemployed lawyer and let him or her do some doctoring instead. In a perfect society, of course, there is no unemployment so the tendency of thinking such thoughts was banished from many minds. Anyway, if a person was smart enough to be a lawyer, he or she was certainly smart enough to be a doctor or nurse. Besides, a lawyer is a Doctor of law.

As already mentioned, in the perfect society there would be no need to have courts and prisons. On the other hand, some citizens may want to be in prison because of the free room and board. Should these citizens be denied such a basic request? Suppose that persons outside the perfect society sneaked in past non-existent border guards and created mayhem. Citizens would be incapable of defending themselves since they had no knowledge of the use of weapons or methods of criminal detection.

Does a perfect society need religion? People do not sin and hence there is no need to fear an unpleasant afterlife. If there is no sin there are no sinners. How do religious leaders of the many one-and-only true faiths handle such a society?

The perfect society lasted for a while but was abandoned, more or less, because of the experience gained. In the short or long run, such a society had too many imperfections.

Moral: Man does not live by perfection alone.

Plants And Philosophy

A PHILOSOPHER WALKED through a meadow. When he found a boulder of the proper size and contours, he sat down to rest. He looked at the grasses, the wild flowers and the other plants around him and the sight moved him to meditate:

"A plant is two things, yet one. One part strives toward the light, always seeking it. It seeks the light with its leaves, using its stems and branches to lift the leaves toward the light. It savors the dew in the morning, the heat of the day, the raindrops of the storm, and the chill of the night."

"And one part crawls away from the light, seeks its way into the earth, burrows through it, pushes it away. It seeks out the hidden wetness, the nourishment in every crevice consuming decaying fragments of life past. This part steadies and anchors the part seeking the light. It nourishes, yet is nourished by its inseparable twin above the ground. Each part lives for and by the other. A harmony exists where each helps and is helped to sustain their life together."

(A very good way to live)

Poetry And Pottery

WHO BUT ME could have thought such a thought? Who but me could have done it? I traveled to the West Coast to find a place to sit down and look out over the Pacific. I saw the sky, I saw the ocean, and I saw the horizon separating the two. At sunset, the three merged and then disappeared. With the stillness, the colors, the gradual fading of day, it seemed as if creation was performed in reverse.

My days went by as peaceful as could be until one day something or someone moved in the distance. I heard a slight rustling sound, I saw the vague outline of a silhouette, I sensed a disturbance in the universe. Since the rustling thing definitely moved, I decided to confront this intrusion and get it over with. When I moved against it, it moved away. When I retreated, it came closer. When I stood up, it sat down. When I sat down, it stood up. When I turned around, I couldn't tell what it was doing. However, if it could sit down and stand up just like myself, it should be something similar to me. So I cast away all my fears and resolutely marched toward this thing. But, contrary to expectations, the thing marched toward me, as if it was getting tired of our games.

As it turned out, this rustling thing, this disturber of the universe was just an ordinary, smallish man. He was so ordinary that he looked like anybody else. It was as if humanity had duplicated itself so often that it had run out of new variations. His looks didn't seem to bother him because he seemed rather cheerful. "Call me you," he said - at least that is what I thought he said. I can listen to the universe with my sense of hearing, but otherwise I am rather deaf. Perhaps he had said "call me Joe" or "call me Yu", and so on and so on. I was tempted to say "my name is I", but he would probably confuse that with "eye" or something else.

So, what was he doing here I asked this smallish man. "I have found a place" he said, "where I can sit down and look out over the Pacific". That said, we sat down and looked out over the Pacific. He had a rough mind and rough hands. I say that because he began to recite what was probably poetry, since I couldn't understand it; it seemed abstract to me. His rough hands, he explained, were due to the pottery business he had left behind when he decided to walk west. He talked about his life before he began gazing at the Pacific. It was hard to phantom where these other places might be since he was so nonspecific, as if anything specific would reveal state secrets.

He became my mentor. He taught me about this place where we could sit down and look out over the Pacific. The most amazing fact that he revealed was that we were not alone; he told me how to see or sense these multitudes. In the West, all the hills, all the coastlines, all the meadows, all the mountains, all the deserts, all the riversides - all that you could imagine - there were others just like him and myself who were sitting down and looking out over our Pacific.

Moral: If you have to choose between poetry and pottery, gaze at the Pacific instead.

What Politicians Have Said Or Will Say Eventually

We will stand up and march forward; we will not lie down and march backwards.

We must do what we have to do even if we had to do it anyway.

I will tell you now and I will tell you tomorrow that in the future I will tell you the same thing.

We must have courage. Without courage we lack courage; without courage we get discouraged.

The only thing we have to fear is something else.

I must, regrettably, withdraw. Regrettably, because my competitors will no longer have my wise counsel.

This is a competition between the scrupulous and the unscrupulous. The choice is clear. Who can ask for anything more?

You must vote which means that you have to remember to vote. And then remember who told you so.

They say that patriotism is the last refuge of the scoundrel. I am a patriot anyway and I will always be a patriot.

Next year, when I walk into the Oval Office, I will remember you. Afterwards, I will be too busy.

I have no ambition for higher office. Should it be thrust upon me, I will probably accept it. The people's wisdom must be respected.

We stand here today, just before the seas part and the rivers overflow, to accept the judgment of history by which we must all abide. In a few months we will know.

If God lets me win this race, it must me mean that he agrees with me.

If we can't agree on something, the least we can do is to disagree.

 Character is an elusive thing. That's why so few have it.

I do not seek power and position just because I like power and position. It's only natural that if you achieve a position, power sort of sneaks in the back door. Once you have power, position sort of follows you through the front door.

Should I win this election, which I will, it's only natural that the result will be pleasing to all of you. You worked long and hard on my behalf for little or no money which is very puzzling to me.

I don't really understand the opposition. If I win, all of them will in trouble with the federal government.

 Responsibility is one thing, irresponsibility is another. So, always remember the thing and forget the other.

Our cause is right as it is mixed with dignity, hope, love of open spaces, and increased governmental assistance for reproduction.

Look hither! The mountains, the hills, the lakes, the rivers. That's America for you, always there, always beckoning.

Nature is God's way of reminding us of nature.

We are fighting the good fight so don't fight it.

I want you to meet my wife. My trusted confidant when I need confidence.

On Tuesday, November 2nd there will be great joy. No more slogans to polish, no more sentences to un garble, no more promises that can't be kept.

Consider this vision thing. Everybody has a vision these days, but only I have visualized my vision.

Please pray. Pray for all those candidates unfit for office.

This is a win-win situation because if we win we win.

Don't run America down; run it up instead.

Don't sell America short; instead buy her long.

On this great occasion great things will happen because that is what great occasions are for.

Being president is serious business. You need leadership. I will gather around me lots of leaders. That's what leadership is all about.

We must protect the weak and the innocent such as women, kids, grand kids. If we don't fight for women they will fight back. We need them at home more than ever.

Should marriage be allowed between two women or two men, you ask. For the time being, why don't you ask somebody else?

Ideals are OK but at times we must be flexible. Idealistic flexibility is often required in our complex society.

Our society could be an ideal society if not so many opposed idealism as we see it.

We must struggle on. Then we will still be struggling on because as Americans that's what we do best. Struggle is good for character and for friendly relations with neighbors.

Even during the antiquity of Greece and Rome, parents worried about their kids. We can do no less.

Last night, in a dream, I dreamt that the things that ought to come to pass had come to pass. That is what this campaign is all about.

And finally, don't despair. I shall return.

(... an experiment ...)

(... and/or a collection of puzzles ...)

A Group Of Presidents Travel To D.C.

The presidents were selected by themselves, by history, by sentiment, by those who care and by those who don't care.

There were no sequences, no drawings of paper slips out of glass bowls or anything else.

At the first stop on the trip to D.C., the first president was remembered because he fell down stairs in public.

On the second stop on the trip to D.C., the second president came aboard still crying because he had been denied a second term.

On the third stop on the trip to D.C., the third president was greeted as the one who loved women but not his wife.

On the fourth stop on the trip to D.C., the president was remembered as the one who believed that the killing of wildlife was therapeutic.

On the fifth stop on the trip to D.C., one president was superior in intellect to the others, but he had no common sense.

On the sixth stop on the trip to D.C., the president believed it wise to save his tape recordings for posterity.

On the seventh stop on the trip to D.C., the president believed that in a Federal election it is adequate to win with ten votes.

On the eighth stop on the trip to D.C., the president loved freedom but kept slaves.

On the ninth stop on the trip to D.C., the president saved his nation, but could not save himself.

On the tenth stop on the trip to D.C., the president believed in the power of sleep and the importance of human reproduction.

Having reached the goal of D.C., one of the presidents suggested that a group picture should be taken. The suggestion was rejected because they were all dead, with some abstentions. Yet, they will always be remembered.

Observation: *The writer seems to be fond of numerical numerations. Is there a cure?*

President By Acclamation

ELECTIONS, IN GENERAL, as practiced these days are fair enough but they take up a disproportionate share of time, time that most of us don't have. We are too busy doing other things such as earning a living with an income beyond and above the average.

It occurred to Robert A. Filbert, a name he had made up early in his life and career, that there was a better way. Filbert could say so because he had by steady, hard-charging work earned enough money and accumulated most of it, so that he had wealth beyond and above the average. Now, he felt, was the time to participate in voting at a level commensurate with his accomplishments. Filbert was not interested in local elections, state elections and most federal elections. The presidential election aroused his interest in the sense that he was appalled at the time required to "run", as it was called, although it hardly required any physical activities beyond "sitting", "looking" and "talking". --- Filbert got the idea that most if not all presidential elections could be simplified by a method of "acclamation". He set out to practice what he later would preach. The method, as employed by Filbert, consisted of visiting all the fifty states, or at least as many as he could manage. In each state he would call a meeting and then he paid each of the voters showing up a sum commensurate with their cost of attending the meeting such as lost income and lost economic opportunities. The honor system was used to great effect and Filbert was pleased with the efficiency of his method. As the delegates were seated, Filbert suggested that they should vote, by acclamation, that he should be president. It was done.

After having been elected president by acclamation in most of the fifty states, Filbert completed all the paperwork and he was very careful that it was in perfect order and in perfect sequence. He presented this perfect paperwork to each state's secretary of state, or a reliable deputy, to verify that he had been properly elected to be president by acclamation. Finally, Filbert registered his claim of having been elected president by acclamation with the federal secretary of state or if the secretary was not at his or her desk, a suitable assistant was found somewhere.

Having registered with the federal secretary of state, it was now a matter of fixing the date and time of his inauguration. He was notified that his inauguration would take place no later than 7 A.M. at a date to be determined later. The date was determined and the time of the inauguration came, but nobody showed up at the Capitol steps except Filbert and his wife. Filbert, of course was flabbergasted. How could he, elected president by acclamation, be treated in such a sordid manner?

When the president by election heard of Filbert's mistreatment, she was furious and then invited Filbert to the White House. She told him that she would give her secretary of state a good talking to. She further revealed that, at the moment, she was not married. She told him that she found the job as president by election a heavy burden to bear and she was very lonesome living in this big White House all alone. There were times, she admitted, when she was ready to jump out of the window of the Oval Office to get it all over with. It was obvious to Filbert that what she was talking about was that he could be president by marriage. Filbert thought of his wife, he thought of himself and he thought of the lonely president. He was sure that he would make the president by election very happy. Filbert was sure that the two of them would one day be judged not by their passions but by the content of their characters.

The Princess And The Tennis Balls

ONCE UPON A time there was a princess who wanted to marry a real commoner. She traveled all over the world but nowhere could she find one. She wanted a real commoner, not just a commoner. Her requirements were so stringent that by the time she was middle age, she still had not found one. There were commoners enough, but it was difficult to find out whether they were really real commoners. Would they obey and execute her wishes? Were they capable of living in real castles without complaining? Would they eat whatever the castle chef put on the table? And above all, would she, the princess, always be first in their thoughts and would they always be her constant companion? How much, how long, how articulate would they be during a royal intercourse?

When the princess had given up her active search, her one-time beauty began to break down here and there, particularly there. Never mind, she thought, I still have time and endurance to brood as much as required. Then, on one horrendously dark and stormy night, she heard, or thought she heard, a knock on the front door of the castle and she made her father the king open the door. Gracious, what spectacle did he the king, confront! The knocker was a middle-aged man, it seemed, who was in an absolute mess, all covered by dirty clothes barely hiding the corpulence of his body. And water running out of him everywhere. He was carrying a beaten-up suitcase that he could barely carry. What the king saw, then, was very disappointing, but what the king thought, was that here was a real commoner; never in his reign had he seen anybody so messed-up.

The king got hold of the queen and she had to agree with the king's assessment, but to be sure the two of them directed the staff to prepare the most horrible guest room possible, indeed it was the castle's torture chamber. Not often used these days, but it was available under special circumstances. The queen made sure that all the nails of the bed of nails had been properly sharpened, that the stretch-and-quarter apparatus was set to go and that all the five-finger nail pullers were ready. The suspected real common man was only too happy to get a room on such a dark and stormy night.

The next morning, the king and the queen and the middle-aged princess asked the candidate, real commoner, how he had slept last night. Wonderful, was the answer, can't remember I ever slept so good. While there might be evidence to the contrary, the royal triplet concluded that this was indeed a very real male commoner.

The princess, and by now her prince consort, took great pleasure in sharing the royal beds. After some bliss, however, came some hiss: the prince consort tended to interrupt everyone's sleep by his loud snoring. After many arguments pro and con in the upper echelons of state, it was decided that in order to remain a consort, he had to submit to modern torture. While in bed, he was ordered to always wear a contraption that covered all his back by as many tournament tennis balls as possible. That would keep the commoner from sleeping on his back, thus preventing all the soft stuff hanging down from the roof of his mouth cavity from flapping to and fro which caused all that infernal noise. Not only that, if you sleep on your back you can develop sleep apnea which in turn can cause heart problems which in its turn can cause death. No wonder the prince consort submitted to modern-day torture in return for a life-long consortship. It was generally concluded that while the consort might be a commoner in the flesh, he was not a commoner in spirit.

Disclosure: *Part of this stuff can be traced back to H. C. Anderson - somehow.*

The Prodigal Son Revisited

THERE WAS A rural family of modest means with a mother, a father, and two sons. The younger son had a restless nature; he wanted to see the world, among other things. He persuaded his parents to give him his inheritance now, so that he could live his dreams while still young and energetic. So it came to pass that the younger son left home to gamble his inheritance away, not use it at all, or multiply it by discoveries and investments.

A decade or two later, the younger son returned home, still vigorous and apparently very wealthy. He showed his parents and his brother all kinds of documents showing all kinds of investments worth millions in all kinds of currencies. The parents rejoiced and praised their wealthy son; now they could retire from the daily strife against nature and men. Now they could enjoy their autumn years in comfort. The older son, however, thought that all this attention to his younger brother was misplaced. How about his work and devotion to duty, so much so that he did not even have the time or energy to have a family of his own? Had they not noticed his calloused hands and his worn-out body? His efforts had kept them all in modestly comfortable circumstances. His parents pretended to hear his complaints, but they really thought that such thoughts were thoughtless. Now they should all enjoy their good fortune and relax.

It came to pass that one day an elegant lady showed up at the family place. She showed her husband, as he, the younger son, had to admit that he was, all kinds of court papers showing all kinds of liens against all kinds of properties and all kinds of unpaid bills in all kinds of currencies. She, the wife, wanted what was left of her husband's wealth or she would inform all kinds of government agencies, all kinds of courts and all kinds of lien holders about his whereabouts. So, the younger brother was broke after the wife had taken what was left of his wealth. Now it was his turn to feed the pigs, milk the cows, dig the ditches and struggle with all the other pleasures of rural living. Before long, his hands were calloused and his bones afflicted with all kinds of pains. His wife divorced him.

The older brother, on the other hand, was smart enough to court his brother's former wife and to propose marriage. The former wife probably accepted, so that she could keep an eye on her former husband in case he should reveal some part of his estate that she didn't know about.

Except for the younger son, those two rural families led a life of modest affluence. Their favorite pastime was to sit on the porch and watch the former man of means do the chores with the other hired hands.

Moral: Being a prodigal son isn't what it used to be.
(Suggested, of course, by Luke 15: 11-32)

Reeds

A FAMILY OF reeds was living along a river bank. As in any reed family, some family members were stiff and unyielding while others were flexible and bent with the slightest breeze.

A terrible storm came in from the ocean. The reeds that were stiff and that would not bend before the storm were broken or torn up with their roots. The reeds that bend with the wind, survived the fury of the storm.

One day, a group of men came to harvest reeds. The surviving reeds bent themselves as they had done before the wind to avoid the fury of the men. But all the reeds were cut down. The men wanted to cross the river and they needed pliable reeds that could be woven into a raft.

Moral: Experience is no guide either.

Respect For Life

WE HAVE RESPECT for life, but we kill off bacteria and viruses by various means such as disinfectants, radiation, sterilization, penicillin, and other concoctions. We have respect for life, but we are ambivalent about sharks, rats, snakes, and other unpleasant creatures.

We have respect for life, so we don't hunt whales anymore - with some exceptions. We have respect for life, but we keep domestic animals to give us products we need for our nutrition, most of them on a postmortem basis.

Where is the dividing line between respect for life in all its forms and the wanton killings of the smallest creatures among us? First, it seems to be a matter of size. We are not eating whale meat, but don't reflect on the means of getting rid of bacteria and viruses by the billion billions that make a living off our bodies, inside or outside. These creatures, small as they are, threaten our bodies and our existence.

There is the story of the Hindu holy man whose servant walked ahead of his master to warn him of any living creatures in their path so that the holy man could avoid stepping on them, thus avoiding causing their death or maiming. The holy man did not consider: Who warns the servant of any living creatures in his path?

But, back to the dividing line between the living creatures we do see versus the living creatures we don't see. It seems to be a matter of one's vision, excluding the blind and the partly blind. Also, it seems to be a matter of the size of the living creatures. Some of us may be able to see the smallest insects at close distance, but nobody can see dust mites without optical or electron microscopes.

One must conclude that sight and size matter when we profess to respect life in all its forms. Besides, respect for life has to be modified here and there if we are to have adequate nutrition.

Moral: Morality, regrettably, is not an absolute.

A Note: "The (nuclear) chain reaction is analogous to the growth of bacteria - one bacterium splits into two, two split into four, four split into eight. They say that a single bacterium reproducing under ideal conditions could cover a football field with a foot-thick layer of descendants in twenty-four hours". ("Adventures in the Atomic Age" by Glenn T. Seaborg, Farrar, Straus & Giroux, 2001; page 96)

Revolutionary Furniture

YOU MAY NOT have noticed it, but furniture, in its broadest sense from kitchen utilities through armchairs and beds, are not just lumber, nails, screws, springs, fabric and whatever else is needed. Any assembly of parts is more than just the whole. As someone once remarked, human beings have their physical ingredients but a whole human body is more than the sum of its parts. The body is said to have a soul.

To a degree, furniture of various kinds has, if not a soul, at least they have a sense of compassion, if that is the proper word. Take an armchair. It doesn't take long before it adjusts itself to the peculiar contours of your body. The interface of man and armchair becomes so intimate that it is hard at times to know where man ends and the armchair begins. I ought to know because I have had many armchairs so far in my lifetime. When they are apart, man and armchair miss each other to such a degree that one is attracted to the other as much as the other is attracted to the one. More simply put, the two parties are attracted to each other.

Consider my last armchair with its exquisite leather, its solid frame, its firm but still gentle feel, seemingly anticipating my every twist and turn. I was tempted at times to sleep my eight hours in the armchair, but I couldn't help feeling that my bed would miss me. Consequently, I usually spent my nights in my bed, enjoying all its comforts while also building up a very good partnership between the two of us. But I had to be careful not to offend the feelings of my armchair. As it got older it seemed to get more and more possessive. At times, I found my armchair close to the door to the bedroom; the only thing keeping it out of the bedroom was that its width was greater than the door opening. If it hadn't been for the narrow door opening, I was convinced that my armchair would follow me all the way to my office, up and down stairs and elevators if it had been possible.

I loved my bed as much as I loved my armchair. On the other hand, I had other responsibilities that I wanted to fulfill. One of them was to give life to my succeeding generations. I met a girl who had the same sense of duty toward posterity and she willingly offered to cooperate with me in that great endeavor. Unfortunately, my bed would have nothing to do with it. It made itself so narrow that one person, usually the girl, fell to the floor. And if that wasn't mean enough to get our attention, the bed broke a leg or two thus diverting our thoughts from anything else having to do with motion. In several extreme cases, the bed let loose a spring or two which snapped viciously at us, usually hitting the girl.

My girlfriend and I finally decided that this was no way to live. So she brought her bed from her apartment and installed it next to mine, hoping that life would get itself into a more-mellow phase. That is not what happened. When we came home from our jobs, we found the bedroom in serious disarray. It looked as if the two beds had been fighting each other while we were gone. As before, legs had been broken, springs had snapped, mattresses had been torn and who knows what else had happened.

With the beds and the armchair out of control and the table in the dining room beginning to be more aggressively inclined, we decided to do something. My girlfriend said that we should cut up the armchair and the two beds into small pieces and to haul those pieces to the public dump. No sooner so said, the whole apartment went into a deep chill. It was as if everything in the apartment, major stuff and minor stuff, were preparing to do us in. My girlfriend and I were not accustomed to such strife; all we wanted was to do our part for the future of mankind. Some of our friends suggested that we hire a priest or two to conduct furniture exorcism. And then what, we said. How long would the exorcism last? - days, weeks, months, years and so on? Was the priest or priests willing to give us some sort of guarantee? Did they have the proper credentials?

Encouraged by the revolt of the major pieces of furniture, the minor pieces of furniture decided to join the revolution. While the tactics of the major pieces were essentially brute force, the minor pieces apparently had a more subtle tactic, the tactic of extreme attraction. My girlfriend and I could hardly move around in the apartment before two or more minor pieces began to follow us around, some even attaching themselves to our clothing; it was impossible to brush or shake them off. Strangely, most of the minor pieces stopped at the entrance door of the apartment; it was as if they wouldn't or couldn't leave home. We had the situation that the major pieces were unable to pass through the narrow doorways and thus couldn't leave, while the smaller pieces could leave the apartment but chose to stay put - for the most part. We faced a situation where a revolution had two very distinct factions, that is, the majors and the minors. How can an apartment stand, so to speak, when it is so divided?

How to end this revolt of the furniture? As usual, the divide-and-conquer tactic seemed to be the proper choice. Borrowing some of the ideas of the French Revolution, my girlfriend and I discreetly suggested to the minor pieces that since everything minor would include butcher knives and other deadly assault weapons, they could easily exterminate the majors. To the majors, the royalty of furniture, we suggested that by their overwhelming advantage of weight and bulk, they could smother or crush anything that the minors could put up against them.

Everything went as we expected. With the minors and majors annihilating each other, the apartment was no longer divided against itself. It showed a little wear and tear here and there, it was again a nice place to do some living and a pleasant place to contribute to posterity. Afterwards, my girlfriend and I bought a new set of furniture, all virgin stuff. This new set caused us no trouble at all; the majors and the minors had accepted their lot in the universe. Sort of like dogs.

Romance, Adventure, Suspense

AFTER THIRTY YEARS of sitting before a typewriter eight hours a day seven days a week, he was asked by his publisher to write his memoirs. The writer considered the request but the eight hours a day before a typewriter gave him pause. He hardly knew anybody, he seldom went anyplace. He was rarely exposed to any ideas other than his own. Various girlfriends over the years got cranky and left after a few months, not being able to take the constant clatter of his typewriter.

It would be embarrassing, of course, to face the fact that he had hardly any memoirs to write about. He could write about the typewriters he had used over the years, their looks, their feel, their ups, their downs, but he knew that the publisher did not have typewriters in mind.

Since he had hardly any memoirs to write about, he decided to make some adjustments. After all, the time he spent just looking into empty space trying to think about the next paragraph, took at least four hours a day. He could say, truthfully, that he used the typewriter not more than four hours a day.

During those four hours, he could do many interesting things. To stretch the truth a little bit further, he could say that on the seventh day he rested from his labors. If he took interesting things from his many books on romance, adventure, and suspense even the publishers would notice. So, rather than inventing any more, why not experience something in those three areas himself and spread it over 30 years?

He contacted all his former girlfriends and told them that he had reduced his workweek to six days a week and only four hours a day. None of them were interested in his reduced workweek. Instead, he hired some stunning young ladies as escorts, but they insisted on being paid before any escorting was done. After the escorting, a substantial tip was expected. Except one; she seemed awestruck by his literary life and refused any tips.

Next, the writer took a trip abroad, always carrying his typewriter. In Paris, he followed the footsteps of Hemingway and Fitzgerald. All he accomplished was to run into other Americans following the same footsteps. Rather than getting discouraged, he continued on to Pamplona and the running of the bulls. Among those running, several were gored and all those gored were Americans. In Pamplona his typewriter got stolen and he returned to the States.

Back in the States, he bought himself a new typewriter and went to his daily and weekly routine of eight hours a day seven days a week. But one day there was a knock on his door. It was the young lady escort who had refused tips. She asked if he would let her be his secretary; she wanted to leave the drudgery of escorting for the suspense of literature. The writer sensed an opportunity and did hire her as his secretary. Her 30 years of life could not be stretched to cover the 30 years of his memoirs, but it was a beginning. He had several rejected manuscripts on romance, adventure, and suspense that he had put away here and there. He set his secretary to edit these manuscripts as if they were his memoirs. The memoirs completed, the writer added a note: "Edited with the assistance of Ms. So and so". The publisher accepted his memoirs, the public accepted them, and his secretary accepted her entry into the suspense of literary life. Henceforth, both of them spent eight hours a day, six or seven days a week in the production of literature. How things have changed, mused the writer, watching his secretary before her word processor.

Moral: Life and literature are mirror images of each other - some say.

Selfishness

A DECENT MAN was an international servant specializing in refugees. The pay was not good, dangers were ever present, the locations were terrible, but he got to see parts of the world he could never have seen otherwise and he knew that he was doing important work. This decent man rose in the hierarchy since he was so effective in administration and in getting things done. Eventually, he was promoted to be commandant of a refugee camp. Still, there were hints of selfishness in taking the position because you could live a life not possible for the refugees.

This decent man decided, as he surveyed his camp, that unselfishness was to be his guiding principle. He would not eat until the last refugee was fed. He would not sleep under a warm blanket until everybody could lie down to sleep without freezing. He would concern himself with every detail no matter how trivial it might seem.

He wore himself out. His vaunted ability to get things done was compromised because hunger made him weak, deprivation of sleep made him lethargic and inefficient. Feelings of guilt occupied his mind. He was no longer an efficient international servant. The refugees suffered from his self-imposed ethic of unselfishness. He was too concerned about the individual refugee. He had to be dismissed as a camp commander. This decent man was flown back to headquarters. Before the plane took off, there were the usual instructions on how to behave in case of a cabin decompression and how to use the oxygen masks that fell down. If you were responsible for anybody next to you, you must first apply the oxygen mask to yourself so that you will be able to help others.

Moral: Selfishness can be a virtue.

Serendipity

A BOY AND a girl grew up in the Kentucky horse country. They met, married and were employed by their families' businesses which were concerned with the conception, training, and racing of thoroughbred horses. After a string of spectacular victories over a number of years in various derbies, their considerable wealth gave the young couple the opportunity to pause and to reflect on their lives. Was it really a worthwhile endeavor to be in, this manipulation of the sexual lives of horses, this almost industrial production of race horses? Being stuck, until now, in an entirely rural setting with few opportunities for a sustained cultural life, the young couple got restless for a city landscape.

They decided to abandon horse life and enjoy city life in the biggest city of them all, the Big Apple. In a prestigious building, they bought an apartment a few floors below the penthouse that had a view of Central Park. All went well for a year or so when both the young woman and the young man began to suffer allergy symptoms. After extensive tests on the young man, the doctors concluded that he was severely allergic to concrete. Parallel tests on the young woman revealed that she was allergic to steel reinforcing bars and structural steel beams. Together, they were allergic to every building in Manhattan.

What should the young Kentucky couple do? After some

thought, they decided not to go back to Kentucky. After extensive research, their doctors suggested cities with much smaller volumes of concrete, steel reinforcing bars, and structural steel beams such as Stavanger, Norway and Wermelskirchen, Germany. The couple decided to give it a try. They flew to Stavanger on a Boeing 737 jet plane. Surrounded as they were by aluminum in various forms, they both felt much better. While Stavanger was OK, the couple did not adjust well to that city. One trouble was the language; it was so different from English. Also, there were so many variations and dialects of Norwegian. How could you be sure that if you learned one variation of Norwegian, that that variation would prevail?

Next they tried Wermelskirchen, Germany. They took the train, but the steel tracks and the concrete ties caused an allergic relapse for both of them. Wermelskirchen itself though was pleasant enough; a town of about 50,000 inhabitants surrounded by the hills of the Bergische Land. The main trouble with Wermelskirchen was that the inhabitants spoke German rather than English. Also, each German town seemed to have its own informal language. You had to learn two languages, one useless in the U.S., the other useless elsewhere in Germany. It was a nice city with nice bakeries and nice cafés, especially one called Café Wild. That café served a delicious Napoleon cake in memory of Napoleon and associates who had passed through town some two-hundred years ago.

Having more or less exhausted the possibilities in Europe, they flew back to the U.S. on a 737 jet plane, again surrounded by aluminum. The trip did the young couple some good. They decided that to avoid a life of constant misery, they would become assembly workers at the Boeing's plant in Long Beach, California which produced the 737 plane. Close by, on a large round hill was the city of Rancho Palos Verdes, a delightful little town with views over the Pacific and Los Angeles. Most of the homes and commercial structures were made of wood and thin layers of stucco. The steel and concrete content of the city's structures was minimal. If it hadn't been for their allergies due to steel and concrete, they would never have discovered the city of Rancho Palos Verdes.

Moral: Serendipity works.

Smell, Future Tense

I HAD KNOWN him since our boyhood. We were not exactly friends, but we kept in touch now and then mostly, I believe, to satisfy the curiosity that each of us had for the other. From my point of view he was a little strange, but from his point of view I was probably stranger yet. He had a strong interest in the senses possessed by the human body. He articulated this interest not as a doctor or as a scientist, but as a reasonably competent observer of the human species, based on his everyday experiences of the world around him. For example, he was very interested in the sense of smell. To what extent was it inherent in our genes and to what extent was it self-taught? Consider a dog, any dog. This lowly creature is far down any list of worthwhile organisms. Even so, a dog has a sense of smell more sensitive by a factor of 2,000 than that of the human body, a body which tops the lists in any non-smell categories. He suggested to me that if you looked at photographic portraits of bloodhounds and then compared them to photographic portraits of human beings, it will strike you very strongly that as far as smell is concerned, it just can't be. If on the other hand it turned out to be true anyway, human beings had to compete in a different arena, that of the future. By common observation, no dog thinks about the future or how to get there or what to do once it is there. ------ So, according to my sort-of friend, humans must compete in the future. In the semi-scientific circles that he wandered in, it was generally agreed that as far as smell was concerned, he had no peer when wandering about in the future. Somewhat by accident, I believe, he was made aware by members of the community, that every morning there was an annoying smell which could not be pin-pointed. He taught himself to smell in the future and he discovered his life's work: to smell tomorrow's newspapers. Not possible, of course, was the general reaction. However, some true believers were convinced that all that smelly stuff in the mornings had to have an origin. The logical source was the newspapers thrown on the porch or on the lawn without regard to whether the subscribers were allergic to newspaper smells or not.

So my friend offered his services to the newspapers. The day before the printing of the newspapers was done, he would personally inspect the printing plants and offer his opinion as to whether the newspapers were likely to smell good or not the next morning. And if not, he would suggest an appropriate perfume to make the smell pleasing to almost everybody. Anyway, my friend advised and the papers tended to follow his advice. There were, of course, those who "smelled a rat" as the saying goes and they pointed out that this amounted to smell censorship. The next step might very well be that smell could easily slip into political censorship; after all, any party would tend to object to the smell imposed by the opposing parties (usually unwashed) while at the same time approving of their own smell. The difficulty was that once you had started with any kind of censorship, other types of censorship would follow. After all, not everybody approves of an early dawn or morning dampness or afternoon haze and so on *ad infinitum*.

For the elite of the community, the obvious solution to the whole dilemma was to get back to the source, that is, the fellow who could smell tomorrow's newspapers. If he lost his sense of smell, wouldn't that solve the problem? Since I knew him reasonably well, I was appointed to be his assassin. I accepted the assignment more or less for this reason: if Hitler or Stalin or Mao Tse-tung and their associates had been assassinated early in their careers, humanity would have been spared a lot of misery; obviously, a worthy cause.

Socks And Clocks

FOR THE MEN and women on the Isle of Paradise living was easy. Trees on land dropped fruit into their laps. The fish in the sea sought out their nets. Men were vigorous and women were passionate.

Then civilization came to the Isle of Paradise and with civilization came work. For those who worked, work sapped their vigor and passion. For those who did not work, guilt about not working sapped their passion and vigor. Missionaries put socks on their feet and merchants put clocks in their cottages.

A prophet arose from the native population. "This socks-and-clocks society," he said, "is ridiculous." By the time you've wound up your clocks, your socks have fallen down. When you've pulled up your socks, it's time to wind your clocks again. Who needs it?" The prophet became a prophet among his own people because he made them see their own foolishness. Civilization was laughed right off the Isle of Paradise and it never dared to come back.

Moral: Wishful thinking is engaged in everywhere – even in fables.

Sofar's Box

AS FAR AS I was concerned, it looked like an ordinary box with a lid. Measuring its width, height and depth and taking the sum of the three measurements would yield about 40 inches. In other words, it was just small enough to qualify as a carry-on item on most domestic airlines. Not that the owner of the box, Mr. Sofar, had any intention of putting himself or his box on any domestic airline. Sofar was more comfortable walking, usually at a speed of two to three miles an hour.

I got to know Sofar through some mutual friends which turned out to number very few. Then I got to know his box. It was this box that disturbed so many people and that aroused the interest of so many others. It was rumored that whatever got into the box never came out again; it was a sort of black-hole thing. Anyway, the box was on display on top of a very elegant-looking solid oak table. As Sofar and I got better acquainted, I asked him, very indirectly, about this box I had heard so much about. One day, he showed me, close up, the box with its lid off and it was indeed an empty box. As an illustration of the box's power, he borrowed my Rolex wrist watch and put in the box, then closed the box with its lid. After a while, I began to worry about my Rolex watch; it was not something that you buy on the spur of the moment and then forget about it. Sofar noticed my discomfort and took the lid off the box and asked me to inspect the box. The box was empty. With a Rolex watch involved, it was very empty. Naturally, I was flabbergasted at this turn of events even though it was similar to other events that so many people had been so uneasy about. I asked Sofar, very politely, if it was any possible way of getting my Rolex watch back again. He reassured me that that was quite possible; he was going to personally take care of the matter.

Taking care of the matter turned out to be not so easy. Sofar maintained that it was just a matter of filling up the box and then everything deposited in it would be spewed out again and everybody would get their fair share. If this event should occur after his death, his last will and testament would state that all those who had been so patient would be richly rewarded. I was willing to do my part, but I was not willing to contribute another Rolex watch. It would be much cheaper to fill up the box with rocks, say, to hasten the day of return of all the stuff that had been put into the box. However, no matter how many times I filled the box with rocks, closed the box with the lid and then waited, when the lid came off, the rocks were still there.

Sofar pointed out the various errors in my handling of the box. First of all, I didn't allow enough time for the rocks to disappear. Secondly, the box didn't have the capability to process rocks. And thirdly and most of all, the box recognized value. Pearls, diamonds, gold bars, money, caviar, the more expensive, the better. That is, to fill up the box at any reasonable speed, you had to be willing to sacrifice in the short turn in order to gain in the long term. Some of us were too impatient for anything past the short term. Since Sofar had written up his last will and testament and promised us rich returns, why not get the whole thing over with, it was suggested. Someone took one of the non-disappearing rocks, put Sofar's head on the hard place (the oak table) and then banged away.

Later, it was rumored that Sofar had written in his will and last testament: "My last conscious thoughts will be of the box, the box, ..." And indeed, it came to pass.

(Recall Ben Jonson's play "Volpone" and MacArthur's last West Point address.)

Sooner Or Later

THE JUDGE SENTENCED the defendant to death. He let the defendant chose the method by which he was to be executed. The defendant was also allowed to choose the time of the execution. The time would be "sooner or later" as the judge put it. The defendant, naturally, choose to die "later". He was somewhat apprehensive about being allowed to set the time for his own demise. Did the judge have something up his sleeve, so to speak? Was it safe to choose the "later" option? Nevertheless, the defendant told the judge: "I choose to use the "later" option as being the day of my natural demise". "That's OK", agreed the judge. "Where would you like to live while you wait for your natural death?" Encouraged by all these developments, the defendant said: "At home". "OK", agreed the judge, "you are free to go home to wait for your death by cancer, heart problems or whatnot."

The defendant was released, walked out of the courthouse and began to cross the street to get a streetcar home. When he was in the middle of the street, a car at high speed came from out of nowhere, hit the defendant and then sped off. He was declared dead at the scene.

What was up the judge's sleeve was an electronic device that signaled the crew of the execution mobile to get to work. The judge was tired of being reversed by the upper courts. As a taxpayer, he wanted to avoid the state's enormous costs of a life-long prison term and the endless appeals associated with a formal death sentence. An informal execution, however, saved time and money and it also spared the convicted much anxiety. It was a win-win situation for all parties involved.

Moral: Some things are too good to be true.

Space Travel

A star of the trampoline
Is that tramp, Pauline?

Up and down she bounces
With all her many ounces.

Soon, one is not enough
On which to do her jumpy stuff.

Trampolines on floor and ceiling
Are to her much more appealing.

But, the distance is too short
And the neighbors go to court.

So, elevator shafts are cleared of cable
To show that she is able.

To bounce from penthouse and basement
To everyone's amazement.

Then all buildings are too small,
No longer does she have a ball.

But, she is a national treasure
Beyond all earthly measure!

A trampoline is put on the moon,
And that not a minute too soon!

She bounces back and forth
Especially on the Fourth.

In the race for outer space
She is the Nation's ace!

But, she gets bored with all her travel
And the moon's dust and gravel.

She wants to go to Mars
And end this moony farce.

But Mars, Pauline,
Has no trampoline!

She says: So What!
I shall correct that blot.

I'll take one along
I shall return. So long!

But, Mars she misses
And into deeper space she swishes.

Reflections off the trampoline's shiny metal
Remind us of her mettle.

Moral: Ambition is not bad
Just temper it a tad.

Disclosure: Based on notes From 1977

Square Dreams

ONCE UPON A time there was a country so small that the Earth's curvature could not be detected by its citizens. This country was so small that the gravitational force tugging on it was ten percent less than would be expected. In general, a country needs to have at least three things: a national railroad, a national airline and a national steel mill. Since it was so small, however, this once-upon-a-time country had only one of these attributes; it had only a proposed railroad. Since the country was so small, that proposed railroad would have only a single proposed track which, more or less, would circumscribe the country's area. Naturally, there were discussions about whether the proposed track should form a circle or a square. Most of the citizens felt that a circular track would be very boring for any passengers taking the train, forced to constantly looking at the same bushes for each revolution. The decision to run the proposed railroad in a clockwise or counterclockwise manner was put off for the time being.

After considerable discussion it was decided that it would be far more interesting to any passengers, as well as railroad personnel, to have the proposed track in the shape of a square. There would, of course, be certain difficulties associated with having a ninety degree angle four times in a complete circuit. In between those right angles, the ride would be smooth and straightforward without anyone having to deal with constantly changing directions as you would with a circular track. The only problem, of course, was that no one had ever constructed a track where ninety-degree angles occur at regular or even irregular intervals. One suggestion was to have a roundhouse device at each corner, but the personnel required to make it work would make it impossible to carry any passengers. Another suggestion was to call crew members passengers. A third proposal was to close the curtains in the passenger section and having a pre-recorded message announcing that the train was now making a ninety-degree turn even if it was not true. A fourth method would be to produce a video that would explain everything. A fifth method would be to keep quiet about the ninety-degree turns and instead promote the national airline and the national steel mill. After much study, it was concluded that having an airline as well as a steel mill was not feasible. It was also concluded that the country was not big enough for an airline since it was not big enough to have room for a terminal building in addition to having a single runway. If a steel mill was constructed, there would not be any space left for one runway and one terminal building. Also, there would be no place to put the steel ingredients except on the single runway.

The small country eventually came to the conclusion that all plans had to be scrapped. The conclusion, such as it was, was that having a national railway system where the track was in the shape of a square, while desirable, and made everything else impossible.

If there is a Moral hidden somewhere in all this, it must be: *It is not easy to be square in a small country.*

Suite Dreams

SINCE I HAD to stay in the city for a while, I rented a suite in an extended-stay hotel. It was a very nice suite with living room, bedroom, kitchen and bathroom, almost all the comforts of home, albeit on a smaller scale. The suite was on the second floor with access to the suites provided by a broad veranda-like passageway wide enough to allow chairs and other conveniences and yet not obstructing anybody from walking through. As I passed a couple lounging and catching some sun, the male half looking, somewhat youngish, said: "You have a surprise coming." I ignored his remark and went to my suite. Another male was sitting in my chair who I asked what business he had to be in my suite. He answered that he was only doing what he felt like doing and if I didn't like it I should talk to the management. Before doing that, I took a peek into the bedroom. Instead of one bed as before there were now two beds and in one bed there was a youngish-looking woman who seemed to be all excited. Before I could ask her what the hell she was doing in my bed, she asked me to tell Oscar that she was waiting for him.

The rest of my patience evaporated; I went down to the office and complained. The office manager couldn't quite understand what I was complaining about. I had a large suite and there was plenty of room for three people. Besides, I had paid the rent in cash. Nobody paid cash anymore; it made everything too complicated. In another beside, the manager said that, how could he know that the bills I had given him were not counterfeit? So, just to protect himself, he had added a few tenants just to be sure that he got his money's worth out of that suite. Naturally, I went back to the suite carrying with me a very strong fury. As I passed that guy in the lounge chair, he said again: "You have a surprise coming". Again he was correct. In the bedroom there were now two young-looking girls, each in their own bed, both looking very excited. Again, both of them now, asked me to tell Oscar that they were waiting for him. So I told that Oscar in the chair that the two girls were waiting for him. The guy in the chair said that his name was not Oscar. So I went back to the bedroom telling the girls that the guy in the chair was not Oscar. The girls could hardly stop laughing. "Of course he's Oscar - he is just kidding you," they said. The one they were kidding was probably me. I sort of wondered if the girls would be satisfied by the combination of Oscar and me. Then, I rejected the thought. Even if I told them that I was willing to substitute for Oscar, how could I handle two girls at the same time? On the other hand, maybe that guy in the chair would help by doing his part, so to speak.

Anyway, I went back to the manager's office to press my complaints again. The manager brought up the possibility that the bills I had rendered could be counterfeit. Besides- the manager's favorite; why would I complain about having two girls in the bedroom, particularly when Oscar was nowhere to be found? Even though he had a point, I resolutely went back to the suite. Sure enough, when I passed the guy in the lounge chair, he said: "You have a surprise coming". The surprise this time was a guy who claimed to be Oscar. The girls in the bedroom told me that the new guy was not Oscar either and they said that without even looking at him. The new guy showed me various types of identification and they clearly showed that at least his first name was Oscar. I suggested to the guy that claimed to be Oscar that since the girls had no interest in him he should leave. He refused; he was set to stay as long as it took just to experience how these odd things would come out in the end.

I went out to talk to that guy in the lounge chair to ask him if I had more surprises coming along. The guy in the lounge chair was no longer in the lounge chair. I bid my time for a while; maybe the guy was just going to the bathroom. Or, perhaps, he had run out of surprises. The guy never showed up again. I went to the manager again and asked him who that guy in the lounge chair was. The manager didn't know who he was, besides he had not paid for a suite anywhere on the premises so he hadn't bothered to pay any attention to him. The essence of what the manager said was that he didn't know that guy in the lounge chair. But, how could the manager know that there was not a guy in the lounge chair, if he had not paid any attention to him?

Back to the suite again; the guy in the second chair in the living room said that he knew a guy named Oscar; maybe he should call him up and sort of entice him to participate in a pleasant adventure. Before he could call his friend named Oscar, a messenger asked me to go down to the manager's office. I did and the manager said that Oscar had called and he left me a message. The message, in essence, said that he, Oscar, had fallen so severely behind schedule that he couldn't possibly be at my suite before some time tomorrow at the earliest. I went back to the suit with a heavy heart. How could I tell the two girls that Oscar wasn't coming any time soon? How could I keep them occupied while Oscar tried to catch up with his schedule? Perhaps I could find out where the girls came from? At the latest count we were three guys, those two in the chairs and me with hardly any place left to sit. As a group, three men and two girls had an asymmetry that made it very hard to figure out what the proper thing to do would be. And if the real Oscar would show up, the imbalance would be even worse. At this point, for some reason, I began to think about that guy out in the lounge chair who gave me all these surprising comments, the one the manager had not paid any attention to. Suppose he was Oscar? That would explain a lot of things. He was close enough to my suite to see, or at least hear, what went on in my suite. He could have left to make a telephone call to the manager, pretending he was Oscar just to mess up things even more, just for his own sinister enjoyment. On the other hand, how about that girl in the lounge chair next to the guy; that would explain a lot of things too. Since she never spoke a word in anybody's presence, it is certainly possible that she could have talked on the phone to the manager convincing him that it was Oscar calling. The manager would have no voice reference in a manner of speaking.

The conclusion to this tale, so far, was that I gave up on my suite with those two girls in their separate beds. Instead, I rented a similar suite in a similar establishment across the street. Now all I had to do was to keep an eye on my previous suite to learn what was really going on. I couldn't help worrying about those two girls, each in their own bed, waiting for Oscar.

Suite Business

HERE I WAS, installed in a suite in an extended-stay hotel just across the street from the hotel where at least two people seemed to be waiting for Oscar. But, I had to get down to business and not worry about Oscar. I was working for an outfit that insisted that all employees had to use the smallest possible paper clips with a particular emphasis on cost. So, not to embarrass my company and myself I shall call the company the Widget Company. The company has all kinds of widgets from those which are manufactured to those which are farmed such as carrots. The most interesting widgets are those that span the space between manufactured and farmed widgets.

As instructed by the company, I paid the rent in cash for the second suite. It was the policy of the Widget Company that whenever possible, all transactions and services should be paid for in cash. Occasionally, I wondered about this peculiar way of conducting business. Were the cash bundles all counterfeit or not? Or just a few bills here and there? On the other hand, I didn't know of any instance that the Widget Company had been caught using counterfeit money. Then again, if all commercial entities agreed that fake money was acceptable, who would have any incentive to worry about it? If everybody accepted counterfeit money, then counterfeit money was just as good as money printed by the US Treasury Department. What is money anyway? A suggested definition that I came across some time ago was that "monies are numbers written on pieces of paper and then stuffed into a black box somewhere". The modern equivalent is zeros and ones floating around in cyberspace. But, back to work and selling widgets. I put a few ads in the local papers that featured financial news and data. Soon, contact men were lining up outside my suite trying to snatch their pieces of the action. I wasn't too impressed by some of the contact men. They thought I was gull- ible and I thought they were gullible so we had some trouble doing business with each other. Just to give two examples: The first contact man through the door to my suite said that his company paid for purchases by cash only. As he put it, non-cash transactions mess up everything. Continuing now down the line of contact men until number 9 came in the door. His suggestion was that we do nothing - in a manner of speaking. All his company and my company had to do was to release information and data on the extensive business dealings between his company and the Widget Company. That way, the stock prices of both companies would increase and everybody would be happy. No expenditures were required for either company. Not quite perhaps, some token amounts of cash should be directed toward a few chosen stockbrokers and stock analysts to make them aware of the tremendous amount of business that would be gener- ated as a result of all the activities of our two companies. If nothing else, contact person number 9 had a knack for generating wealth where there was little or no wealth before. I told number 9 that I would consider his proposal. By next morning I should have consid- ered it long enough. In business, you have to create anxiety among the opposition before you proceed. Finally, I had enough of dealing with all these contact persons. I told them to line up again next morning. One of the contact persons that had not managed to get through the door yet asked me if he could stay in my suite overnight so that he would be the first in line the next morning. I made up some plausible excuse to get rid of him.

Now that my business was done for the day, I had other things to do. All day, even during the most exacting and exhausting business dealings, I could not help thinking about the two young girls, each in their own bed, waiting for Oscar. Now that I had voluntarily given up my suite across the street, it was none of my business what was going on in that suite. In a way, that made those thoughts even more exciting. It was getting dark, this being wintertime or at least as much wintertime you could expect in Southern California. I went across the street and sneaked past the manager's office. Not far away, I happened to notice an elegant car with California vanity plates that displayed the statement "Oscar Jr". Anyway, the "Junior" sort of implied that there was a senior Oscar somewhere who was less vigorous than "Junior". No wonder that the two girls, each in their own bed, were so excited at the thought of Oscar Junior even if they had to wait.

I went up and peeked through the window of my old suite. I saw a dark and stormy suite. I say that because no lights were on and two or more voices were having a stormy time of it arguing and arguing. I thought I heard a girl's voice scream "You cheated on me!" The whole situation was difficult to analyze. Perhaps Oscar had finally arrived and he had concentrated his attention on one girl and now the other girl felt slighted. I did not want to interfere, but at the same time I feared that inaction on my part could lead to a catastrophe or something less. So, I went down to the manager's office and talked to him about a possible crisis in my old suite. Let me add that the manager was the night manager. I found out that he was Oscar Junior and this Oscar said that it was none of my business. Besides, he said, the suite that I was talking about was empty. He told me that some suspicious guy had paid the rent in cash according to a note the day manager had left for him. Just to get to the bottom of this, I offered to pay the rent for the suite for one night. Oscar Junior refused. Cash may be legal tender here and there, but it was too much of a nuisance for him personally. What could he do with all that stuff? So I gave up and I went back to my second suite, went to bed and had some very annoying dreams, mostly about Oscar Junior but with a few glimpses of Oscar Senior. The older Oscar seemed to be in good health and vigorous considering his age.

Next morning, it was back to the business of wheeling and dealing. First in line outside my door was the guy who had asked me to stay overnight in my suite so that he would be first in line the next morning. So, out of a sense of fair play, I let him in first. He said he had spent the night in a suite across street. I asked him to describe that suite for me and when he did I quickly realized that the described suite was my first suite. I asked him, how many persons were there in the suite? He seemed puzzled by the question; he was the only person there. He had had an anxious night since somebody had tried to get in. He turned off all the lights and piled all the furniture he could lay his hands on in front of the door. Not that he merited it, but I let him in on some small-time business deals to get rid of him as well as some of the cash. At this point, I wouldn't have been surprised if his name was Oscar. His initials on his attaché case were "O. N." so that was certainly possible. It was also certainly possible that he had turned off the lights and then he had made a lot of noise by moving the furniture, in the dark, to block any entry through the front door. Perhaps I had misunderstood that noise as conversation. Not having a strong sense of hearing, I suppose that was possible even if it was implausible.

After a long day's work, I wanted to relax. Then, as always, the phone rang. A girlish voice asked if I would care to come back to my old suite. She and the other she were still waiting for Oscar. While they were waiting, maybe I would like to hear about all the strange things that had happened to them the last couple of days.

Suite Girls

OF COURSE, I could not understand how the girls knew that I was in a suite in the hotel across the street. And not just the hotel but the suite number too. Anyway, I went across the street with mixed feelings, part curiosity and part concern for the girls. The girls let me in and gushed all over me. It was the first time that I had seen them out of their beds, before I had only seen their heads. Out of bed, their bodies were sights worth looking at too. I asked them about the contact person who had told me that he had rented this very suite last night and that this person had heard quarreling voices. Their version of last night was that my contact man had not been there. Besides, the two of them would never quarrel about anything.

The two girls wanted to talk about Oscar. They were worried because they had not heard anything from him. I pointed out to them that they must know Oscar in some sort of way or how else could they even know that there was an Oscar. In other words, Oscar would have a phone number, a street address, an e-mail address, or some other way of making contact with the world. The girls said that to contact Oscar wasn't that easy. There were all kinds of men who passed themselves off as *the* Oscar. I mentioned that the day manager at the hotel had passed on a message from Oscar saying that he was so far behind schedule that he couldn't show up until the next day. Since that was yesterday, the "next day" was today. In other words, Oscar wasn't that far behind his schedule since it was still today. Repeating myself, I asked the girls who that guy Oscar was anyways? It was hard to get a sensible answer out of them even when they both contributed to one. Finally, they vaguely hinted that Oscar was a musician. How nice I thought, what the world needs now are more musicians. What sort of music and instrument did Oscar play, I wanted to know, classical, flamingo, folk music or what? No, they said, Oscar wouldn't play anything like that. He was a real musician, he was a rock-and-roll musician. When I had rented that first suite, they thought that it would be a nice touch to have two girls in my suite with no effort necessary on my part. They had e-mailed Oscar, carefully copying his e-mail address as given in a fan magazine, telling him the correct name and address of this hotel and also the suite number; that sort of explained Oscar's message to the day manager that he passed on to me.

The girls continued to worry about Oscar and at the same time that they were waiting for him, excited as usual. The girls asked me to make payments for the suite rent for a few more days. I explained to them that I had tried to pay the rent for longer than a few days, but the day manager had sort of refused to take payment in cash. Now that it was evening, I said that I would try to convince the night manager to take cash. One of the girls suggested that maybe the night manager would be more inclined to take cash from a young woman. The night manager, however, refused her attempts. Cash was too much trouble, he said; besides he had no place to put it. Later, a thought occurred to me that since the night manager had a car with vanity plates displaying "Oscar Jr." maybe he was the Oscar we were looking for. I had to admit that this thought had a certain flaw; if he was working nights how could he be a musician? And if he had been really interested in the girls, why hadn't he revealed himself to the young woman with a handful of cash?

My thoughts on Oscar had, perhaps, other flaws as well. Oscar, the night manager, seemed too young to be a successful rock musician. These days, to strike it rich, to be a rock musician in the really big leagues, you had to be in your sixties or seventies before you were considered mature enough to be able to entertain teenagers. Such were my thoughts, but I didn't want to upset the girls so I just kept those thoughts to myself. Clearly, they were unhappy and worn down by all this waiting for Oscar.

Since the unhappy girls made me unhappy, I decided to break the rules of the Widget Company and pay the rent for their suite using a credit card. From the company's point of view, this was allowed only if there was some miscalculation of the cash supply by the auditors at head quarters. However, miscalculation and cash supply are both open to interpretation. On my own initiative, then, I paid the night manager using my company credit card. He was unusually suspicious about accepting a credit card from a person who preferred to pay cash. However, since the credit-card thing spewed out all the necessary paper slips, the night manager couldn't deny what he saw with his own eyes. Thinking that I would catch him off guard, I asked him: "How's the rock and rolling business going these days, Oscar?" He didn't bother to answer. My question, of course, could also be open to interpretation. I went back to the suite, reassured the girls that everything was OK except we had to be patient in the matter of waiting for Oscar. I suggested to the girls that they get some sleep, each in their own bed. Just a few dreams away was another day, another day with, perhaps, no more waiting for Oscar.

The next morning, when I opened the front door of the second suite for another day, the two girls were first in line. They had spent an almost sleepless night worrying about Oscar. I got rid of most of the contact men standing in line behind them as fast as I could by dispensing cash. I sent the girls back to the first suite and assured them that as soon as I had the time the Oscar matter would get my undivided attention. I had a thought that I thought was a good one. One of the contact men in line seemed old enough to be a top-tier rock-and-roll musician. When I had dispensed with the rest of them, I invited him into my suite. Wafting several handfuls of Widget Company cash in front of him, I told him that there was big money to be made with very little effort if he followed a few simple instructions. They were: 1) Go and find out what the current craze in guitars is. 2) Buy one and have it lettered, very prominently, with the name "Oscar". 3) Get some crummy clothes suitable for a man in his sixties or seventies. 4) Walk back and forth in front of the suite hotel across the street carrying the guitar, being sure that "Oscar" is visible from practically any angle. 5) When you see two youngish girls running toward you, run away as fast as you can. 6) As soon as you have outrun the two girls, come to my suite and I will give you the cash I am now wafting in front of you. ----- Everything through 6) went according to my instructions. The guy ran his best race, but the girls almost caught up with him. The running oldster made a final effort and he outran the girls, the girls having spent too much time in bed lately. The oldster eventually showed up to claim his price. I gave him a bundle of cash and he put it in his inside jacket pocket. That last movement, stashing the cash away, was an effort too much. Without warning, he dropped limply onto the floor. I called the emergency number, took the cash envelope out his inside pocket and waited for the paramedics. When they arrived, all they could do was to declare him dead. Perhaps I was a little callous about that running oldster, but a better outcome in 6) would have been if he had dropped dead on the street. That way, the girls would no longer be waiting for Oscar. On the other hand, the girls were so persistent that they would have switched their attention to another oldster carrying a guitar.

Sun Tax

THE BELL RANG. I opened the door and saw two youngish men in uniforms which had all kinds of insignia, among them US in several places and US flags at short intervals. "Good day, sir" said the presumed leader of the team. "We are here to collect the sun tax that you owe the federal government." "Sun tax," I answered, "I have never heard of anything like that". Then the second fellow spoke: "Ignorance of the law is no excuse, sir". I asked them for a phone number that I could call and inquire about this sun-tax business. They did and I talked to a pleasant-voice female that assured me that the sun tax would have to be collected from all residents of California as well as a number of other sunshine states. Still not convinced, I called my Congressperson who explained to me that the recently passed energy bill was expressed in small type with single spacing on several thousand pages. For all that Congress knew, there could be a sun tax hidden somewhere in that legislation. "Why don't you pay that sun tax" the Congressperson advised. "Then, if you don't owe any sun tax this year, the US Treasurer will refund the tax next year."

Still, I was skeptical about this sun tax. It didn't seem reasonable; I told the two-man sun-tax team. Their contra arguments pointed out that it is not reasonable to assume that sunshine is free. Is water free? No! Is clean air free? No! Is food free? No! So, it is not fair to tax only three of the four life-sustaining elements. Besides, while sunshine has many good qualities, there are also significant costs associated with it. A lot of people suffer sunburns. Many people develop skin cancers after having been exposed to sunlight. If you look at the sun directly, you can damage your eyes. Sun glasses are expensive as are sun lotions. In general, sunshine can lead to any number of debilitating conditions. You can get sunstroke, just to mention one. And who, ultimately, pays for all this misery, asked the tandem team. The taxpayers do. So, what the sun-tax law does is simply to recognize these costs and to collect the funds necessary to alleviate any suffering due to sunshine. Everybody should pay their fair share.

We were still standing in my doorway; the two team members seemed too young to be in need of sitting down. Anyway, being able to think on your feet is so valuable that it should be encouraged. The two tax collectors seemed to express certain logic in their arguments. In particular, I was intrigued by their emphasis on the societal benefits that the sun-tax law would impose on the nation. Residents of California and Florida, say, would be taxed at a much higher rate than North Dakota, Wyoming, and Montana, say. These Northern-tiers states would hardly pay any sun tax at all, thus convincing the residents of such states to stay put and not migrate to California, Florida, Arizona, and so on. These Southern states already have populations far in excess of what is reasonable. The sunshine states' severe population growth is threatening the very quality of life.

Again, all this stuff seemed reasonable up to a point, but the problem is where is that point? Being a Californian, I was sort of convinced that I ought to pay a sun tax to keep the populations of other states from showing up here and then spoil the good life enjoyed by us who are here already. So, I asked the two-man team to compute what my sun tax would be. They showed me various tables and charts and explained to me how they computed my tax to be $1999. Being of a generous mind that day, I told them that I would add a dollar to make it an even $2000. To settle my tax, I told them that I would have to borrow $2000 in cash from them. I would then pay them $1000 now and the other $1000 in half a year when they came collecting again. I went into the house to snatch some paper that I needed to write out my IOU, but by the time I returned the sun-tax team had disappeared. Why would anybody run away from my very generous offer?

Moral: Confidence men without confidence are a nuisance.

A Postscript:

Remarkably, a few days later my Congressperson called back and told me that his staff had located sections in the energy bill that seemed to imply that certain states could impose sun-tax laws. Most of the thousands of pages of the energy bill had been written by a Congressperson from one of the smallest Northern states with a district electorate of a few hundred voters. This person's epic efforts had reduced him to exhausted incoherence so that he could no longer remember what he had written. Hence, it did not seem possible to ask him for clarifications of any sections of the energy bill. If nothing else came from this incident, at least the person who had written the bill had risen in the esteem of his colleagues to such a degree that he had begun his ascendency in the party leadership.

A few weeks later, I talked to my Congressperson again and he told me that Congress had sort of agreed informally to ignore the section of the energy bill that was concerned with sun taxes. Since nobody could recall that sun-tax legislation had passed Congress, it simply followed that Congress had not passed a sun-tax bill. Besides, it was really the fault of the president and his staff who had not bothered to read the whole bill before the president signed it into law.

Still, that leaves one puzzle. How did the two-man team that visited me know that there was a sun-tax section in that bill? A further puzzle is that if they knew that, why didn't they exploit it? All they had to do was to wander around on Capitol Hill and remind members of Congress of the sun-tax law. They would then ask for donations of proper magnitudes from the members that would be spent for the public good. There was no need to collect sun taxes in person from individual taxpayers all around the country.

Telling Weather By Clocks; Pros And Cons

A FELLOW BY the unlikely name of Smith claimed that he could tell the weather by looking at clocks. The only requirement was that the clocks had a minimum diameter of one foot. Naturally such a claim upset a lot of people, particularly those who had anything to do with forecasting the weather. If true, such ability would wipe out a whole profession in its many manifestations with dire consequences: providers thrown out of work, children facing starvation, mortgages left unpaid, cars repossessed and other disasters. However, the manufactures of clocks with diameters more than a foot rejoiced. No longer would there be any out-of-work clock makers thus providing many beneficial consequences: providers could provide, children would be taken care of, mortgages could be paid with ease even after buying a sufficient number of cars.

Obviously, the Nation stood at a fork in the road; should telling weather by looking at clocks be allowed or not? To try to settle this question, a national board of inquiry was appointed; half the members being pro-clock, half the members being anti-clock. Hearings were held and a sort of summary of the proceedings was made public. To save time and space, let us imagine that a neutral **Moderator** conducts the discussion between two board members, **Pro** and **Con,** respectively.

Moderator: Let us eliminate the obvious. Mr. Smith would be in a room with a one-foot-diameter clock; let it be stipulated that the room has no windows.

Con: Mr. Smith could go into the next room which has windows. Or, he could be in electronic communication with an aide outside the building.

Pro: Why all this suspicion? We should concentrate on Mr. Smith's unique ability to tell the weather by clocks only and try to learn how we might be able to do it too.

Con: Mr. Smith is a charlatan. He has aides running around outside collecting all kinds of weather data. They can slip him a note now and then so that he is up to date.

Pro: I have not noticed any such activity at all. Besides, being a human being he needs nourishment as we all do. We should concentrate, I repeat, on Mr. Smith's unique abilities and reach a conclusion on how to utilize it.

Con: Mr. Smith's unique ability is to lie and confuse the nation. This is not telling, it is story telling. Suppose we ask Mr. Smith what the weather is in New York City, say, while he is in this room.

Pro: I suggest that whole board of inquiry gather outside while we leave Mr. Smith with a proper clock in this room. Then we can tell the weather and he can tell the weather and then we compare the two tellings.

Con: That's laughable! You know perfectly well that we all have a different sense of weather. Some of us get cold when it is warm; some of us get warm when it's cold. Why can't we see if Mr. Smith can tell the weather in New York City or, if that is unacceptable, let the board draw a city or whatever out of a hat and then ask him what the weather is there just by looking at a proper-size clock?

Moderator, Pro, and Con: We finally agreed that we can't agree. Besides, Mr. Smith's time is valuable. Henceforth, he will be at the side of our President whenever and wherever he travels.

The Alligator And It's Afternoon Meal

ON A BRIGHT and sunny afternoon, a man was limping along a river bank, trying to forget his infirmity and to seek his peace of mind in nature.

An alligator came out of the river and said to him: "I shall take you out of your misery, first by one leg, then by the other leg, and then by the rest of you." The alligator easily snapped off the limping leg, but before he could snap off the other, the man was already far away; fear, having given him the speed of a gazelle even with only one leg.

The alligator had to return to his den with a single leg. He soon discovered that it gave him no nourishment at all, since it was made of metal, wood and plastic.

Moral: Eyes can be deceived, but not the digestive system.

The Bird And The Fly

THE BIRD WAS sitting in its living room and tried to relax, but a housefly kept buzzing around showing off its aerial acrobatics. The bird was of a good mind to have the fly as a late-afternoon snack. As it studied the flight of the fly, waiting for the opportune moment, the bird became fascinated against its will by the virtuosity of the fly. One moment the fly was in level flight as a bird, the next moment it had landed on the ceiling feet first.

"How did you do that?" The bird asked the fly.

"How did I do what?" asked the fly.

"How did you land on the ceiling?" the bird wanted to know.

"Before you land, do you make a loop - the - loop or do you roll half of one revolution, right or left?"

"I don't know," said the fly. "I just do it."

"Show me how you take off and land on the ceiling," the bird commanded, "and we will get this settled once and for all."

The fly did as it was told until its wings were sore and it could hardly flap them anymore. The bird watched intently, but the fly was so quick at the crucial moments that its movements were just a blur to the bird.

"We'll never get this settled," said the bird, "until you slow down. Until you land and take off from the ceiling in slow motion."

"It can't be done in slow motion," protested the fly. "It must be done quickly or not at all."

But the bird persisted and the fly was in no position to argue. The fly did as told and it tried to land on the ceiling in slow motion, but of course it stalled and went into a tailspin. The fly was so exhausted it could not get out of its spin, so it hit the floor and broke its wings.

"Now we will never know," whimpered the bird.

Moral: If at first you succeed, try, try and try again to fail.

The Carpenter And The Poet

ONE MORNING, A carpenter agreed to build a roof over the head of a poet if the poet would write him a poem. The carpenter worked vigorously, straining his every muscle and giving the raising of the roof his complete and total effort.

The poet was sitting around doing nothing, staring ahead, once in a while taking a nap, at other times watching the carpenter work. In the afternoon the poet gathered his strength and wrote down the poem he had composed in his head using perhaps five minutes for the task.

The carpenter became very upset. "Here I work all day to raise a roof over your head, and all you do is spend five minutes to write me a poem," he complained. "That is not fair!" The carpenter was so upset, he did not finish the roof, he just grabbed the poem, even though he knew he would not like it, and he went home to sulk. The carpenter swore he would never do anything for a poet again.

The poet was angry at the carpenter for having built him an unfinished roof, shoddy and leaky, in return for a perfectly good poem.

Moral: Among men, division of labor is a source of friction.

The Death Of A Pelican

A PELICAN HAD caught a delicious fish in his pouch and he was about to swallow it.

"Stop!" one of his friends cried. "You're about to choke on something. Open up so I can have a look at it!"

The Pelican opened up his bill as wide as possible so that his friend could help him.

"Just what I thought," said his friend.

"Now let me take care of it!"

The friend snatched the fish out of the pouch. In his eagerness to swallow it, the friend was too careless and he choked on the delicious fish.

"What a friend!" marveled the pelican that had caught the fish. "Sacrificing his own life so that I may live!"

Moral: Many an unheroic mistake appears as a heroic act.

The Earthworm And The Bird

AN EARTHWORM DUG its way to the top of the soil and had a look around. Another creature looked back at him.

"Hello there!" said the earthworm. "What sort of creature are you?"

"I'm a bird" said the creature. "I'm interested in creatures like you."

The earthworm felt flattered. "Anything you want to know about me?" he asked.

"Is what I see all there is of you?" asked the bird.

"Certainly not!" said the earthworm indignantly.

"There are at least four inches of earthworm behind me."

"I don't believe you" said the bird."

The earthworm was annoyed.

He crawled out of his hole and stretched himself out to at least four inches.

"Now I believe you" said the bird and picked him up with his beak.

Moral: Beware of Skeptics.

The Gull And The Grasshopper

A GULL AND a grasshopper lived at the shore of a great, but dead, salt lake. The two became friend and spent their days together. The grasshopper often asked the gull: "Other gulls eat grasshoppers. Why don't you?" "Because now there is enough to eat, but just in case, I am saving you for my last meal", answered the gull.

One day, a swarm of locust came to the shore of the great salt lake. They ate the grass and the plants on the ground, the leaves on the trees and the crops in the fields of the religious settlement above the lake. The gull saw the multitudes of locust and he said to the gull: "There will always be something to eat. I might as well eat you now." And the gull did.

Prayers from those who had planted and tended the crops at the settlement sent the swarm of locust away to places where no one lived, or perhaps, where no one prayed.

After the locust had left, there was nothing left for the gull to eat at the shore of the dead salt lake. The gull starved to death without its last meal.

Moral: There is no safety in numbers.

The Hare And The Tortoise

"SO YOU BEAT me once," said the hare to the tortoise after their race. "But it won't happen again. Let's race once more!" "If you think it will make you feel better," answered the tortoise.

So, they had another race and of course the hare won. He had learned his lesson.

The next day, the hare said to the tortoise: "Let's have another race!" "If you think it will make you feel better," said the tortoise.

Every day for weeks the hare challenged the tortoise to a race, and every day the hare won.

One day the tortoise had enough. "I can't go on making you feel better day after day after day, "he said. "I wasn't built to sprint, even at my speed. What's the point? You'll win every race anyway."

The hare had to agree. He knew that whatever was gnawing at his heart, he could never run away from.

Moral: You remember best what you want to forget.

The Hen And Her Brood

THE HEN WORRIED all day and all night about her chickens. Her worries gave her hardly a moment rest or sleep. "Suppose something happens?" she said to the rooster. "It is a wonder something <u>did</u> happen," he answered.

The hen checked her brood constantly. She worried if they were too pale, too flushed, too active, too inactive, if they ate too much or too little. Did they have any pains? How did their stomachs feel? Any aches in the feet? Any split feathers? If any of her brood reported the feeling of the faintest pain or the vaguest of irregularities, immediate and prolonged attention was applied. Her chickens could not do this and they could not do that. They could not go there, they could not go elsewhere. Why?; because obviously anything might happen anyplace.

What the hen dreaded most of all was a report from any of her brood of feeling good, of being in perfect health, because feeling good and being in perfect health always preceded an illness.

As her chickens grew up, they tended to become listless, brooding, introverted, inactive, quiet, fearful young adults. When it was time for the management to decide who should join the adult flock, every young from the hen's brood was sent to the block.

Primary Moral: If you fear the worst, the worst will probably happen.

Secondary Moral: If you don't fear the worst, the worst may happen anyways, but in the meantime you can at least enjoy yourself.

The Inventor Of Writing

IT HAPPENED A long time ago. In fact, once upon a time there lived a man, or a woman, who thought that words were important. In his head, as long as they remained unsaid, they were like pearls, rich in substance, perfect in structure. Words could be strung as beads on strings, short or long, straight or twisting, in knots or in loops. Or, one by one they could be placed in regular and beautiful patterns or in a dizzying chaos, both pleasing to his mind.

Yet, when these words passed from his head and passed his lips, a metamorphosis occurred. No longer pearls, they turned into lead shots, pitted, discolored, resembling little lumps of dirt. Individually, they fell unnoticed to the ground. Collectively, only their ugliness in the aggregate was discernible. He was ashamed of them and of himself.

This man of long ago despaired of ever saying words or sentences that would retain the beauty and the perfection they had before their birth. Once born, words were irretrievable, they even ceased to exist.

In his despair, he began to invent symbols for his perfect words and through them; he struggled to recreate his perfect thoughts and feelings, joys and sorrows. Once in a while he succeeded in putting together brief strings of words that imitated and approximated the ideals dwelling in his head. In such moments, few as they were, he felt a sort of happiness, a feeling he could not yet identify with his written symbols.

He came to distrust speech, his and others, so he gave it up completely. If he was asked a question, he did not answer but pulled out his pad. Meticulously and laboriously, he began to make notes toward the answer that he wanted to make as perfect and concise as he could make it. He wrote and he rewrote, crossed out and added, shortened and lengthened, rearranged, changed tenses and emphasis transposed and juxtaposed. When he was satisfied that he had done his best, he showed the response to the inquirer. But, during his absorbing toil, the inquirer more often than not had drifted away and consulted others who would give him an answer at the spur of the moment or if he did stay, so much time had passed that neither of them really remembered what the question was any more.

So, once upon a time, this chiseler of words and phrases and sentences was left with a nearly perfect answer without a question. Yet, although it happened a long time ago, it still happens every day, now and forever, as long as men invent writing.

Moral: The perfect answer no longer has a question.

The Inventor

SCIENCE HAS DECLARED that there are about 85 different ways to tie a knot, commonly used in Western civilization. By trial and error, an inventor set out to construct a machine that would be able to tie all the known knots. He was an adherent to the Edisonian edict that an invention is "one percent inspiration and 99 percent perspiration." tried out his invention on window-display dummies and the knots were perfect and even beautiful. As the next step, he tried out the machine on himself. Unfortunately, the dummies had idealized dimensions befitting their display function, including very small neck sizes. However, the inventor's neck measurements were on the sturdy side, a minor discrepancy one would think. Contrary to his expectation, the first machine-tied knot on a human subject choked the inventor to death.

Moral: He should have invented a shoelace-tying machine instead.

(A mathematician has calculated that there are 40,000 distinct ways to lace up a shoe with two rows of eyelets each, according to Petroski, American Scientist, May/June "03)

August 24th 2010

The Owl And The What

ON A STARRY night, a what was fleeing from an unseen terror.

For the what, the darkness covered the whole world with its black velvet. The what accidentally stumbled into the owl. "Watch where you are going!" said the owl indignantly, "are you blind?" "Please help me," said the what, "something terrible is following me." The owl looked. "My dear what?" it said "it is a field mouse who happens to be traveling in the same direction as you." The owl took care of the what's terror.

The what decided to stay close to his sharp-eyed benefactor. When daybreak came and his own sharp sight returned, he still trusted the eyes of the owl more than his own. In midmorning, the what thought it saw a tiger approaching, but he asked the owl to be sure. The owl squinted sleepily into the morning sun and said: "It is a little striped field mouse lost in the woods." So the what paid no more attention to the tiger stalking him and he laid down to rest. He never rose again.

Moral: The owl said it best: So what! At least it wasn't me.

The Power Of Laughter

IT WAS THE grandest shopping mall ever, easily the world's largest mall. If it wasn't, there was plenty of land around the mall complex to make up for any shortcomings later should there ever be a challenge to its stature as the largest mall ever.

As one former president had put it; "The business of America is business". Hence, it was entirely proper that the current president should attend and bless the formal opening of the grandest and largest shopping mall ever. The official blessing would take place in the mall's atrium, grander than any atrium anywhere. The layout of the atrium included a large fountain at its center, almost the size of a small lake although the use of "small" was not considered a proper description.

The atrium, being at the center of the mall, served as the hub for the spokes radiating out from it, the spokes having such features as up-and-down staircases, up-and- down escalators, up-and-down elevators and up-and-down chandeliers as required for proper lighting. The president would come down an escalator to the floor of the atrium. On the big day, he stepped onto the down escalator. Hardly seconds went by before the escalator turned itself into a slide. The president fell on his back and slid with an ever increasing speed toward the fountain into which he was submerged in its waters. This event was witnessed by reporters and photographers from the print and electronic media as well the general public with its cameras as well as other devices. The event was forever fixed on paper and the zeros and ones of Cyberspace.

It was as if the world had come asunder and the president with it. As the event happened, there was subdued laughter as if everybody was trying not to laugh. In a second wave, the laughter came full blast. Ashamed of their own behavior, the public went back to being subdued then back to full-blast laughter again. The two modes of laughing alternated until the president was retrieved from the fountain and was dried off and hustled away to somewhere.

The escalator company was scrutinized. The company readily admitted that saboteurs could have caused the escalator to turn it into a slide; it would take only limited technical know-how. It was possible that the design team had been infiltrated by terrorists. All they needed then was to change the intelligent design by a creative blend of mechanical engineering and electronics know-how. Then, on the day of the event, all a terrorist had to do was to use a cell phone to activate the escalator-to-slide mode. The reaction was that, if the terrorists were so smart, why didn't they just blow up the president?

The president also, at the beginning, asked the same question. But as he moved around the capital, several states of the nation and several states of the world, he couldn't help hearing the laughter behind his back. The president wisely concluded that he could no longer govern effectively if at all. He resigned and he was not missed. It was as effective as any assassination.

The grandest mall of them all fell into disuse and disrepair. Eventually, it was bulldozed into oblivion and the land was returned to being farmland again. This incident became known as the "Improvised Escalator Malfunction" or IEM for short. IEM is easy to remember because it is pronounced as "I am".

The Raven And The Cuckoo

THE RAVEN AND the cuckoo were summoned before the Council of Birds to show cause as to why they should not be expelled from the Order of Birds.

The resolution of expulsion read in part: "The raven gives birds a bad name by stealing pieces of silver and shiny trinkets from the species of Man, the principal benefactor of birds. The cuckoo's behavior presents a detrimental image of birds by its rejection of the sanctity of family and family life, an attitude that members of the species of Man find abhorrent."

The raven was asked how he pleaded to the charges. "Guilty!" cried the raven." "But I shall of course reform. I shall never steal again; never more!"

When the charges against the cuckoo were read, she was asked how she pleaded: "Not guilty!" she said. "It's my nature – and it's yours to accept my eggs and rear my young as your own. I know you really don't mind; mine are more vigorous, healthier and better looking than your own."

The Council of Birds then decided on its verdict: It accepted the guilty plea of the raven. His silver and shiny trinkets were confiscated and divided among the members of the Council. The cuckoo was reprimanded for her insensitivity toward her fellow birds and she was placed on probation. A condition of her probation was that members of the Council could return all her eggs and young to let her carry the burden of motherhood herself.

At the time, the raven and the cuckoo had no choice but to accept the verdict of the Council of Birds.

Moral: If you are different, your equals may not like it and you get into trouble.

The River Of Life

ONCE UPON A time, there were two villages separated by a river but connected by a bridge. Here lived a couple in love; a young man from the East Village and a young woman from the West Village. One day, they met on the bridge and looked at the current of the river and the beauty of its eddies. They agreed to marry.

As they returned, each to their own village, doubts began to whisper. Idle tongues on both sides of the river spun tales of past loves and betrayals, hints that their characters were as deeply flawed as crevices and had qualities of deceit as barren and lofty as empty space. The young man and the young woman began to spy on each other as the whispers rose above the background noise of the river.

The young couple forsook each other and, perhaps in spite, married other partners soon to be forgotten. One marriage begot a girl, the other begot a boy, and then the two marriages begot their demise.

That girl and that boy did not grow up in the same village. Yet, they fell in love and one day, standing on the bridge and hearing the murmur of the river and seeing the randomness of its eddies, they decided to marry. They knew the anger, even hatred that each parent had for the other. Nevertheless, they each asked their parent for the blessing of their marriage. The unexpected happened, the father of the boy and mother of the girl agreed to the marriage. At the wedding of the young man and the young girl, the once young man and the once young girl found themselves on talking terms. Said the father, "I'm so happy today! Your daughter could never have found a more miserable, evil, and good-for-nothing boy than that son of mine". The mother of the girl said: "I'm so glad your son married my daughter because a more trashy, conceited, and impossible wench you'll never find".

As any predictor could have predicted, the marriage between the boy and girl would become the worst in the two villages separated by the river. But their parents found true happiness and would live together in love and harmony for the rest of their lives, because now they had a common bond. The river and its eddies had nothing to do with it.

Moral: To bond or not to bond; that's the question.

(Suggested by a 1891 story by the Norwegian author Jonas Lie)

The Room

NOT SO LONG ago, somebody invented the room. It had a floor, four walls, and a ceiling, hence an apparent improvement over previous practices. A structure with just a floor exposed the occupants to the weather elements. Even a floor with two or three walls would still give inadequate shelter. If there were four walls but no ceiling, the rain could not be kept out. If there was no floor and no ceiling, occupants and guests would walk around in mud.

The inventor of the room sensed that he had solved a number of problems associated with shelter. But, how could a person get into the room? Make a hole in a wall and crawl in, make a hole in the ceiling and drop in, or tunnel a passage underneath the room and then break into it?

The inventor could not decide on a solution. Later generations invented the door and the room concept became practical. Further inventions included hinges, doorknobs, and peepholes, floor coverings, means to attach things to the walls and lamps to the ceiling. Thus, the invention of the room made civilization possible.

Moral: Even inconsequences have consequences.

The Rooster And The Hen

THE HEN SAID to the rooster: "You don't chase us around anymore."

"I never did," answered the rooster. "You and all the other hens made that up. An old wives' tale; now, leave me alone!"

"You never kept to yourself when you were younger," said the hen.

"I have always kept to myself," said the rooster. "All roosters keep to themselves."

"But what is the point of you being around if you do not chase us around?" the hen wanted to know. "Ask the other hens, that is part of the fun!"

The rooster was getting angry: "If you chase for fun, why don't you chase me around for a change!" He bristled his feathers, shook his head, crowed three times and turned his back to that silly hen.

When the hen told the other hens what had happened, all the hens decided to chase the rooster – just for the fun of it. But the chase was too much for the old rooster, he dropped dead before the hens had hardly any fun at all.

Moral: You won't live long enough to regret words spoken in anger.

The Weaned Leech

A LITTLE LEECH lived in a shallow pond with his parents, his sisters and brothers and their whole extended family. One day, his parents told him:"It is time for you to be weaned. From now on, you have to suck for yourself. The first pair of legs you see coming into the pond, just pick one of them and start sucking."

"Suck, suck, suck!" came a chorus from all over the pond.

Sure enough, a pair of legs did come into the pond and the little leech picked one of them and started to suck. But, no matter how hard he tried, his sucking didn't seem to work. It was such a skinny leg. It had such tough skin. Inside the skin were heavy tendons, a big bone and hardly anything else. The leech kept on trying anyways; he did not want to disappoint the whole extended family crawling around in the pond.

Even when the two legs were taken out of the pond, he kept on clinging and sucking. He only took a short break to ask the owner of the leg: "What sort of a dry thing are you?" "I am a flamingo," was the answer, not that the answer did him any good. The little leech was out of his element and soon his pond disappeared out of sight. He was never to be seen again. When asked about him, his family said he had gone abroad to suck.

Moral: Giving advice to the young is useless – say the old.

The Woman And The Bee

A WOMAN WAS picking flowers in a field. A bee flew up to her and said: "These are my flowers. Please, do not pick them." "You silly little thing!" answered the woman. "I will pick as many flowers as I please! Now, get out of my way!"

"Please, do not pick my flowers." repeated the bee, "or I shall be forced to sting you."

"Do not make me laugh!" hissed the woman. "A little thing like you can't hurt a big thing like me." And she kept on talking, ridiculing and abusing the bee with her tongue.

When the bee had lost its patience, it deftly put its stinger into the tip of the woman's tongue. Her tongue swelled up to fill her mouth and she was lucky to lose only her power of speech and not her life.

Moral: A swollen tongue fits a swollen head.

(fragments)

Various Thoughts and Items

A Day In The Life Of Somebody, Somewhere

In the morning, I walk clockwise around our cul-de-sac.

In the afternoon, I walk counterclockwise around our cul-de-sac.

In the evening, I walk straight to bed.

Other Items Worth Considering

Thinking back, I now regret that I did not regret more.

Whenever I am going uphill, I know that I am going downhill.

If you live in Maryland, can you call yourself an MD? US Postal Service thinks so.

If you live in Massachusetts, can you call yourself an MA?

I think I forgot to remember that I had lost my memory.

Thinking is something I do when I am not doing anything.

I think I have a habit of having habits.

I think I admired him when he ate the burning candles right off the birthday cake.

A thought: What is the numerical difference between some and a few?

Thought two: What is the numerical difference between many and numerous?

Thought three: When I am awake, I can't sleep.

I think *you* will be better off by not being better off'

Another thought on life: Why all this dressing and undressing?

There is no absolute nonsense except life.

Be pessimistic and you won't be disappointed.

Being run over by 13 steamrollers brings bad luck. (F. Stabel)

If you drink ten gallons of grape juice for 1440 months,

you will live to be at least 100 years old. (F. Stabel)

To Whom It May Concern: Change

CHANGES CHANGE EVERYTHING. But before we change we must be willing to change. There can be no changes if others don't change. Hence, from the beginning of change there must be a willingness to change so that the vision of change doesn't change. Otherwise, there will be an exchange of changes and change will not change. Change must be judged by the speed of change because it is critical to conserve the momentum of change so that the changes inspire broad signals to change. Next, we have to be sure that to change the future we must change now or else the change of changes in the future will have no chance of meaningful changes in the present. After all, what is the point of changes now if future generations don't change as we change as we get more mature? So, let's change because change is needed and not because it is just to change. We must be sufficiently changeable so that our visions can grow from changelings into full-blown changes.

Tom Thorsen

February 2008

Trading Time (I)

A PART OF some faraway city that I often visit dates from medieval times. It does not have streets in the conventional sense; it does have lanes, paths, warrens, and so on whose names imply passageways of narrowness. There is not a single lane being straight for any longer than one-hundred feet, nor are there any two lanes intersecting at a right angle. In contrast, the surrounding city has broad streets and rectangular blocks.

One afternoon, I happened to be in the vicinity of the old town and by some unknown impulse, I entered it to walk its narrow lanes. In the maze of it all, I got lost. As I tried to orient myself, a shower made me look for cover. Not far away was a shop called "Time" according to a very weathered sign. I entered the shop and found a place full of clocks, all ticking and tocking away. I noticed that all the clocks showed different times, certainly very strange to me. Time passed and a man short in stature with a weathered complexion came in from a back room. He was not young, not old, or even something in between. "Can I help you," he asked. "The rain" I indicated vaguely. "Do you sell clocks?" I asked. "No", he answered, "I'm a time broker".

To make a short story even shorter, I will omit all those "I asked" and "He answered" stuff. I will just summarize what was spoken. First, I asked him to please explain what a time broker did. The weathered one thought that should be obvious, but he explained it to me anyway, pointing out that some have more time than they need while others have too little time. The obvious answer is time-trading. Just to give a trivial example to illustrate the process. Suppose someone wants to extend his vacation while someone else wants to get married as soon as possible. So, the latter sells time to the former. The clocks that you see and those you don't see are keeping track of the times traded. If you listen carefully, the whole building is ticking and tocking away. Indeed it was.

On a more serious note, some want a few days more of life while others want a suicide deal. The potential suicider sells his time and the value of the trade passes onto his heirs; both parties get what they want. As is reasonable, the time trader charges more for time-extensions than for time-reductions; there will always be more potential time- extenders than time-reducers. But, buying and selling time have consequences; once a contract is signed it cannot be broken. Consider a young couple that has inherited much time from their parents; they want to use the time as efficiently as possible. They decide to bypass their younger years and add that time to their middle ages where, statistically, they would possess the best combination of experience, knowledge, and vigor. She died in childbirth as a very middle-aged mother while he died of stress as a very middle-aged stock broker.

The time trader went on and on; the ticking and tocking didn't seem to bother him. It certainly bothered me; I never wanted to be faced with anything so mind-boggling. The rain stopped and that was my excuse to get out of that place. After some days of reflection, I wondered if that weathered man in the shop called "Time" had a few points after all; I could certainly use more time now and then if somebody was stupid enough to sell it to me. I went back to the old town, but I couldn't find that shop again. When I asked for directions, I got the impression that the locals thought I was mad.

Moral: Time was. Time is. Time will be. Don't fool with it.

Trading Time (II)

ON MY NEXT visit to the city with the shop called "Time", I tried once more to find it. I wandered through the old town inspecting every building for any signs of any shop with clocks ticking and tocking away. My search was futile. When I asked for directions to this shop, the locals still looked at me as if I was quite mad.

Somewhat obsessed by my search, I decided to hire an artisan to construct a model of the old town to such a scale that it would fit onto an average-size table top. The idea was to jog my memory by having a birds-eye view of the three-dimensional model; maybe I would notice something which I couldn't see at ground level. Once I thought that I heard a ticking-tocking sound from a specific place of the model. I asked the model builder to listen to it. He got himself a stethoscope with a sound amplification that would have induced deafness for any medical practitioner. The model maker told me that all he heard was wood glue drying. So, the model did me no good. .

Next, I did some thinking. What would be the purpose of having a time-broker shop if nobody could find it? Where else than the old town could a shop be located? Why not somewhere in the modern part of the city? Wouldn't a time broker be licensed? Wouldn't there be a bureau that would grant licenses?

Couldn't the time-broker shops be located in office towers, in shopping malls, in mini shopping malls? Not all of a sudden, but after a while, it occurred to me that why not try to find men short of stature and weathered faces, neither young nor old nor in between?

I began to roam the streets trying to find a weathered one. That was very easy; the weathered ones seemed to be all over the place. I began to shadow one weathered one but it didn't take long before another passed me by that had an even stronger resemblance to that fellow in the old town, then another one seemed a better prospect yet and so on and so on. This continued until my legs refused to follow any more of these look-alikes. Eventually, it occurred to me that almost all of these weathered ones were decoys. I decided to fool them back. I rented a small shop on a main street with surprising ease and set out to be a time broker. In the beginning, I had a few potential customers, but they didn't seem to understand the concept or if they did, they just walked away laughing.

Then, on the seventh day as I had expected, one of the weathered ones struck back. This particular weathered one came into the shop heavily disguised as a young basket ball player. His face had a fair complexion but it also had a brutish expression. The disguised one told me to close the shop or face the consequences. Courageous as always, I chose to face the consequences. The tall one pointed to the window view of the outside world. There, on the sidewalks, on the streets, up the trees was a virtual army of weathered ones. Still courageous, I called the city's police department. The tall and the brutal one disappeared first, followed by the multitudes on the sidewalks, the streets, and the trees. I stepped outside, being courageous as well as curious, and easily noticed that they were all gone with the exception of one.

This weathered one was quite flat; in its stampeding hurry, the crowd had trampled him into a two-dimensional shape. I sensed that this weathered one was the one I had met in the old town. Curiously, the police never showed up. What is it about time trading that make people behave this way? Did they know that they were frauds ... just like me?

Moral: He who lives by time shall perish by time.

Tumbleweeds

THE NEWS THAT arrived at the National Catastrophe Control Center in Las Vegas, Nevada became more and more ominous. The tumbleweeds were growing larger and larger. First, they sucked most of the nutrients out of the soil while they were growing, then they tumbled eastward. They filled up every canyon in sight, clogged all rivers, including the Mississippi, sank into and filled up dams, reservoirs and lakes, including the Great Lakes. The tumbleweeds invaded the cities, first getting stuck at street level between buildings, then gradually filling up these manmade canyons and eventually burying each city, leaving a dome-like structure of tumbleweeds behind.

The whole thing had started innocently enough. At a federal research station on the east slope of the Rockies, somewhere in Wyoming, genetic research was conducted on several species of tumbleweeds. The object was to breed smaller tumbleweed, one that would stay put and not roll, and one that over a span of generations would shrivel up next to nothing and hence be less of a nuisance. But, something went wrong, a genetic accident happened. A mutant of tumbleweed came into being that grew significantly larger with each generation. One day, a whole generation of these mutant tumbleweeds was large enough to just roll across the fence around the research station and continue to roll downhill along the slopes of the Rockies. Rolling eastward, following the prevailing winds, the tumbleweeds were slowly but surely advancing toward the Atlantic and Gulf coasts, obliterating canyons, cities, dams, lakes and rivers, covering the landscape under a brownish tumbleweed cover, hundreds of feet thick.

It was a national catastrophe and the Center in Las Vegas, Nevada was asked to do something about it. The staff pondered the unusual situation. The odds on such a catastrophe occurring was practically nil – yet it was not impossible as events had shown. After some hectic and concentrated pondering, most of the staff shook their heads and gave up. They went back to shooting craps or shaking hands with one-armed bandits. The prevailing attitude at the center became one of what can be done, after all, about the impossible?

The states east of the Rocky Mountains were declared a disaster area, thus making federal loans and grants available. Despite this precaution, the Eastern Establishment was wiped out, smothered under millions of giant tumbleweeds. The injunction: "Go west, young man!" was now heeded not just by young men, but by young and old of both sexes.

Moral: Despite the complaints about the wickedness and the lawlessness of the West, everybody knows where to run when they get into trouble.

(Note: This is what may be called an allegorical fable, where the West is the West and the East is the.....)

Uncertainty

AT THE RECENT Olympic Games, the javelin competition was expected to yield a new Olympic record, even a new world record. As a precaution, the officials at this event stationed themselves at a distance beyond the world record. At the other end of the field, the discus competitors did warm-up throws. Suddenly, a javelin official turned around responding to a cry of "Fore!" from a discus thrower. At that instant, a javelin entered his back, avoided his vital organs and then the steel tip of the javelin came out of his chest. This official, by force of will, determination, and excellent health, staggered about the area beyond the world record, bewildered by it all.

One of the rules of the javelin event is that the steel tip of the javelin must hit the ground first, belly landings are not allowed. Yet, it was obvious to the officials and even some of the spectators that the world record had been broken, except that the steel tip had been prevented from reaching the ground.

Some officials suggested to the pierced official that he should fall face down, hence making it a valid throw. However, the official in question was too bewildered to follow the suggestion. Other officials argued that since the pierced official was staggering around the field, the length of the javelin throw would still be uncertain. The strength and the determination of the pierced official finally gave away and he fell to the ground, unfortunately on his right side. The other officials ruled that the javelin thrower should be allowed an extra throw. The pierced official was reprimanded and disqualified for his negligence.

Moral: Uncertainty is certain.

(a fable?)

(a parable?)

Value Of Signs

EARLY IN THE morning, I went shopping at my favorite store. Next to some items of merchandise there was a sign that said $19.99. That seemed like a good bargain, so I told the sales person that I would like to buy one. I gave her the $19.99 plus sales tax. All done, I thought, until the sales person wrapped up the sign and put it in a bag and gave it to me. I was afraid to ask what an item of merchandise would cost. Not to embarrass myself in front of strangers, I took the wrapped sign valued at $19.99 and went home.

That, of course, was not a good idea. My wife had a hard time understanding why I would buy an ordinary sign that couldn't possibly have a value of $19.99. My wife, bless her attitude, took the $19.99 sign back to the store and demanded an explanation or at least $19.99 plus sales tax back. That was not a good idea said the sales person. There was a great scarcity of $19.99 signs and their value had doubled every hour since early in the morning and it would probably go on doubling in the hours ahead. In view of the great scarcity of $19.99 signs, why not instead invest in signs worth $39.99 and in particularly the $59.99 signs which were almost guaranteed to triple or quadruple in the next few hours? My wife, of course, didn't consider any of these suggested bargains, bargains. I could tell even though I was watching all the sign bargaining from a distance. Still, I could observe the flavor and the intensity of the arguments pro and con.

Finally, my wife and the sales persons called a truce for a while. My wife wandered around in other parts of the store with me following in the distance. Since I was so far behind, I could take my time and peek into nooks and crannies where I had never thought of looking before. Almost inadvertently, I asked a sales associate where the Sign Department was and probably by a slip of his tongue, he told me. Sure enough, the Sign Department was well hidden but the constant stream of people in and out of the solid access doors revealed its existence. So I sneaked in, of course, looking deceptively like any other sign person and, sure enough, a multitude of sign persons were making signs in all price categories from $19.99 to beyond $999.99 at a very good pace. I gathered together a variety of signs, among them a lot of $19.99 signs which I regarded as investments.

Back to the initial pile of merchandise with that $19.99 sign that was supposed to be so valuable by now. My wife came to the same place and I revealed myself also but the sales person who had wrapped my $19.99 sign and put it in a bag was nowhere to be seen. At the end of the shopping day, my wife and I cashed in our sign investments. Next, we spent our time and fortune traveling around the country. We spread the word about the value of signs and if at any particular place there was no knowledge of it, we used our investments to give us more investments.

Why buy any merchandise at all when you can invest in signs? Or, put another way, a sign is identical to itself - most of the time.

Watersheds

AND SO IT came to pass that in a year divisible by four, the two candidates for president were both women. One political analyst stated that that was a watershed. Another analyst wrote that it was a tremendous watershed. Yet another analyst spoke to his mother and said that it was the mother of all watersheds. You could hardly blame anybody who pointed out that it was a watershed since it was a watershed and so it was impossible to write a sentence about the watershed without mentioning that it was a watershed.

The campaign began and it was polite; each of the two candidates emphasized that they understood the other's point of view. That didn't last very long because something went terribly wrong. One candidate held a great rally on a plain somewhere in Texas. The weather turned ugly but the candidate didn't want to disappoint her supporters so she spoke with fire and brimstone on her breath. To conclude, she raised her right hand and closed its fist in some sort of power salute. The Texas weather by now was vicious. Lightning struck her arm and she became part of the earth.

About the same time, the second candidate was touring a watershed in Wyoming, preaching the gospel that all watersheds should be inspected and made safe for human habitation. Unbeknownst to her, or anybody else, there was a tremendous thunderstorm pouring waters on the surrounding mountains and these waters joined together into a flash flood. The candidate was inspecting a shed in the watershed and suddenly she was carried away with the shed. Later, no traces were found of the shed or the candidate.

The nation stood in awe and disbelief that both candidates were no more. Some with conservative religious bents suggested that the Heavens were upset by the two female candidates participating in an election. Secular liberal advocates pointed out the need to install lightning rods and have yearly inspections of all watersheds, preferably financed by the federal government no matter what the cost might be.

Next came the concern that the elimination of the two female candidates smacked of male conspiracy. After all, the two vice-presidential candidates were male so any suspicions began with them. The two candidates pointed out that they had no powers to call down lightning and flash floods, certainly a reasonable response; but, who then?

The two vice-presidential candidates were promoted to presidential candidates. Both avoided any visits to Texas or Wyoming. Otherwise, life returned to normal and as was unavoidable, only one of the two candidates was elected president.

Came the next election in a year divisible by four. The two presidential candidates were male and the two vice-presidential candidates were female. It came to pass that the two presidential candidates succumbed because of their derring-do financed by election funds. One went off into deep space and the other took a deep-ocean dive. They were accidents and both perished. The female vice-presidential candidates were promoted to presidential candidates. As was unavoidable, one was elected president.

Was there a female conspiracy somewhere deep in space or deep in the ocean? Not very likely, yet who knew? Later historians would point out that these events showed that when females come to power, if that is the word, they tend to choose the indirect route. Indeed, a historian wrote that conquering the flank first, rather than a direct assault on the main goal, is their tactic. A sort of tactic reminding one of McArthur landing his troops behind the enemy's lines at Inchon.

We Didn't Meet, Even Eventually

THIS HEADING, OF course, is grammatical nonsense because if we didn't meet we didn't meet. There is no use in expending time waiting for things to change since "even eventually" cannot change the fact that we didn't meet. The obvious question then is: now what? The obvious answer is why don't we just ignore the heading? What does the heading know any way that we don't know?

After this step forward, we must be concerned about what direction any further steps we should be heading. The problem now is what is the meaning of "direction"? Direction, relative to what? The best bet is that by "direction" we shall not mean anything in a geographical sense, such as North and South. We shall mean a direction toward a goal which, as the heading suggest, is to find someone to meet even if that someone probably couldn't care less. The task, then, is to try to make that someone care or at least care a little bit. As it turned out, geographical directions had nothing to do with it. Confusion, as always, is part of the human predicament.

To be more specific, suppose that I am a young man and you are a young woman. I can recall, in clear detail, the first time we didn't meet. I was sipping from a glass filled with Concord grape juice and as usual I spilled a portion of it on myself. Any sort of cleaning, dry or wet, couldn't prevent a permanent stain. You wore a beautiful spring dress and you drank a glass of juice just a few feet away from me. You didn't spill anything of it. I like that ability in girls, the ability to do something right and still not feel superior about it. With my stain in progress, I couldn't approach you even if I had had the nerve which I never had.

Even though I stopped at every juice outfit that I happened to pass by, you were never there with a glass of juice in your hand. Of course, I looked at the other girls even though they were not you. The girls that I looked at were, I'm sure, wonderful in all respects except, of course, they were not you. Months went by with no sighting of you. Since we lived in a city of several hundred thousand inhabitants this was to be expected. What I didn't expect was that one day we didn't meet for the second time. You were walking on the sidewalk on the other side of the street, on its sunny side. I have always appreciated girls in their summer dresses, but seeing you in a summer dress was like a revelation, a mirage, and a half-awake dream. I crossed the street, against the traffic, disregarding my life and limbs. By the time I had reached the other side, you were gone. Yet, the image of you in your summer dress will always be with me.

So, did we meet or didn't we meet? In a sense I think we did because in the future all the girls that I would like and love were, in a sense, you. But, in the real world, if we had met, we would both have been disappointed. True love is to reject mirages. True love is to live each ordinary day, in the here and now, without regrets.

We Met, Eventually

HOW DO YOU find that someone that you want to meet? Even narrowing the search to the United States and Europe, there would be more than half a billion men and women to search through. Narrowing the search further to men and women in the age bracket of 20 to 30 years, you still have a number in the order of one sixth of half a billion, generously rounded off to about 100 million. Separately, then, we are dealing with 50 million men and 50 million women. So, just to emphasize, in the United States and Europe there are those 100 million souls roaming those areas in search of a mate.

Hence, the odds of meeting that someone is so close to zero that there is little point in even trying to search for him or her. Still, to a few it doesn't matter what the odds are. In addition to low odds, another difficulty is the Atlantic Ocean. How can North Americans and Europeans mingle with each other in any meaningful way and hence be able to search for that someone when they are more or less confined to separate continents? But, discouraging numbers aside; they are not necessarily discouraging. The fifty million Americans divided over fifty states come to one million per state. The odds are improving; one in the million only. Concentrating on the Western and Eastern states where half the population live, the odds are now one in half a million. As an illustration only, one may arbitrarily pick a major city like Seattle in the state of Washington. The population of Seattle is about half a million. Now the odds of finding that some-one is about one in one – or almost certainty; so, now you know that that someone is somewhere in that city.

At this point, applied mathematics is no longer a useful tool. What the one-on-one search needs now is something like serendip-ity, something out of the ordinary. Researchers have researched this final phase, but there are still many questions to which there are no answers. Nevertheless, there are some things that you can do. You could, for instance, advertise your presence in the Seattle Times. Or you could take one of the Washington State's ferries where so many people commute and enjoy themselves. Or, you can shop at Pike Street Market for salmon and other sea life. Or, probably your best bet, get to the top of the Space Needle where, on a clear day, you can see the area that the 500,000 inhabit. Let me now intrude into this narrative to at least hint what worked for me. I shall leave out the details and specifics, but it had something to do with walking down a staircase to a ballroom featuring a Saturday evening dance where now and then the orchestra played, and the audience danced to tunes connected with Scottish waltzes or whatever they called them, dances which required athletic ability as well as physical endurance. Just because it worked for me doesn't mean that it will work for you. But then again, who knows? Anyway, serendipity knows.

Wet Socks, Dry Socks

THE OTHER DAY, I noticed that my socks were wet. Today they are both dry. Thinking back, I remembered that on that other day when I took a shower, I had forgotten to take my socks off. This incident shows that at the moving present, time's arrow is pointed in the direction of the future, that is, from wet to dry, for example. On the other hand, by thinking back to the wet condition of the socks after that shower, the arrow is now completely reversed, a neat 180 degrees turn.

So, while the moving present moves toward the future, at the same time when recalling something at the present, this recalling moves in the direction of the past. The trouble with the past is that we don't remember everything that happened. Consequently, the past has gaps in itself; the past is incomplete.

Another troubling aspect about the past is that we have no control over what we remember and what we don't remember. It is certainly a very common observation that what we really don't want to remember is what we really will remember. Take the example of the wet socks slowly drying while on your feet. Who would want to remember that once I, or some other person, took a shower with the socks on? You feel ridiculous and you want to forget the whole incident. It is almost guaranteed that I, or that other person, will never forget the wet-sock incident. And so it goes, mine or your mind goes on collecting and storing all kinds of ridiculous happenings that persist in being remembered with the utmost clarity despite all efforts to get rid of them.

Hence, it is very comforting that, as of today anyway, nobody can read your mind. Your secrets are your secrets as long as you have a sense of the present. Yet, as is frequently recorded, strange happenings and doings carry themselves involuntarily to the present from the past in a disguised manner. Take the present example of going into a shower with your socks on. Many sources, other than me, have made the observation that now that the present industrial civilizations can produce shoes at affordable prices, everybody who wants to be shod can be shod. Yet, from infants and up through those in their second childhood, there is a compulsion to tear off shoes as soon as they are put on and then walk around barefoot. Considering that shoes and socks can't get any closer than they already are, it implies repressed incidents of not having taken off socks in showers or tubs. Shoes are just repressed symbols for socks expressing itself in the present.

When one grasps the idea that manifestations in the present reflect incidents stored in the past, it is easy to draw various conclusions. One conclusion is that don't do anything whatsoever that tends to stick to the past. A slippery past is the best defense. Throw the past a banana peel and watch it making a fool of itself. The past has made fools of us often enough.

Moral: To remember or not to remember, that is the problem.

Wet Socks, Dry Socks (II)

THE PHONE RINGS, it's her again. She says: "I see that your favorite magazine published something you called "Wet Socks" and so on.""Yes", I agreed, "it did". She is my former girlfriend and my current estranged wife. As soon as the divorce is final, my hope is that she'll be my girlfriend again. Anyway, to summarize part of the conversation:

She says: You have embarrassed me again; this wet-socks dry-socks business is ridiculous.

I say: Why should you be embarrassed, I'm the one who wrote it.

She says: Apropos embarrassed, being Mrs. Hereandthere is embarrassing.

I say: It's due to my grandfather's sense of humor. Besides, you last name is spelled with an extra "o"; Mrs. Hereandthereo, which disguises any hidden meaning whatsoever.

She says: Really? How about Mrs. Whatsoevero? Neverthelesso? But, back to the socks business; why would you want to write such a silly thing?

I say: To plumb the depths of my consciousness.

She says: Who wants to know that depth? I don't.

Obviously, we got sidetracked. So I tell her about our future plans. We get a divorce and we are girlfriend and boyfriend again, respectively. After a digesting period, we move back to high school where we were classmates. She suggested that we go at least as far back as kindergarten or to the time when we were living in different parts of the country and had no idea whatsoever of the existence of the other. She had a point; but moving that close to our birth events sort of obscured the progressive aspects of our early existence.

Anyway, how about this traveling back in time? As always, she was stubborn. When we reach the marriage and divorce states again, do we do a second time travel, she asked. This is not time travel, I pointed out to her. It is just going back to what we were; we will just watch our steps more carefully the next time. As for Mrs. Carefullyo?; she is as feisty as ever. This wet- socks and dry-socks stuff must be erased for all time, she said.

We divorced; we were girlfriend and boyfriend again, respectively. But the road of time, as always, reached a fork. I took the road that would lead to wet socks; she took the road that would lead to dry socks. Either way, there were no ways of getting rid of socks. Why there were wet socks on one road and dry socks on the other road was never clarified by Fate. No one could explain what the socks were seeking after that fork in the road. Perhaps the explanation was that these roads were less traveled and nobody had bothered to keep them clear of rubbish. Or, perhaps, someone like me had taken showers with his socks on and he wanted to conceal the evidence, the concealment based on the theory of hiding something in plain sight.

Moral: (I have always wanted to write something I couldn't understand.)

Where Art Thou, Vice President?

IT HAPPENED A few days after the inaugural which was at the end of January. It was discovered that the Vice President (VP) was missing. Part of the fault for not having kept track of the VP fell to those who were installing the new Administration and who wanted to get rid of the old rascals as soon as possible with more than deliberate speed. This led invariably to all kinds of shuffles, trying to clean out numerous bureaus, agencies, secretariats, ministries and so on while working at top speed to fill out the necessary forms to create the new society. So many contributed to these efforts that the case of the missing VP could be looked at from many and various points of view.

Anyway, the VP had not been issued a correct photo identity card. When the VP presented himself at the portals of power, he fully expected to be admitted. Instead, he was admitted to a mental institution in the nation's capital. You can't very well have vice-presidential pretenders presenting themselves at the portals of power with improper, even erroneous, photos with no visible means of verification. It did take a few days before a photo was discovered in the archives showing the VP arising out of the Tidal Basin wearing a pair of slightly brown swimming trunks. On the back of the photo was the inscription: "*This is the Vice President*".

The President scraped together some time and invited the VP to the White House. The President had to admit that the VP sounded like the fellow he had talked with on the phone. So, let bygones be by-gones, said the President and took the VP on a tour of White House and its treasures. The VP thought that it was only fair that he should be put in charge of the Bureau of Engraving and Printing so that he would be able to pass the time as Vice President. The President agreed to that, although he pointed out that it would entail a lot of travel to the burials of foreign dignitaries as well as peddling the products of the Bureau. Finally, the two of them were joined by the President's wife who the President called his treasure. This prompted the VP to ask if he could spend the night in Lincoln's Bedroom. The President reluctantly agreed because he had heard so many rumors about this VP. He wasn't just handsome, he needed hardly any sleep and he could hear footsteps on soft carpets as well as any noises passing through walls, floors and ceilings. It was rumored that the First Lady appreci-ated anybody having such attributes. The President couldn't very well deny the VP's entry to Lincoln's Bedroom. But, why should he have to wander the corridors at night just because the VP was a light sleeper?

A few days after the Lincoln's Bedroom incident, the VP was lost again. From the archives arose the photo of a young handsome man shown in almost black swimming trunks arising from the depth of the Tidal Basin. On the back of the photo was the note "*This is the Vice President*". The brownish and the blackish swimming trunks were both of proper size but the startling differences of the two colors had to convince almost anybody that the VP had not yet been found. On the other hand, all that the Administration required of its VP was that he could be declared dead or at least incapacitated. The question arose, how do you get rid of a VP? The correct question, however, is how do you get rid of the Tidal Basin?

<... if it can happen it will happen; it was either this opus or another nothing poem ...>

Woman Against Serpent

WOMAN SAT IN the Tree of Knowledge and tasted its fruits.

The Serpent slithered by on His way to visit His wife. Woman picked more of the fruit and threw it at the serpent.

"Stop and listen when I am talking to you," She commanded.

"What did you say?" asked the Serpent.

"I said: Why don't you take a bite of this delicious fruit?"

"No thank you," said the Serpent. "They told me never to touch that stuff – as you surely know."

Of course Woman knew and She also knew how this fable was supposed to continue and end. But, She was not satisfied with that knowledge.

Woman jumped out of the Tree of Knowledge and began to kick the Serpent around. "Now you take a bite or else!" She screamed at Him.

Just to get rid of Her, the Serpent took a bite – and then He also knew that Woman had tricked Him. "Aha!" cried Woman. "Now you know! Get out of the Garden! On your belly you shall crawl and dust you shall eat for the rest of your days!"

"What do you think I have been doing up to now?" asked the Serpent. Woman pretended She did not hear Him. She chased and kicked Him out of the Garden and She made sure that He did not slither back. The Serpent did not really mind. He knew He would not be alone very long.

Moral: Anticipation of sin is more enjoyable than sin itself.

Semi-Poems On Worms In Apples

By: Thomas Thorsen

(...not serious?...)
Two worms in an apple
One green, one blue,
Wanted to grapple
As wrestlers do.

It was a messy chore
To get room to wrestle in,
They ate apple from its core
And out to its skin.

But after all that apple
They didn't want to grapple.
The blue worm turned green,
The other got a bluish sheen.

The bluish and the green
Both took an aspirin
And they took a rest
So they could digest.

(...serious?...)
A worm
used an apple
as its dorm.

Another worm
With a different dapple
Also invaded this solid form.

Such were their needs
That they fought a battle
Between skin and seeds
Until the apple became a rattle.

Hunger made them into
string-like things
So neither one
Would ever fly

As a moth or as a butterfly.
Soon they would both expire
In their little hollow empire.

But still no room to grapple
In that really wormy apple.
When you eat, your figure
Just naturally gets bigger.

Each should've used its little head,
They should have planned ahead.

About The Author

THOMAS THORSEN WAS born on June 13th 1931 in Oslo, Norway. He and his younger brother, Carl Johan, grew up in a loving family with their parents Nicolai Olaf Thorsen and Gunvor Christine Thorsen.

His education there consisted of elementary school, high school and a year at a technical institute. He experienced the years of the German occupation of Norway during World War II and served in the Norwegian army for the compulsory one year with the occupation troops in Schleswig Holstein, Germany, during 1950-51.

He came to Seattle, Washington in June of 1953, when he had just turned 22, to attend the University of Washington. He earned a B.S in 1955 and a M.S in 1956 in Mechanical Engineering.

While in Seattle, he met Inge. They got married in 1956. In 1958 they moved to California and lived in a small apartment in West Los Angeles. Thomas got a job working as a research engineer at U.C.L.A. while also attending classes.

In 1963 they adopted their son, Steven. A year later, Thomas started teaching Engineering at El Camino College in Torrance, California. In 1965 the family moved to Inglewood and while living there, they adopted their daughter, Tanya. After ten years, they moved to their present home of 38 years in Rancho Palos Verdes.

Thomas stayed at El Camino for 35 years and eventually also

taught Mathematics. He had a heart attack in 1995 and retired in 1999. The children got married and the family got bigger. There are now five grandchildren.

For about ten years, after Thomas retired, he and Inge did a lot of traveling until in 2010 he was diagnosed with Parkinson's dementia, although we believe it started a lot earlier. He died at home on July 3rd 2013, with his family around him.

He was a wonderful, loving husband, father, grandfather and brother. He is greatly missed.

You might have heard that Aesop was not Aesop

and that Shakespeare was Marlowe, but if you

ever hear that Thorsen is not Thorsen, it is

a fable, pure and simple.

CPSIA information can be obtained at www.ICGtesting.com
Printed in the USA
BVOW07*0458131114

374807BV00001B/1/P